Un-NappPily
in LovE

Un-Nappily in LovE

Trisha R. Thomas

St. Martin's Griffin
New York

Published in the United States by St. Martin's Griffin, an imprint of St. Martin's Publishing Group

UN-NAPPILY IN LOVE. Copyright © 2010 by Trisha R. Thomas. All rights reserved. Printed in the United States of America. For information, address St. Martin's Publishing Group, 120 Broadway, New York, NY 10271.

www.stmartins.com

The Library of Congress has cataloged the first St. Martin's Griffin edition as follows:

Thomas, Trisha R., 1964–
   Un-nappily in love / Trisha R. Thomas. — 1st ed.
     p. cm.
   ISBN 978-0-312-55763-8
   1. African Americans—Fiction.   2. Married people—Fiction.   I. Title.
   PS3570.H5917U56 2010
   813'.54—dc22

2010014436

ISBN 978-1-250-62390-4 (trade paperback)

Our books may be purchased in bulk for promotional, educational, or business use. Please contact your local bookseller or the Macmillan Corporate and Premium Sales Department at 1-800-221-7945, extension 5442, or by email at MacmillanSpecialMarkets@macmillan.com.

Second St. Martin's Griffin Edition: March 2020

10 9 8 7 6 5 4 3 2

Un-NappPily
in LovE

Any man who makes a claim of finding true love more than once in a lifetime hasn't yet lived long enough to know the difference.

—*Anonymous*

Jake Parson could say for certain he had been in love—real love—and knew there was no greater joy or, for that matter, no greater sorrow. There was no getting over that first woman who left an indelible stamp on your heart and mind. It was easy to pretend to be free in his waking thoughts, but when night came, when darkness stilled the mind and quieted the noise, her face would appear. Her touch, her kiss, her laughter all rushing in to fill every space.

He sat on the edge of the bathtub and rubbed her back with the wet towel, watching the bubbles trail down her bronze skin.

"When do I get the surprise you've been promising?" she asked.

He brushed wet tendrils out of her face before kissing her shoulder, and trailing to the soft flesh of her breast. She tilted her chin upward, enjoying his touch.

"Trust me, you don't want to rush this."

"Cut." The director's edgy voice boomed with the echo of the spacious bathroom. The ten-million-dollar home was the same one used in countless other films set in Harlem, New York, but shot in Toronto, Canada. "That's a wrap." Johnson Landry had written the script specifically with another actor in mind. He took a chance on Jake as a favor. Hopefully, Landry wouldn't regret that decision. They were on their sixth take. The bathwater was cold. Both he and his co-star were shivering. She suffered more than he, sitting in the stale water for hours.

"Remember, you are in love, head over heels. You'd do anything for this woman." Landry threw up his hands. "Let's try this again tomorrow. You're not feeling this at all."

The director had it wrong. If anything Jake was feeling it too much, and it scared him. Trying to even out his feelings, control the surge he felt, afraid he'd lose it in front of all these people.

"Nah, I'm cool. I can do it." If Landry wanted real, he'd give him real. He knew love. The kind that broke you down and swallowed you whole. He took a long deep breath. "I'm ready."

"All right. Let's go one more time," the director called out over the crew. "From scene four. Let's roll."

When they were finished filming, Jake stood up and moved quickly off the set. He felt someone grab his sleeve and knew before he turned around who it was.

"Where are you going? I thought we had an understanding?"

He leaned in close so no one would hear but her. "You don't get everything you want. Someone should've told you that a long time ago."

"No, you're the one that's not going to have his cake and eat it too. Looks like you can say good-bye to your son."

He gently removed her hand and made his way to the street for a taxi, hoping he'd still have a family when he got home.

The Incredible
Shrinking Wife

Several Months Earlier

"This way, over here, JP." The long lens of the camera pointed our way. The frenzy of photo hounds jostling for spots to get better angles made me nervous. I squinted from the bright flash and saw a long slender arm reach toward me. I recognized the garish diamond-and-ruby bracelet before I saw the rest of Jake's publicist, Ramona Scarsdale. She bore a striking resemblance to the actress Lynda Carter circa 1975 as the comic-book heroine Wonder Woman. Her dark hair freeze-framed high and away from her face cascaded down her back. Her cheekbones and red lips were artificially enhanced, making her look like a wax figure instead of the real thing.

She slipped her cold fingers around my wrist and gave me a tug. "Wait over here," she growled, adding a nudge that made me lose my balance.

"Owww." The wail came from behind me, though the young woman was expressing my sentiments exactly. "You stepped on my toe," she squealed.

My ankle had twisted awkwardly in the five-inch heels I'd yet to master, so I was only half concerned with her pain and thinking about my own. Four inches used to be the legal limit until someone had upped the ante, making it even more difficult to walk, talk, and look beautiful at the same time. "I'm sorry. I fell off balance."

"I had the perfect shot and you got in my way." She had a ring in her nose, one in her bottom lip, and three in each ear. She held up her phone, which was in camera mode. "Okay, so like, move," she ordered with a lisp, indicating a piercing on her tongue too.

"Sure." I scooted a bit to the right while she took the picture.

"He is so fine. Even cuter up close and personal. JPeeee . . ." she sang out.

"Yes, he's gorgeous," I said, watching proudly as my husband stood against the gold backdrop poised and looking like a million bucks. His tux was custom designed and fit over his toned physique.

My hubby's new world was filled with flashing lights and admiring fans. Exotic locales for filming and promoting his new career as a movie star. One day he was my house husband, basically sitting around waiting for tomorrow and more broken promises from his agent, and the next he was being asked to co-star in a movie with Sirena Lassiter, the Billboard-topping "it" girl turned actress. Jake and Sirena Lassiter knew each other back when Jake—or JP, as everyone knows him—had been a rap artist.

We met six years ago when he'd hired me as a marketing consultant for his hip-hop clothing line, JP Wear. At the time I was engaged to another man but Jake didn't see that as a hindrance to getting what he wanted. At the time it was me, Venus Johnston, thirtysomething, with—as Jake described—"hips you can't miss, lips that you want to sink into, and eyes that save the day." He's a songwriter by nature, so he's a bit poetic in his descriptions. But on the inside I was closed off and a bit lost. He found me.

Till this day I question his good sense, especially since I'd just found out my mother had breast cancer and my fiancé was under investigation for securities fraud. I was hardly considered an ideal good time. But that didn't stop Jake. He stepped right up to the plate determined to hit a home run. He was confident like that. Forget about a base hit, getting to second, and hoping to slide into home. He was an all or nothing kind of guy.

Looking at him now, thinking about all we'd been through together, made me puff up with pride. The man was smooth, elegant, with integrity to boot. I slid the tear aside that escaped, threatening to mess up my airbrushed makeup. In such a short time, our lives had come so far. We had a daughter, a beautiful home in Atlanta, and enough history, love, and intrigue between us to make a Friday-night movie on a steamy channel seem pretty tame.

We fought for each other when we had nothing left to fight for ourselves.

The minute the crowd started cheering and screaming I knew why. Sirena Lassiter had arrived at Jake's side. He slipped an arm around her waist. She kissed him on the cheek. The on-screen couple oozed chemistry, the kind that made it easy to believe he'd take a bullet for her the way he had in this sure-to-be box-office hit, *True Beauty*.

"Sirena, JP, over here. You guys are hot." The cameraman with the best pictures would get the most money from the celebrity-filled magazines. JP gave a sexy smile then turned toward Sirena, who was already staring up at him.

Perfect shot. I could already see the headline, especially since she was engaged to be married to Earl Benning, CEO of Rise Records and also producer of the film. Anywhere Earl Benning walked, a camera followed. Anywhere Sirena Lassiter sneezed, a newshound reported and offered tissue. Having Jake in the fold gave them something about which to speculate. Was Sirena Lassiter falling for her co-star even though she was engaged to one of the most powerful men in the business?

Not a chance. It was all an act. The way she looked at him was planned and rehearsed simply to keep everyone speculating long enough to get them to the box office. In a nutshell, I wasn't worried about Sirena Lassiter or anyone else. Jake and I were locked and loaded. Nothing could come between us. We'd proven it time and time again.

"Okay, this way. Let's move." Ramona waved the order and her two assistants closed ranks. Each assistant took Sirena and Jake by the elbow. We were on the move until I was suddenly stuck behind a barricade.

"Wait a minute. I'm with them," I told the large man wearing a suit jacket over a yellow security T-shirt. Jake stopped abruptly as if he'd forgotten something. I lifted my arm and waved, glad I'd been waxed under the armpit instead of my usual cheap shave. "I'm over here, baby."

I knew he wouldn't leave me behind. After six years of a rocky marital ride, we'd made it through the storm. The official report was in, we were no good without each other. Side by side, ready to get through any crisis. I was the index finger and he was the thumb, or vice versa. I tried not to quibble about who was in charge.

Ramona whispered something in his ear. He nodded and then kept marching as she'd ordered.

"Ramona, I'm over here."

She looked back and barely swept her eyes across the crowd. How many fans were dressed in a red shiny tight dress? I stood out like a chili pepper. It was my first thought when the dress had been sent over by the stylist, hired by Ramona, *handpicked especially for you,* the note read. The stiff fold on one side kept poking me in the ear. "Ramona!" I screamed, the same way I'd done a few hours ago squeezing into this damn dress. And now she couldn't see me. Beautiful.

I scooted to the last pole of the velvet rope. I tapped a female security staffer on the shoulder. She was mountain-large with a melon-sized hair bun.

"My husband is Jake Parson."

"Who?"

"Can you please let me through? My husband is JP," I confirmed. J-P—just two initials, like the diamond-laced bling he wore with a swoop on the end. Sirena had it custom-made for him as an end-of-filming gift. I thought about him wearing the chain around his neck. Not until this very moment had it bothered me.

The female security guard kept her eyes straight ahead. "Sorry, not without ID."

"Do I look like one of the gang? I'm freezing out here in this dress with shoes that are killing my feet."

Her eyes rode me up and down, then focused on my glowing shoulders. I'd been spray tanned with Honey Gold #6, the darkest color on the chart, yet I still turned out radioactive red. Enough said. She unclipped the velvet rope and stood aside to let me through.

Close Your Eyes
This Won't Hurt a Bit

Two things you never forget: the first time your period started, and how you met your husband. Everything in between fades to obscurity. I tried to emphasize this very fact to Mya, our five-year-old daughter, when she's having a kiddy breakdown, recounting when someone was mean to her at school or her socks didn't match in the bright light. Or one shoestring was longer than the other. Or when, by the end of the day, she's counted how many times her teacher has called on Suzy more than her.

In twenty years you won't remember. Life becomes a figment of your imagination. I reminded myself of this fact while tiptoeing in my high heels down the aisle to the front of the theater, where as soon as I got there, I realized there was no seat open for me.

Ramona sat on one side and Sirena was on the other. I stood on the edge of the aisle and gave a baby wave to Ramona. "Remember me?" I even forced my lips to curve in a not-as-angry-as-I-feel smile.

Jake stood up. "Baby, I was worried about you." He gave my hand a gentlemanly kiss then pulled me forward, until I nearly stumbled over Ramona's pressed knees. I landed in his lap.

"Oh, sorry," I said, having nearly landed on her as well. I pulled myself up but Jake gave me an exaggerated kiss, making me fall back again.

I heard the very familiar sound of a camera clicking, but what I was most aware of at that moment was Sirena staring and examining every kinky spiraled strand of my hair up close, doing her uncertain best at trying to make me feel insecure.

I'd defected from the ritual of chemically straightening my hair years ago and happily accepted my nappy tresses for what they were. And like my grandmother used to say, *"God don't make no mistakes, baby. You are who you are."* I wasn't born with natural curly locks. Then again, seeing as how my mother started chemically straightening my hair when I was only three years old, I wasn't sure what I was born with. I wasn't old enough to write my own name, but I knew how to spell Ultra Sheen, the white jar that housed the creamy product that made my hair shiny and straight. I was one of millions of little girls who would grow up not knowing any other way. All was good and right in the world as long as our edges were straight and our ends were clipped and flipped.

Of course, it was hard to explain all this on a first meeting with someone. They generally thought I'd gone cuckoo and was rebelling against the status quo. Partly true. I was born and raised in the late boom of middle-class Los Angeles.

Californians were normally known for being open to change, and new lifestyles, not withstanding the scorned hope of Proposition 8. I'm going to go out on a limb and say the people who opposed the gay marriage bill were from somewhere else and had secretly invaded the California ballot boxes. There was really no other explanation. It was an embarrassment and made me stop telling people I was a Southern Cali girl, plain and simple.

All I knew was that I'd learned early to accept change, roll with the tremors, as it were. You had a different outlook on life growing up fearlessly awaiting the next earthquake to shake you to your core. When I was little, I thought it was God's hand telling me to wake up. Just about once a week, in the middle of the night, the rumbling would start. My mother wouldn't even stir; my father's snoring would stay steady. While I would be on my feet standing in my flannel nightie in the doorway as I'd been trained since kindergarten. At school, we were prepared for the Big One, emergency snacks written with your name on the plastic bag so no one else could claim your canned tuna, crackers, and bottled water. At the end of the school year you got to take it home and were reminded that summer didn't mean you could let down your guard. The Big One could strike when you least expected. Always be prepared.

Eventually I stopped following earthquake preparedness protocol. I stayed tucked under the cover and waited for the shaking to stop like everyone else. It was never the Big One.

I felt a nudge and realized Sirena's elbow had conveniently connected to the back of my head where I'd invaded her space; I also realized I'd been waiting for her all along, like the earthquake. *She was* the Big One.

"Oh, I'm sorry," she almost mimicked in a sweet melodic voice like a high school cheerleader you'd better not turn your back on.

"It's okay." I sat up, best I could with the constraints of a dress that had no give in the fabric.

Ramona stood. "I was just going over a few details. Please—" She opened her hand, offering the warmed seat.

"I think I'll stay here." I kissed Jake on the nose.

"You'll save that for when you two are alone," Ramona chastised, checking over her shoulder for random looky-looers.

Jake gave me a lift on my bottom with his wide palm. I took my seat, feeling scolded by the teacher and sent to the principal's office.

The lights dimmed and the screen came to life. I'd seen *True Beauty* five times. Breaking things down to numerology takes the emotion out of it. Tonight would be the sixth time I've seen my husband use those same wide palms of his to lift Sirena off the ground while he steamrolls into her against the wall. The skin of his moist muscular back flexing with every movement. Twelve unbearable seconds and then a cutaway to morning while they bask in each other's spearmint-sprayed breath.

The bedroom scene floated around in my head and I repeated to myself, *In twenty years you won't remember.* I hoped and prayed it didn't take that long. I hoped it only took me not having to see it again and again, every time I closed my eyes, or drove my car, or took a shower, or ran on the treadmill. I'd memorized the way Sirena's hands trailed Jake's back then stopped at the base of his head, massaging in between moans. I'd even imagined myself in the shot up to the moment he whips her around and her hair cascades over her shoulder and down her back.

"Here we go." Jake's voice sounded even more distant than my mind had ventured. He was already tending to the big screen. His eyes glazed over in the movie light. If I'd seen it five times, he'd seen it at least twenty. I decided to close mine through the entire movie, for whatever good it would do, and told myself, *In twenty years it won't matter.*

The next step was the afterparty, which was hardly a party. More like a train stop—All aboard!—at which not-so-busy actors made desperate attempts for a last chance to made the weekly entertainment pages. Who wore what to what had gotten to the point where real models weren't used anymore to show off fashion. The modeling profession had essentially collapsed, taken over by celebrities whose only job now was to look hot while shopping, walking the dog, or going out to dinner.

One cameraman pointed his lens in my direction, then lowered the camera when he realized I wasn't Jada Pinkett Smith—and even if I was, today didn't seem to warrant a photo op.

"Your flight leaves at six in the morning. You may want to get a move on, catch a few hours of sleep." Ramona sipped her shimmering pink martini, the signature drink of *True Beauty*. "I'll have the driver take you to the hotel."

I could barely breathe in my dress so I stayed with water and a wedge of lemon. "No, I'd rather stay." I peered at Jake, who was yucking it up with a popular celebrity who'd gone from female rapper to actress. Sirena stood in the middle like they all went way back, and I'm sure they did. Good memories for all. Since Jake wasn't the type to name-drop after spending many years in the music industry, I wasn't privy to who his industry friends were. He never talked about the celebrities he knew. He always said everyone knew everyone but no one really knew anyone.

Sirena Lassiter's name especially never came up. Not once after watching one of her many movies on DVD did he roll over and say, *That Sirena's a cool gal. She and I used to party together. You'd like her.* It was only when Jake was faced with a life-or-death situation that Sirena miraculously appeared in our lives.

About a year ago, henchmen in a case of mistaken identity had accosted me. Before Jake could come rescue me he had to make sure Mya was safe. He had no one else. Sirena was the first person who came to mind, someone he could trust. The famous Sirena Lassiter had picked up my daughter and brought her home safely. No one could've been more grateful than me. I thanked her profusely. I had her over for dinner. She came bearing gifts—for Mya a princess Nokia doll, for me a Marc Jacobs bag, one she was given for promotion, for Jake, a pricey aged cognac that made him nervous just holding the bottle. I'd made lasagna that night. She cleaned her plate like it was her last meal. The girl could eat.

We made small talk. She asked about the flower business. I asked about her next movie, still impressed to have Sirena Lassiter at my dinner table. Four hours later, and I just wanted her to go home. I stretched and yawned, and started cleaning up the kitchen. Sirena didn't budge. She stayed at the table laughing and talking with Jake as if I were the busboy.

"These things can go on all night. It's best if you—" Ramona stepped toward me but stopped talking abruptly when she saw an editor she'd yet to nail down for an interview.

I gravitated toward Jake and his small group.

"So you must be JP's better half?"

I smiled and did my best to contain my giddiness. Seeing someone in the flesh after seeing them in movies was a huge deal, and never got old.

"Queen Latifah," I mouthed with no sound. "I love everything you do. I have your last album too. Play it all the time."

"Call me Dana." She peeled her hand out of my death grip, then put a hand on Jake's shoulder. "Glad to see somebody made an honest man out of you."

"That she did." Jake tilted his head, offering a sexy grin. "A better man."

"Now ain't love grand."

"Nice meeting you," I said to the Queen's back as she was already moving toward the comedienne who had a late-night talk show. I hadn't seen it and didn't want to pretend I would. Staying up past ten was a feat I'd yet to manage since running my floral business. And being a mother, wife, and occasional super freak in the bedroom left little time for TV watching.

Sirena remained by Jake's side as if her life depended on it. No one would guess she was the main superstar. She'd sold millions of albums before she'd even stepped foot in the movie business, but she clung on to Jake like he was the center of attention.

"I didn't have time to tell you earlier, I love that shade of red on you." Sirena reached out and tried to help my one-sided tulip stand erect.

"This dress has been nothing but a nightmare," I said. "Yours is gorgeous but I bet you can't breathe either."

Jake's arm slipped around my waist. "You look beautiful." He nuzzled my ear. Sirena looked away as if witnessing his show of affection toward his wife was too much to bear. I snuggled closer to him. If I could sit through their love scene countless times she'd have to acknowledge some real-life husband and wife romance. I reached over and straightened his tie.

Ramona came back worse off than she'd left, slurring her words after the many martinis she'd drank. "Your wife has a six A.M. flight. She should be in bed, 'sleep right now." Her right eye flittered. She was the one who should've been in bed.

"I can sleep on the plane. It's a straight four-hour flight from Los Angeles to Atlanta. I'll be fine."

"I'll make sure she makes her flight," Jake affirmed.

"And you need your beauty rest, young man," Ramona said to Jake.

"Right."

"That's not going to happen," I said, giving him the sexy eye.

Again, obvious discomfort from Sirena. She excused herself and briskly moved to go talk to someone else.

"Let me say good-bye to a few folks and I'm ready to roll." Jake kissed my hand before heading off. The afterparty crowd had thinned. He made his way around thanking everyone.

"I know you're not trying to leave without talking to me." LL Cool J announced. Over the years, he'd transformed himself from a gold medallion, wife beater–clad sex symbol to now Todd Smith, wearing a clean, tapered black suit. He threw out a hand and shoulder-bumped Jake. This was the first time I'd seen him at any of the promotional events. He played Jake's brother, who died early in the movie. Jake's role was to avenge his death by taking up with the woman responsible, only he actually falls in love with the femme fatale, played by Sirena.

He was taller and overall better looking in person. I tried to act unaffected, but damn he was fine . . . if you liked that sort of thing. *Please, not the one-dimple smile.*

"This is my wife, Venus."

Oh, the smile.

"Very nice to meet you. Your man here is going places. Betta hold on tight."

"Don't worry. I have the only key to his ankle bracelet. He won't get far."

Jake kind of choked.

"Nice." Todd winked. "All right, man. Take it easy."

Jake leaned in my ear. "You're too much, you know that."

I watched him slowly making his way around, offering thank-you hugs and handshakes. Everyone wanted a piece of Jake these days. His phone buzzed constantly with offers to be at one place or another. Funny how one little film and the hit song on the soundtrack could change everything. From invisible to a name on everybody's lips. Extraordinary.

Well, he'd always been extraordinary to me, movie or not. I gazed back to Sirena and she was watching him too. No surprise there.

"All right, baby, let's hit it." He took my hand and I rushed to keep up with his elegant stride. Sirena watched, cognizant of the fact Jake hadn't directly said good-bye to her. I waved for him as a good cocaptain should. She gave a slight but disappointed smile.

"Honey, say good-bye to Sirena."

Jake squeezed my hand. "It's cool. It's not like I won't see her to-morrow."

And the next day, and the next, I was thinking. But it was also out of Jake's character. Trouble in paradise for the screen lovebirds. I'm not sure if it was a good thing or bad since it would mean emotions had spilled over into real life. My life.

Cinderella's Coach

A bright-eyed little boy faced me over the seat on the plane. He stared at me with cherub cheeks and intense brown eyes with infinitely long lashes that refused to blink. Our son would've been about his age. I still counted the months since the date of his birth. Twenty-eight. He would've been two and a half years old. It used to make me sad to be in the presence of other people's babies. Not anymore. I'd see my little guy in their eyes, I'd hear him in their laughter. After a minute or so I smiled; he smiled right back. I closed my eyes after having a staring contest with him. He won since I blinked first.

I shoved the iPod headphones in my ears and pushed PLAY on the playlist Jake made for me. I slept the entire way once my seat belt was snapped. I think I woke up once when they served omelets, croissants, and sausage. It smelled good. They served real food in first class, not the rickety stale peanuts and pretzels I was used to. But I wasn't hungry, only exhausted. The whirlwind partying and schmoozing had left my feet aching, and my big and pinky toes throbbed from standing around in high heels.

The fairy tale was over as quickly as it'd started. I was back in my Cinderella castle cooking and cleaning.

I kissed Mya on the forehead where she sat eating her breakfast. "Hey, sweetpea."

"I saw Daddy on TV with that lady again." Mya stuck a spoonful of oatmeal in her mouth. "She's pretty."

I scooted around in my house slippers, sat on the breakfast stool, and eyed my mother, Pauletta. "Mom, I asked you not to let Mya stay up watching television. Were you up with her? Or did you let her watch anything she wanted, flipping channels with reckless abandon?"

"I was in the room." She averted her eyes.

"Don't tell me, you fell asleep."

"You didn't ask me that. You said, was I in the room? And the answer is yes."

"Mom . . ."

"I think I would've heard panting or moaning if she landed on one of those nasty channels," my mother said, pouring herself some orange juice. "I'll tell you what I did see: Sirena what's-her-name sure was looking cozy with Jake. How much longer do they have to globe-trot promoting this movie?"

"I don't know."

"I'mma about sick of her. She's a pretty girl but do I really need to see her every day on every channel, on every magazine, on every—"

"Yes, I know. She's everywhere." And so my day began as my night had ended—with Sirena Lassiter on the brain.

"Well, you need to ask your husband. Like this . . . 'Honey, how much longer do you have to continue backpacking with Sirena what's-her-name?' Then he'll say, 'I see you're concerned. I'll put an end to it immediately.' Then you say, 'You need to bring your ass home.' I think he'll get the message real quick."

Her new bob-cut wig was slightly crooked. She'd started wearing the premiere Star Jones collection over the last year after the resurgence of the cancer she'd fought and, we'd thought, beaten. A full mastectomy on both breasts for safe measure, so it was a shock to learn it was back, this time in her right lymph node. The chemotherapy made her new hair growth come in thin. I tried to talk her into wearing it short and natural. Pauletta was not the one. She reminded me on many occasions that it was hard enough maintaining an air of femininity after what she'd gone through. The last thing she needed was to look in the mirror and see short boy hair staring back at her. In Pauletta's world, a good head of healthy hair and a good man made the woman—contrary to popular belief, it wasn't pricey handbags and shoes.

"Sirena's everywhere because everyone loves her." This was more an explanation for myself. I'd rehearsed it a number of times.

"Apparently *everyone* does." Pauletta grabbed the remote and pushed the volume up.

And so it continued. The entertainment segment of Channel 10 news showed a quick flash of the very event I'd attended with Jake, although no one would know this since I'd been shoved to the back of the crowd. Jake stood with his arm wrapped around Sirena's waist. She flashed her pearly whites and those big doe-in-the-headlight eyes.

My coffee got cold real fast. I poured it down the sink. "Let's go, Mya. We don't want to be late."

Pauletta turned the TV off. "Don't forget my flight out is at four."

I trailed behind Mya, sad at the thought of my mother leaving. As much as my mother liked to point out the brazen truth, I didn't want her to go. She'd come to stay with Mya so I could tour with Jake for a few of the premieres. I'd come to depend on her. My mother had been by my side for every up and every down of life. I knew she had to get back home to my father in Los Angeles. I just wished for a few more days with her and thought about asking her to stay—but why get in the way of love?

Mya's school was a twenty-minute drive. I never believed in private schooling. I thought people who threw away money like that were being show-offs. What was a first or second grader going to learn for an extra ten grand that she couldn't learn in the general population? Addition, subtraction, how to belittle and tease one another, were lessons equally taught amongst children of every income level. There was no getting around it.

However, once Jake got the role in the film, my tune changed. I had an entirely different view now that we could actually afford private school for Mya. I guiltily wrote out the deposit and accepted my new state of mind.

Whitherspoon Academy offered the best in early education. Cookies and warm milk were served at naptime. All the children wore cute little navy blue vests in the spring and blazers in the winter. Best of all, the school frowned upon and discouraged recess beatdowns by playground bullies. You could say I'd studied their brochure way too long.

To top it all off, it's what Mya wanted and begged for. This was the school Jory Stanton was attending, her *best-est* friend. They had survived preschool together, announced their undying love, and threatened to make life miserable for anyone who tried to separate the two. But at the time, we were broke. Jory's dad, Senator Robert Stanton, had even offered to pay for Mya's tuition just to keep the boy from being a first-grade dropout. But money hadn't been the only impediment.

The wait list to get into Whitherspoon was as long as my arm. Thank goodness the young woman who ran the front office was a big JP fan. She knew every song off his first album and couldn't believe her luck that he'd resurfaced in her office. We were suddenly bumped to the top of the list for the small price of an autograph and cameraphone picture with Jake. She nearly wore out her battery sending it out to all her friends.

"Wait for me, Jory!" Mya screamed from her open window.

The children were filing inside. The sprawling estate made of brick and flanked by tall white pillars was built in the 1800s by African settlers, or in layman's terms, slaves. At least there was a plaque at the entrance dedicated to a black man, Milo Redding, 1843–1892, for helping design the building. The inside parlor gleamed with hardwood floors and dark lacquered desks.

Jory's bashful smile lit up when he saw his partner in crime but he tried to keep his excitement under wraps in front of his buddies. The mop of dark blond hair had gotten thicker and curlier in the ripe old world of first graders. He was looking more and more like his father, who I was hoping was nowhere in sight.

Mya unbuckled her seat belt before I pulled to a complete stop at the curb. "Hold on, wait a minute. Kiss, kiss, little girl." I touch my cheek to show her where to plant it. "Have a good day, sweetpea."

"I love you, Mommy."

"I love you three times more," I boasted.

"Four," she yelled before slamming the door too hard. She escaped with her long twisted ponytail swaying with each step. It would be a giant puff by the end of the day. She was growing up so fast. She knew her own mind, kind of like me when I was her age. Except if I'd talked back as much as Mya, my mother would've shown me the door with a red knapsack tied on the end of a stick.

I eased out with caution, then hit the brakes.

"Yoo-hoo!" a voice called through the open window Mya had left down in the backseat. Not just any voice, but that of Paige Lawson, the room-mother who liked to delegate. There was a birthday party every Friday with confetti-sprinkled cupcakes ordered from Fredrica's Bakery, whether it was anyone's birthday or not. I guessed it was my turn to pick them up and distribute them to tiny unwashed hands.

I rolled down the front window to show I was ready to take on my duties. "Hi, Paige. How's it goin'?"

"Wonderful. Can't complain one iota." Her Southern drawl was artificially pitched for happiness. She, like the rest of the mothers of Whitherspoon Academy, refused to acknowledge frustration. There was no just cause for stress when life had blessed you with enough money to send your child to the finest private school in the state of Georgia.

"I saw your husband on TV last night. You must be in heaven right now."

"Yes, opportunities like this don't come often." I preened. But I was running late and hoped she got to the point.

"I guess so, honey, married to a movie star. You are the envy of all the girls." She looked around as if we were the new high school clique and everyone was dying to get in.

"Okay, well, it was good to see you."

"I have a huge favor. Big. Gigantic, so get ready. You ready?"

"I'm ready." My patience was running low like my gas tank. Idle conversation would leave me empty in more ways than one.

"This weekend I have to go out of town to see about my poor uncle who's in the hospital, and I need someone to take over the Hansel and Gretels this Saturday."

"I work on Saturdays, Paige. I would do it, if I could."

"This meeting doesn't start until six. It's only for the girls, so there'd be half the trouble. They're scheduled for a tea party and etiquette class. Please, oh pretty please."

"Okay. Sure," I agreed. Anything to stop her from pursing her gooey nude lips in a fake pout. Pink lipstick would forever be in the *don't* column. I put the Range Rover in gear. The car lurched forward and made a screwy noise.

"Whoa, looks like I know what you'll be spending all that new Hollywood money on."

I started over, putting the car in park then back to drive. The transmission had been slipping. No time to take it in for service. I had a business to run. I rolled up my windows to let her know, conversation over. The car moved forward without a glitch. I did a small baby wave. Paige blinked her eyes too many times, as if she weren't the one bothering me. The Hansel and Gretel Club began in the early 1920s specifically for children of color and privilege so they would have a place to celebrate achievement without feeling inferior. The twenty-first-century version of the Hansel and Gretels made sure to have pictures of children from all backgrounds and races on their Web site, but the underlying message was still clear. If your child wasn't a member of the H & Gs, eventually she or he would grow up without a sense of self, lost in the Barbie and Ken world, without a date to the prom—or worse, no spouse of the correct persuasion. Jake disagreed with putting Mya in the club. He didn't like groups that excluded people based on race, or any other sanctions. What kind of example were we setting? Yet he couldn't help but wince every time Mya mentioned the love of her life, Jory. He was Mya's best friend forever. His blond hair and blue eyes didn't bother Jake at all. He swore it was merely the fact that our five-year-old had already been bitten by the love bug. Wouldn't matter if the boy was green with polka dots, it was just wrong.

As I looped around the embankment and headed for the highway, I noticed the heavy gray cloud, then a loud boom of thunder. But just over the horizon there was a slither of orange where the sun refused to be outdone. I agreed, there were too many beautiful colors in the world to try and distinguish.

Kiss My Blessings

By the time I pulled up to In Bloom, the little flower shop that could, the street was showered with rain. I had two employees and one volunteer, Trevelle Doval, the most unlikely addition. She was my ex's ex. Normal circumstances could have made us compadres, having once loved the same man and then hating him jointly. However, that was not our case.

Trevelle was in the business of rubbing people the wrong way and I'd taken the brunt of it on one too many occasions, making it difficult to be pleasant in her company. Which was the reason I almost hated coming to work.

As expected, her white Jaguar sat in the one and only spot in front of my store. Kind of where paying customers were likely to park instead of out-of-work televangelists.

When she was married to *our ex*, Airic Fisher, she encouraged him to take me to court for full custody of Mya. Jake and I had been married for three years, raising Mya together. In that time Airic hadn't made one appearance as Mya's biological father. Jake was the only father Mya knew. Yet, out of the blue, along came Airic like a spider with his new wife to show us what real parents looked like. The custody battle turned ugly.

The holy duo pulled out Jake's past—his arrest for the murder of his accountant—and mine: my short visit on the psychiatric floor at St. Francis Hospital after I'd accidentally overdosed on antianxiety medication. Anyone on the outside looking in would've agreed that Jake and I were unfit parents. The cards were stacked against us. However, the real motivations were soon revealed. It had never been about us being bad for Mya. Trevelle wanted Mya for her own selfish reasons, to replace the child she'd lost long ago and complete her new perfect family. We almost lost Mya to a bunch of scheming manipulative tricks by everyone involved. For the first time in my life, I was sure God was on my side . . . regardless of what Trevelle's Jaguar license plate said—FAVORED. Divine intervention was the only way to explain Jake and I keeping Mya. Keeping our family together. And every morning I am reminded of Trevelle's high jinks with her presence.

"Good morning," she sang out as she saw me enter. Trevelle's long spindly fingers held on to her steaming cup of coffee. "I saw your hubby on the Entertainment channel last night. He's just a regular Will Smith about to happen, isn't he."

I ignored her.

I set my purse and keys under the granite workspace, hidden away safe. I didn't want another incident where my car keys were accidentally taken by Vince Capricio and I was left to drive Trevelle's car. The last time turned out to be the most traumatic night of my life: kidnapped last summer by hit men, hired criminals who thought I was the famous televangelist since I was driving her car at the time. The memory of the ordeal was as vivid as if it were yesterday. I'd fought for my life, and not in some metaphorical context. I mean kicking, biting, scratching, and punching like my life depended on it—and it did. Every swing I got in sent a message that I wasn't giving up. The night ended with my eye blackened and bruises all over my body, but the other guy looked far worse.

I gave as good as I got.

The kidnappers suddenly dropped me off at the same place they'd originally snatched me. I figured they thought I was too much trouble; only later I learned the reason. They'd simply realized their mistake of taking the wrong woman. I secretly wished they'd gotten the right woman. Nothing Trevelle did, even to warrant a carload of hired hit men, would surprise me.

"Hey li'l lady, I caught a glimpse of you in that red number. You were looking hot." Vince spoke up coming from the backroom carrying beautiful floral arrangements in each hand. He set them down and gave me a welcome-home hug. He was the one and only reason Trevelle wasn't banned from my sight. For whatever reason, he and Trevelle's unholy union was working. And if Vince was happy, we were all happy. He was the glue that kept In Bloom together.

"Yeah, like a hot chili pepper. My dress was atrocious."

"Hey, I wouldn't have seen you if you didn't stand out." Vince had finally let the gray hair show through around his temples. I liked it so much better than the jet-black dye. Now his eyebrows matched his hair.

"You need to hire a stylist and stop winging it," Trevelle interjected. "You obviously have no fashion sense." Trevelle leaned over and picked up one of the many bridal magazines stacked nearby. "I'm going to show you what you should be wearing. Then we'll talk about your hair."

She cleared her throat, preparing us for her amazing words of wisdom. We were her only audience these days. Her following had dwindled after a public scandal. After *our ex* had been caught cheating with an underaged girl, along with news of a sex tape, Trevelle was painted as the wayward wife. Had she been a committed servant in the marriage, her husband would never have strayed, or something completely off base. She was cast out like a leper, while *our ex* got off scotfree.

Airic got half ownership of Doval Ministries Incorporated, which he quickly liquidated. He got a boatload of Trevelle's millions in the divorce settlement, but she still had a good enough share not

to be stressed, or be forced to take up gainful employment. The very
reason she had time to grace us with her presence every single day.
It made one question the whole forgiveness platform of the big Chris-
tian picture. The minute one of our angels fell from grace the
churchfolk stomped all over her helpless body. If it were a man
who'd fallen from grace, say for being caught with another man, or
female prostitute, he simply would've repented and quickly been
put back in the pulpit. But no . . . the powers-that-be left Trevelle
Doval on my doorstep like an abandoned child and simply forgot
about her.

"You see, you need to accentuate your positives. That would be
your legs . . . they're short but they have great definition. You can
make them appear longer and leaner by showing more thigh, like
this." She held up the open magazine to a gazelle-limbed model.
"You see how it elongates the leg?"

"For your information, the publicist picked out that dress," I
said, trying to harness my frustration.

"Obviously this publicist thought very little of you. This is not a
time to let yourself be deemed irrelevant. The significant other can
become insignificant when all the light is shining on your beloved
hubby. Airic was so insecure in our relationship. No light shining in
his direction. That's why he found comfort in another woman's arms."

"Yeah, I'm sure that was the reason."

Vince caught me before I could elaborate and gave a disapproving glare. He was very protective of his lady friend these days, constantly reminding me that she was vulnerable and deserving of
some tender love and care. "She needs our patience. One day you'll
be rewarded for your good deed," he'd said after I'd threatened him
with my *either her or me* speech.

Ignoring my contempt she continued, "Try not to be bitter. But
trust me, you don't want him to dim his light just to make you feel
better. I did that with Airic and you saw where that got me."

"Trevelle, do you really want to give me advice on how to keep my husband happy?"

This time, a sharp cut of the eyes from Vince. "I've got deliveries to make. Coming, my lady?" Code for, we're leaving you alone to stew in your rudeness.

But she started it, I wanted to say.

Trevelle stuck out her hand like a true damsel and let Vince escort her out the door. She looked back at me as if to say, kiss my blessings.

I just shook my head. Regardless of how she tried to hide it, she was hurting, and it wasn't fair to kick her when she was down. Even more cruel was leaving her to find solace here with me and Vince. I'd taken this up with God on countless closed-eye, clenched-teeth prayer sessions, asking Him to restore Trevelle's career so she could get back in the pulpit and I could once again be at peace.

When they left, I pulled out my cell phone and dialed Jake's number. He was still in L.A. He and Sirena had an early-morning interview, the one I'd made sure to miss. Jake answered on the first ring. "Hey, baby."

"Hi there, Mr. Superstar, you doing all right without me?"

"Never. I miss you like crazy."

"Really? I'm surprised Ramona hasn't lassoed you up in her Wonder Woman rope to make you forget about me and focus only on promoting the movie."

He laughed but added nothing to the conversation.

"So where's the party tonight?"

"Party? Come on now, I told you. It's all work and no play."

"Yeah, right. You're forgetting I was there."

He got quiet again on the other end of the phone.

"Babe . . . everything all right?" I asked.

"Guess who just walked by? You'll never believe it. Angelina and Brad."

"Oh . . . first names and all." I smiled into the phone. "So you're still at the news studio?"

"Yeah, but we're about to head out to get something to eat. I'm just ready to sleep in my own bed. I'm officially whooped."

"Well, you don't look tired. You looked great on the interview," I said, even though I hadn't watched a second of it. "So when will you be coming home?" I remembered my mother's endearing words of advice: *"Then you say, 'You need to bring your ass home.' I think he'll get the message real quick."*

"I'm planning on tomorrow. But you know how everything's last minute when these interviews come through."

"I understand."

"Babe, you know I miss you. You know I love you. Say it with me . . ."

"You are my starship." I smiled into the phone again.

"That's right. I'm out here in the sea and there's only one light that will always lead me home."

"Don't overdo it, mister." Still smiling.

He was silver tongued and clever. I was no match for his swift attention to detail. He knew I was nervous about his spending so much time with Sirena. He knew my every fear. He saw me coming a mile away and always knew how to head me off.

"You're all I need, baby."

"Okay, well, I better get to work. I've got a business to run." I snapped out of my love trance.

"Babe, I've been meaning to talk to you about that."

I already knew the next thing he was about to say.

"You know we only moved to Atlanta because I was running from demons. Well I'm not running anymore. I think we should pack it up, make L.A. our home again."

I stayed quiet. I should've been ecstatic to hear those words. I'd wanted to move back to Los Angeles the day we set foot in our new house in Atlanta. Too much space. Everything was so spread out and never ending, including our mini mansion with six-too-many bathrooms. But now Mya was at a good school, my business was doing exceptionally well, and I'd signed a new lease on the building.

"Please, just think about it."

"It's just hard now to uproot Mya."

"I never in a million years thought we'd be having this conversation. I thought the minute I said, let's move, you'd have a truck in front of the house, loading it up like Jed Clampett."

"Funny. Just let me think about it, okay?"

I busied myself clipping stems, relishing in the quiet. A quarter inch off every couple of days kept the flowers fresh and ready for presentation. The bell rang, signaling a customer had come through the door. I usually kept it locked when I was alone but I'd forgotten to lock it after Vince left. I felt safe when he was around, making his worth far more important than how many flowers he could arrange and deliver.

The afternoon sun was harsh in the front of the building, so anyone who walked in looked like a Hitchcock silhouette. Except for this woman. Her broad bony shoulders were held up with a pencil-thin body. I hated to make assumptions based on appearance, but she was definitely not a bride-to-be. I could spot a happy future wife by her rosy attitude, the relief of the search being over. This woman was flat and dull, reeking of stale cigarette smoke. "Hello."

"Welcome. How can I help you?"

She put out her hand. "I'm Melba Dubois from *Life 'N' Style* magazine. You're JP's wife, right?"

"Yes. Did we have an appointment?" I gulped nervous air. Ramona had a clear policy on talking to the media—never speak with anyone without her screening. No ifs, ands, or buts. Clear enough. Besides, Jake's past was easy enough to investigate. They hardly needed me for information.

One Google punch of his name and his life appeared. Chronicled perfectly starting when he went to Morgan State University at eighteen and ended up with a demo after spending all his waking hours rapping on his roommate's makeshift studio equipment. A record deal and an album followed that went platinum. He then parlayed his popularity and money into a lucrative line of urban clothing. When his company began to show signs of going under it was due to his embezzling accountant. The accountant and his crooked pen nearly destroyed everything Jake had built.

When the accountant was found dead Jake was the likely suspect. Jake was eventually cleared, but his business partner and former best friend, Legend Hill, was still sought after for questioning. The story was all upward from there—a contract modeling for Calvin Klein, shortly after his movie with Sirena, and here we are. So whatever Melba Dubois had come for wasn't on the up and up.

"I'm sorry you came all this way. I'm really not supposed to talk to anyone from the media, as much as I'd love to."

"Our magazine wants to find out who you are, what kind of woman snags a catch like Jake Parson. Do you mind if I have a seat?" She had a husky British accent. I presumed a pack of cigarettes a day in lieu of food. Her thin legs crossed while she pulled out a copy of the magazine's current issue and handed it to me.

This month's glossy cover featured Sirena Lassiter, no surprise there. I'd read the gripping article in its entirety in the grocery checkout line, letting people with less items go in front of me just so I could absorb every word. The story revealed another side to the pop princess who'd been abandoned by her mother when she was a young girl. She'd had a bout with drugs and abusive boyfriends before going into rehab and coming out of therapy all shiny and new. There was no mention of her loveable co-star, Jake Parson. When the article had been written, no one knew of Jake's rise as an actor, or that the song he'd performed and produced on the soundtrack would be number one on the *Billboard* chart.

"I can't talk to you without an okay from the publicist, even if it's about me. Strict orders. Sorry."

"Ramona, correct? Assigned by Rise Records. She's a hard nut—and I mean that literally." She sneered. "Trust me, she's not working for you or your husband. Once the buzz wears off about this movie, she'll be a puff of smoke. People have to care who you are, who your husband is, if he expects to sustain a career in this business."

"Really, even if Ramona called right now and said, go ahead, talk away, I don't have anything to tell you. I'm uninteresting. I don't have a great Hollywood tale. I've never been on drugs or had to overcome the urge to put my finger down my throat after a big meal." I raised my hands with nothing else to offer.

She smiled slyly. "But you did try to end your own life after losing a child, correct?" She slipped her tape recorder onto the antique coffee table. She pushed the red button, which was a waste of time seeing as how I was speechless. "Incidentally, it was around the same time Jake was arrested and charged with homicide."

"This is not news," I said coolly.

"Exactly. Our readers want to be connected. They already have the news. The human emotion, what you went through, how you were there for each other in a time of sadness and stress—that's what's missing. Stress . . . probably contributed to the loss of your baby, correct?" She sang out like she was on a game show and it wasn't my life she was talking about.

"You know, it would be nice to rehash all of those wonderful emotions, but like I said, I can't." My throat felt tight and dry. It took everything I had to keep my voice even and steady.

"I understand. I'd be cautious too if my husband and his first love were gallivanting about exotic locales, rekindling old feelings and being paid, to boot. Lovely."

I bit the inside of my jaw to stop from making a fool of myself. First love? If I uttered a single word I might even appear shocked by this revelation. Which was how I felt—shocked, mortified, ready to pick up the nearest object and hurl it in her direction, and scream, *Get out,* like a raging poltergeist. "I think you should go now" came out instead, with surprising calm. I stepped back, giving her room to exit.

"I'm hoping you'll give it some thought." She handed me her business card. "I'm available night or day, whenever the spirit hits you. Everyone needs to talk sometime. Good for the soul." She showed teeth not necessarily in a genuine smile; more like in anticipation of her next feeding. This woman was here to suck me dry of any joy my day had left to offer.

This time I made sure the door was locked. I watched from the window as she took her time getting into the small tan rental car. She flipped open her cell phone and talked for a few minutes. Her eyes darted back at the window and I ducked.

When I peeked back out she was gone.

Lights Out

The parking lot was full. Dance class started at six thirty. If you didn't arrive at least half an hour early you could forget about a parking space. I held Mya's hand and we walked a solid two blocks before the white house with giant lit ballerina slippers came into view.

"Almost there," I huffed, out of breath. There'd been little time for workouts. The in-house gym had the latest and greatest equipment, one of the perks Jake spent a ton of money on when we'd first bought the house. Only problem was remembering to go down the hall and turn right. The house was huge, which was my other workout—stairs, and long stretches of hallway. I got my exercise going up and down the stairs. In the floral shop carrying vases filled with water and floral arrangements, which weighed a lot, left me spent like I'd done a few reps with barbells.

The place was jam-packed with tired mothers wearing sullen faces. So it was a relief to hear my name. "Venus, over here. I saved you a seat." Miriam Rivera was waving. It was cold and rainy outside and she was still wearing a sundress. She claimed her Cuban roots made it impossible to cool down. She kept her shiny thick hair cut short, claiming she would sweat like a pig if she carried a pound of hair on her shoulders.

Mya ran and joined the line of miniature ballerinas in their tutus. I slipped off my jacket and unwrapped the scarf around my neck. I sat next to Miriam, glad to get off my feet.

First thing I saw was the face of Sirena staring back at me. There was no escaping her. She was on the cover of the *People* magazine sitting on Miriam's lap. Her eyes followed mine. She tried to sweep a hand over the magazine to make it disappear. Like a horrible curse, the pages fell open to the center picture of Sirena and Jake posed from one of their many red-carpet nights.

"Girl, I'm sure you're sick of this one." Miriam's slight Spanish accent was full of concern. Most of her early English came from watching *Sesame Street*. When Miriam was seven, her family sailed from Cuba to the baseline of Florida on a inflatable tube boat. Neither her mother nor father could speak English. That didn't stop her. She quickly became an A student. She swears if she could make something out of herself, anyone could and should. I ignored her proud Republican sticker on her hybrid bumper. She had a heart pure as gold.

I reached over and grabbed the *People*. "She's not that pretty in person," I said, holding it up. "If you look close you can see little hairs coming out her nostrils." I handed it back.

Miriam let out a raucous laugh that made every head turn. I was smiling too. The absurdity of the entire situation was laughable. Not many women could stand up to the pressure of their husbands linked arm in arm with a beautiful, popular actress. The pressure was already too great to maintain some kind of self while comparing yourself to the airbrushed beauties of the world. To know one personally and have her infiltrate your personal space was enough to send one over the edge. I was quite proud of how I was handling things, especially in lieu of the special-edition news I'd received from Melba Dubois. *First love.* The words rolled painfully around in my stomach; either that, or I was starving.

"Aren't they cute." Miriam nudged me to focus on the little princesses, and a few princes. "We should go get some dinner after this, just us girls."

"Hey, what about me? I can be one of the girls." Robert Stanton leaned his head between us. His politician smile and movie-star good looks hardly blended in as one of the girls.

"Senator Stanton, you are more than welcome to join us, as long as you ask your wife for permission first," Miriam chided.

"Sure. I'll give her a call right now." He pulled up his phone. I snatched it out of his hand.

"Don't you dare."

"Okay, just kiddin'." He had an infectious Southern accent. I gave the phone back to him. His wife, Holly Stanton, evoked fear out of me and anyone else who came into her airspace. She was a lean, mean former WNBA basketball player who held her head high at all times to balance her imaginary tiara. She probably hadn't smiled since she was in grade school. She took her status as a senator's wife seriously and would cut anyone who threatened the castle.

"Besides, I can't." I looked past him to Miriam. "I'm exhausted. I just want to get home and slide my head under the shower, then climb into bed. Plus, my mother is still here."

"She is? I thought she was leaving."

"I know, but at the last minute she said she wanted to stay a few more days." I hunched my shoulders, trying not to add anything else to the list of bewilderments of my day.

"Then we invite her too. One big party. I'll cook. Ben is on call so we'll have wine and talk, talk, talk a regular ol' henfest."

I caught the tail end of Mya's turn. Jory was her partner. I had to admit they looked like the cutest couple up there.

"*Bahhk,*" Robert made the noise of a bird. "Can't be a decent hen-fest without a rooster. Every hen needs a strong rooster. It's the law of the farm."

I clapped for Mya, ignoring him.

"Oh, I think I'm going to cry," a mother a few seats away announced. "Look at Isabel, she's so beautiful. Isn't she beautiful?"

Miriam whispered, "Good grief, it's a practice recital, not the child's wedding day."

The hour felt like it would never end. The director was a lean older woman who still had a ballerina's body. She finally came and stood in the center of the kids and gave them the closing pep talk.

"You are light angels with wings. You can do all things great. There are no mistakes, only opportunities to learn, to grow, to try again." She tapped the girls lightly on the head as a signal they were excused. Mya was the last one standing. The director kneeled on one knee and must've offered an extra dose of motivation. Mya nodded with enthusiasm before coming toward me.

"Miss Perry says I'll be great."

"Of course you will be."

"She says she'll film it on her camera in case Daddy can't be there."

Miriam gave me a perplexed grin. I hunched my shoulders, not sure how Ms. Perry and Mya's conversation had come about. "Honey, don't worry. Daddy will be there."

"She says if he isn't, I should still do my best because he'll see it on film. I'll be in a movie just like him."

"Yes. Okay." I knew how to end the subject quickly. "Guess what, we're going over Lizzie's house," I decided right then and there.

Miriam's daughter, Lizzie, bounced up and down as this was news to her. The girls reached out and hugged each other. Probably best if I went to Miriam's. If I went home in the mood I was in, I would do nothing but sit and keep thinking about what the journalist had said . . . *first love*. I didn't believe that woman. Jake would've told me something like that. But once a poisonous dart was shot in your neck, even if you pulled it out, the effects were still dizzying.

"I had to park a couple of blocks away," I thought I was telling Miriam.

But it was Robert Stanton's arm around my shoulder. "I'll give you a ride to your car."

I shucked him off. "You're sick, you know that."

"It's the thrill of the chase," Miriam chimed in. "Right? You men like to chase, but once you catch, you want to throw 'em back in the sea."

"Not true. I only hunt what I plan to eat." He made his eyebrows dance. Miriam fake-punched him in the stomach.

"Can I go to Lizzie's house too?" Jory asked, holding on to his dad's hand.

"Now that's not proper to invite yourself, son." Robert Stanton moved with Jory in tow directly behind us.

"Can he come?" the girls asked in unison. "Please."

I looked at Miriam. She shrugged her shoulders, like it was fine with her.

"We'll take the boy," I said. "But you stay. I'll bring him home after."

"Now that's just rude. We're a dynamic duo. He's Robin to my Batman. Tonto to my Lone Ranger." He saw he wasn't getting anywhere. "You know, those two little dashes creased right in the center of your forehead, they're not healthy. Sign of worrying too much."

"Don't you have laws to enact or budgets to cut?"

Miriam nudged. "Just let him come. I certainly don't mind."

"Seriously," I whispered. "If he's invited, I probably should go home."

She nodded. "Okay, okay. I get it. The man's got a serious jones for some mocha, is all I have to say." She then turned and mouthed, "Sorry" to Robert.

I could've explained that Robert wasn't genuinely hurt, to alleviate her guilt. Tomorrow would be like today never happened. The historical cat-and-mouse game had gone on for the past couple of years and would continue. No harm, no foul.

I called my mother and told her I was having dinner over a friend's house. I asked her if she wanted to join us. Pauletta had never been a social butterfly. She kept to herself, except for her sisters and my dad.

"You go, I'll be right here. I have some reading I need to catch up on." That meant another Nora Roberts novel. She read them in two days or less, sometimes not realizing it was a repeat from years ago until she'd finished. "I think I read that one before," it would dawn on her. "Oh well, still enjoyable." I'd tried to bring her to the here and now, show her novelists of the twenty-first century who wrote about characters in *our* world. She absolutely wanted none of that. She had plenty of *our* world firsthand. She didn't need to read about it. Stories of the old black South, or the new black Rich, and anything in between was, by her account, stereotypical nonsense. "Black folks are too entrenched in the hard-knock life. I want to be swept away in romance with a guaranteed happy ending."

Didn't we all.

Miriam's house was completely dark when we pulled up. I'd only been over in the daytime so I wasn't sure if this was normal. Conservatives conserving electricity—that would be a first. The perplexed look Miriam gave me said it was definitely a first.

"My garage opener isn't working."

I kept a close step behind her with the kids flanked on my hip. She unlocked her front door to freezing darkness. She flipped the light switches up and down. "What in the world? I think my power's out."

"I can't believe this," Miriam said as she banged her knee on the foyer table. "Damn it," she hissed.

"Get some clothes and come stay at my house. You can't stay here. It's too cold not to have electricity."

"Ooooh, oooooh," Jory sang out like a ghost. "I'm going to get you." He raised his hands like in Michael Jackson's "Thriller" video. The girls squealed.

"Do you have a flashlight? Let's just get a few of your things and head over to my house." I wasn't about to spend any more time standing in the dark than I had to. After a while the ghost teasing wasn't so funny. Mya grabbed both my hands, letting me know she felt the same way. *I'm scared, Mommy.*

The streetlamp offered enough light to see the glint of moistness in Miriam's eyes. "I can't believe this shit." She stomped off toward the kitchen.

I waited with the kids in the foyer, just in case we needed to make a fast exit. I was no amateur to dangerous situations. Car chases, kidnapping, hostage scenarios at gunpoint—all part of the résumé since being married to Jake Parson.

Most believed once you were man and wife, the excitement sailed out of your life like air from a leaky tire. Not true. Jake and I had adventure. Some good, some bad, but we survived and it only made us stronger and more committed. I was glad to remind myself of this fact. We had and would continue to survive anything. *First loves* included.

"This is like the haunted mansion at Disney World," Mya said to Lizzie. "Have you been to Disney World?"

"Yep, but I can't remember 'cause I'm six and my daddy says I was too little to know what a good time I had."

"I remember. Do you remember, Mommy?" Mya's upturned face deserved a kiss. I planted one right between the eyes.

"Yes, we had a great time. Now let's try to be quiet in case Miriam needs us." I was uneasy and cold. Either could've been responsible for my teeth chattering. "Okay—," I felt a tap on my shoulder. I screamed and nearly jumped out of my skin. "Miriam, you scared the . . . out of me." I clutched my chest. "Where'd you come from?"

"I'm sorry. The back stairs. Sorry." Lizzie held on to her mommy. Mya and Jory clung to me. It was time to leave the haunted mansion.

Dual-edged Hot Comb

Miriam's bag sat on the chair in the kitchen. I picked up the *People* magazine and stared at the cover with Sirena in her skimpy bikini while I waited for the water to boil for our tea. Studying her perfect photo, her bronze dewy skin shimmering with youth, made me a bit insecure. She was only twenty-nine; not even thirty. I was knocking on my fortieth birthday. Jake was six years younger than me. It never seemed a concern until now. Her long signature straight hair floated with the fake breeze made by a studio fan. Her sexy smile was accentuated by two small moles at her laugh line. I studied every lash on her eyes and even counted them.

"You need any help?" Miriam came into the kitchen and stopped abruptly when she saw me holding the magazine. "Oh . . . girl, don't do it to yourself. She's airbrushed. You said so yourself." She helped herself to the cabinet, finding the assortment of teas I kept in a wood tray.

I pushed the magazine back in her bag. I couldn't say what was really on my mind. I'd learned a long time ago to be careful about speaking things into existence.

Miriam realized I wasn't my usual talkative self and faced me with concern. "You have nothing to be worried about. Now me, I've got issues. When your man lets the lights go out in Georgia, there's a problem." She poured the water in both cups. She handed one to me with the bag still steeping.

"Thanks." I pursed my lips and blew the heat before taking a sip. "I'm okay, really. Sometimes I let my imagination run wild."

"Tell me about it. I've been letting mine go crazy from the minute I walked into that dark house. Ben didn't pay the electricity bill. In fact, we've been having money problems for a while now. You know the first thing come to my mind . . . where's the money going? Who's he spending it on?" She let her head fall into her hands and suddenly burst into tears.

"Miriam? Oh my gosh . . . sweetie. It's going to be okay." I rushed from the table around to her side and hugged her. "What's going on? You can stay here till this gets fixed. We have plenty of room."

Pauletta came inside the kitchen, not noticing the angst in the room. "I'm heading to bed. The kids are playing. You might want to keep an eye on 'em. This is about the age they start playing Doctor."

"Okay, good night, Mom."

"Miriam, it was nice to meet you. I was beginning to think my daughter had no friends."

"*Good night,* Mom," I said with tight lips.

"See you in the morning. Keep the noise down. No wild parties," she sang out while going up the stairs.

Miriam covered her face with both her hands and then raked them through her cropped curls. I'd never noticed her beautiful widow's peak. "I'm so, so embarrassed. I really am," she finally confessed. "Ben is responsible for the bills. But lately things have been going unpaid. I worked my butt off to earn my degree in biology. I was going to go to med school too, but Ben convinced me we only needed one doctor in the family."

I reached out and touched her hand. "Tell me what's going on."

"Money issues. I don't know where it all goes. I just know the notices keep coming—pink ones, yellow ones, blue ones too." She chuckled. "I sound like a Dr. Seuss rhyme, ah."

She took a sip of her tea. Ironic how we'd planned the evening for my distraction. Now here I was consoling Miriam.

"You're going to have to take control of the situation. Make him sit down with you and go over all the accounts and bills. Figure out the problem . . . and if you have to sell your house and scale down, so be it."

The tea spurted out of her mouth when she choked on the idea. So much for my advice giving.

"Scale down? No, he needs to stop whatever he's doing. He's seeing someone, I know it."

My eyebrows raised. "Never make that accusation unless you have proof. I know this from my own experience. You can think it all you want, but until you have concrete, real evidence, it's the worst thing you can say."

"It's obvious. Where I come from, there are only two things a man will lose his money on: a woman, or an addiction. He's too smart to be on drugs. The smell of beer makes him sick. So guess what's left? A female . . ." She paused. "Or God forbid, a male. I remember the way this waiter was making eyes at him and he was completely flattered. He should've been insulted, but he was flattered. Oh Lord, I hope it's not a man."

"Stop it. Not another word." The phone started ringing, interrupting our heated debate. Jake checking in, nine o'clock on the dot. "Miriam, I have to get this." Already up on my feet, moving to the phone. "If I don't answer, I may not get to talk to Jake until morning and then he'll worry." I felt small and inadequate as a member of the sisterhood, taking a call from my ruler while Miriam was having a minor breakdown.

I faced the wall like an undercover agent, "Hi, baby," I mumbled. "Yes, we're in for the night, safe and sound, home," I said awkwardly as if there was another place we would be. "We had pizza." Jake was surprised to hear this after I'd put the bad mouth on every chain pizza place within a ten-mile radius. Not one could deliver a hot pizza. "Ahuh, I know, it was kind of last minute. Miriam from ballet class is here, and her daughter, and Jory, so we made it a party."

By the time I'd hung up, Miriam didn't want to talk anymore. Good thing, because I was wrung out from whispering *I love you* and *I miss you* while talking to the enemy. The entire time I wanted to ask him about Sirena and if she really was his first love and why if it was true had he felt the need to keep it from me. But I was taking my own advice. What did it matter if it were true? We were in the here and now. The past was gone and buried.

I'd gotten Miriam settled into the guest bedroom next to my mother's room. The entire left side of the house was filled with rooms I would never use. The house was a monstrosity that seemed to grow bigger every year. The busier I got, the less I ventured beyond Jake's office downstairs or Mya's bedroom one door away from ours. I didn't want cobwebs to accost anyone who crossed the threshold so I had a housekeeper come every other week strictly to vacuum and swipe at the air.

Next, I dialed Robert Stanton's cell number. He picked up before it even rang. "You looking for me?" he asked in a lazy seductive voice.

I put on my professional parent hat. "Senator, I know I said I would drop Jory off, but we ended up at my house kind of in crisis mode. I was hoping you could pick Jory up from here."

"Absolutely not," he said jokingly. "You keep him. That kid's nothing but trouble."

"So about fifteen minutes, then?" I said, ignoring the chuckle in the back of my throat. I looked at my watch. In fifteen minutes I had a date with the information highway.

Taste Like Honey

"Have I told you how amazing you are?"

Jake had only hung up a few seconds ago and figured his wife was calling back with something she forgot to say the first time. Instead it was Sirena's voice in his ear. He grinned into the phone. "Nah, not this week." He yawned. "Wassup?"

"I'm laying here with my eyes wide open."

"Still got that insomnia thing, huh?" He yawned again.

"Yep, and I see you still need your beauty sleep. What time do you usually go to bed in suburbia?"

"Ten, eleven. Suburbia is a big job. Lots of responsibilities."

"Carpool, yardwork, PTA meetings? You'll be back in fairy-tale land tomorrow." Sirena chuckled. "I'm totally impressed the way you've settled . . ." She let the word hit him between the eyes before she finished, ". . . into your life, Jay as a father, husband, and now superstar."

"Just a regular superhero." He could play along. Or he could fight back and say he wouldn't trade his life for a second of hers. But he'd learned a while back not to put up a fight unless there was a benefit, preferably the kind with dead presidents.

There was definitely no benefit in antagonizing Sirena. She had a devilish temper. One snap . . . she was not someone you wanted on your bad side. Once a week it seemed he had to endure her zingers about his marital status, how boring his life must've been before she appeared to save the day. There was no point in fighting back. Insecurity. Hers. Not his. Not his issue. "So what, you want me to sing you to sleep?" he asked, adjusting himself in the luxurious king-size bed.

"God, no."

"Right. Off-pitch."

"Among other things. I just called to say good night." She paused. "And to say we make a good team. Thank you."

"You're thanking me? I wouldn't be here without you, and I know that. But you, you're Sirena Lassiter. You didn't need me."

"That's where you're wrong. If you hadn't written 'Taste Like Honey' for me all those years ago, I wouldn't be Sirena Lassiter. I'd be some no-name wishing for stardom." She sniffed into the phone. Tears. "I need you. I've always needed you."

He had no response. No right answer. "Try to get some sleep."

She stayed silent. Jake had his finger on the button to end the call. Before he could push it, she asked him a simple question. "Do you ever wonder what would've happened with us?"

You mean if you hadn't run off stealing the writing credit on the song that sold a million records?

"Taste Like Honey" had put Sirena on the map, but he never came out and called her on it. One of their many unspoken truths that would remain buried. "I try not to worry about the past. What's the point?"

"Good night, Jay."

"Good night."

Sirena hung up, but kept the phone tightly gripped in her palm. She couldn't come up with anyone else to call. She scrolled down the same countless frennemies in her address book. Her fiancé, Earl Benning, wasn't even on the list. He did not like to chitchat about mundane issues such as emotions, only a black and white world, no area or time for gray matters.

Last resort was her father. She pressed the button and waited for him to answer.

"I saw you on that entertainment news show," Larry said over the phone. "You and JP still have that magic together."

She smiled, finally hearing something pleasing to her ears. "We do make a nice couple."

"Dumpling, he's a married man. I think you're the one who told me that. With a family, a daughter, am I right?"

"That's not my problem," she said, more so to tease. He didn't respond. "I'm just kidding. Really. He does have a beautiful family and I'd never try to come between him and his life. I'm just saying, sometimes, fate has a way of working out. Sometimes things are already written in stone."

Again, no response from Larry Lassiter. If he knew anything about his daughter it was that she hardly left anything to chance. She worked for every scrap and crumb, leaving nothing on the table. If Larry Lassiter knew anything about his daughter, it was that Jake Parson's world was about to be turned upside down.

"I wish you could be happy, just once, babygirl. You have so much to be thankful for."

She laughed. "Really? Happy? Daddy," she sang out with a tsk-tsk, though she never called him Daddy unless she wanted something. She called him Larry, the same as a buddy on the street. He'd always begged her to call him Dad, Pop, or some other false endearment that implied love and protection. "There is nothing I want more. You're right. I think it's about time I found happiness."

"Now listen, this is not the time to start any trouble."

"Thank you. Wise words of advice as always."

"I know what you're thinking. But he's got a life. You don't want to hurt him."

"I'm not trying to hurt anybody. Besides, he's a grown man. No one can make him *do* anything."

"Grown men are nothing but boys looking for the latest and greatest toy. You don't want to be his temporary plaything. I suggest you keep it sophisticated."

Sirena squinted with disgruntled confusion. Larry Lassiter had always thought so little of women, especially her. She wasn't gullible anymore. She thought he'd gotten the memo, especially after she'd instructed her accountant to cut back on the three thousand a month stipend. Instead of taking care of the household he'd been squandering it on Indian casinos for the last year or so. She was the one who called the shots. Sirena Lassiter didn't owe anybody a damn thing.

"Whatever, okay. I have to go."

"Well, you haven't even asked about Christopher. He's got a role in a play. Going to be Romeo. The boy's real proud. Maybe you can come."

"I got another call." She didn't wait for him to say good-bye before hanging up. Again her phone sat silent in her palm.

Information Highway

As soon as I settled onto the couch to impatiently wait for the senator, the door knocker clicked. I thought about rushing to get Jory so I wouldn't have to let the senator in. In that short time, he knocked again. Guess everyone was in a hurry these days.

"Coming."

"I thought you'd never give in. And look, it's after midnight and my dreams have been answered. Take me." He opened his arms.

I snatched him inside. "Would you stop that?"

He stuck out his lips. "I bet if you kissed me, you'd like it. Then we could carry on a passionate love affair for about three months," he whispered.

"And then what . . . after the three months? Tell them what we've won, Bob." I raised my arms and announced, "Divorces for everyone. Broken homes, sad and depressed children, and a lifetime of bad memories." I folded my arms over my chest. "Now you need to stop it, you hear?" I poked him in the center of his chest. "You're setting a bad example for your son."

He stroked the area. "I will never wash this shirt again."

"Go. Sit. Over there. I'll get your little prodigy."

When he was wrapped in his jacket and scarf, Jory gave me a long hug good-bye. I ran my hands over his dark blond curls and told him he was welcome anytime. For his dad I simply closed the door,

nearly catching his shoulder in the doorway. After I'd sent the dashing duo off I rushed to the laptop computer with eager fingers. I
needed more information on Sirena.

According to what I found, Sirena Lassiter knew she was going to be
famous. Her mother, Tammy, only eighteen, had entered Sirena into
a baby pageant when she was still in diapers. Her father liked to be-
smirch Tammy's good name, calling her a gold digger and opportunist. She abandoned her baby and husband after all, for a backup
singing gig with Sly and the Family Stone. Obviously Sirena's mother
had believed in her . . . at one time. So it didn't matter what her father said. She kept the first-place trophy sitting on her mantel to
show proof to anyone who doubted her story, right behind the album cover. The sepia-toned image of Tammy's face half covered by
another band member's shoulder was the only picture she had of her
mother. The picture and the trophy were what kept her going. Some
called it destiny. She called it determination.

When her father heard her sing, he first wanted nothing to do
with it. No daughter of his was going down that road. Eight years
old and all Sirena wanted was to be Janet Jackson. The music was in
her head night and day. If friends came over, she ushered them
downstairs in the basement and made them her audience while she
performed. She'd let her long hair cascade over her shoulders and
hold the comb as her microphone. By the time she was twelve, she
had given up on school altogether. Her father opened the report
card and saw failing marks and asterisks of unused potential. He finally agreed to take her to her first audition in exchange for her to
try harder in school.

Unbeknownst to Larry Lassiter, his daughter would never see
the inside of a classroom again. After a nine-hour drive from their
home in Detroit to New York, she arrived fresh and ready to take on
the world. She was the fourth picked for the preteen girl group, New

Sensation. After a year of training, recording in a studio, and being groomed for stage presence, the group was on their way. On the road with tutors and handlers, Sirena was on her way and no one could stop her, not even her father, who she'd left behind. Punishment in a way. She'd show him what an opportunist and a gold digger really looked like. Speaking of her mother that way, all those years, was like speaking directly to Sirena. She'd show him and everyone else.

But the girl group never made it out the door. All the practice and studio time had been a huge waste of time. Sirena had to go back home. Disgusted and determined to be free, this time she got on a bus with the advance money she'd gotten from the girl group and headed to Hollywood. She forged her father's name on her worker's permit and attended auditions nearly every day. At sixteen she was living on her own, supporting herself with video work.

When a music producer finally gave her a shot in the studio, she came ready with song in hand. Overnight success only took a decade, but she'd arrived—and not a mention of JP, Jake Parson.

I was satisfied, and found a new appreciation for Sirena. She worked hard, she persevered, case closed. Not something you could be mad at; if anything, she deserved more of my respect. Whatever that journalist was trying to stir up wasn't worth a minute more of my worry. I closed the laptop, and slept like a baby.

Good Morning, Heartache

My mother was fixing breakfast and offering her wisdom when I arrived in the kitchen. Miriam stared straight ahead as if she were listening but I knew what was going through her mind.

Pauletta scooted the eggs in the frying pan from one side to the other. "I'm telling you, men will do the right thing if you give 'em a chance. You can't always be their shadow. You've got to give 'em their freedom—that way it takes the fun out of their sneaking. It's the getting away with something that brings the thrill."

"My mother knows everything," I said sweetly to Miriam.

"I do know everything. And what I don't know hasn't happened yet."

"How'd you sleep?" I squeezed Miriam's shoulder.

"Very well, thank you."

"I have to get to the floral shop but you're welcome to stay here. I'm sure my mom would love the company." I was feeling chipper and as fresh as the orange juice sitting in front of me.

"Absolutely, stay and visit," Pauletta said with so much conviction it kind of scared me. Thinking about all the wonderful things she might say to Miriam that she couldn't say to me, since she swore I stopped listening a long time ago. Starting with the time I cut off my high-maintenance straightened hair and decided to go natural. "Don't no man want a nappy-head woman, I can tell you that right now."

Wrong. The first words out of Jake's mouth when we met were, "I like your hair." He may as well have been on one knee proposing a lifetime of bliss at that very moment because I think that's when I fell in love with him. I'd been wearing it natural for a couple of years but kept it cut pretty short. I got the hang of what kind of products to use to keep it moist and light. I was a far cry from the video vixens Jake had been surrounded by in his lifestyle of rich and famous, but the way he looked at me made me feel like the most beautiful woman in the world.

I guess I shouldn't judge my mother's advice too harshly. If anything, I hated the fact she was right more often than she was wrong. Like the fact that she could see through Airic from day one. She said he had shifty eyes, which meant he was either thinking of a new lie or figuring out how to keep the old one a secret. When he came to pick up Mya for his bio-daddy visitations, Pauletta never hesitated giving him a piece of her mind. But in the end, she liked to point out, I was the one who chose him.

Miriam flipped a hand, trying to appear relaxed. "I appreciate your hospitality, but I'm going home. I have plenty to do. I have everything all figured out."

"You know what would be fun: if you came to work with me today. I'll pay you. I have a huge wedding to prepare for this weekend."

"Pay me? I'm not destitute."

"I wasn't implying—I'm sorry." I sipped my orange juice and decided I should keep my mouth closed. Besides, call me selfish, but I was way too happy about not finding any proof to coincide with the journalist and her lies to let Miriam bring me down. And even if it were true, I'd decided that the past was the past. All that mattered now was the life Jake and I had made for ourselves. Nothing could tear us apart. We were solid as a rock.

"No. Really, I have something important to do today." The dullness of her tone matched the lifelessness in her eyes.

"Sure," I said, feeling like I'd run out of offers. Pauletta set plates down in front of us.

"You two eat up. I'll go get the girls."

As soon as she was gone I leaned forward to get Miriam's eye.

"Listen, I know you're hurting right now, but everything is going to work itself out. I'm sure it's all a misunderstanding. He forgot to pay a bill, it's not the end of the world."

Her high cheekbones pulled up in a smile that didn't match the sadness in her eyes. "I'm fine. Don't worry about me."

"Too late for that. I'm a dedicated member of the busybody society. I get it honestly. You've met my mother."

"Well, don't," she exclaimed firmly. "You certainly can't worry about what you have no control over." She added with a bit more reason, "Besides, you may like being in the dark, but I don't and I never will again."

Ouch. It only hurt for a minute. I kissed Pauletta on the cheek, snatched up Mya for school, and headed out the door to In Bloom. Even seeing Trevelle couldn't ruin my day.

I dialed Jake's number while I was driving. He didn't pick up. "Hey, Mr. Rockstar, just reminding you of Mya's dance recital tonight. Please tell me you're on your way home. I love you." I hung up without a doubt in my mind. He'd be there. Jake had never let Mya down, or me.

Captured Audience

Sirena picked up the vibrating phone to see the incoming call. Jake had left his phone on the table right next to his fork, next to his plate where he'd hardly touched his breakfast.

Wifey calling again.

They'd finished their morning radio interview for the popular 90.1 FM. The call-in lines were lit up and never went dead. They made a great team, bouncing off each other's lines, knowing how to finish each other's sentences. Too bad there was the small problem of Venus. Sirena knew the depth of Jake's commitment. No half stepping. If he was in, he was all the way in.

She held the phone until it stopped ringing, then set it back down exactly where he'd left it between the cooled coffee and plate of half-eaten egg whites. She noticed how he obsessed over every piece of food he put in his mouth. Worse than most of the women she knew. No red meat or pork. Olive oil and lemon juice on his salads. No mayonnaise, sour cream, or any other creamy condiments. She had to admit all the effort was worth it. His body was chiseled perfection.

"Anything else for you?" The waiter stood over her, blocking out the sun that broke through the clouds.

"Another one of these." She held up her empty glass with a celery stick and lemon wedge still attached. Sirena loved Manhattan this time of year. Late fall meant it was cold enough to wear her Tory Burch boots without worrying about the humidity leaving water spots on the leather. The morning crowd was already cleared out of the French bistro.

Well, nearly empty, with the exception of the older couple who'd wanted to know how long the two of them had been married. "Hardly," she'd scoffed while flashing the eight-karat ring on her finger. She was engaged to one of the richest men in the world. She hadn't worked her ass off to be married to some actor-slash-ex-rapper, with no guaranteed future—at least that's what she kept telling herself. But it didn't stop the yearning, the wish for a second chance.

Sirena looked around when his phone buzzed again. She picked it up and saw that a message had been left. It was instantaneous, sliding her finger across to unlock it and then pushing DELETE. Like she had no control over her fingers. Way too easy. They had the exact same phones given by the product placement sponsors as gifts. The new slick styles came in shimmering colors. Hers was bronze with rhinestones, his was solid silver. Good thing or she'd never have known to delete the deleted calls too. Few men would've left their phone behind in a woman's presence, Jake especially. When she'd first started in the industry, he was the one who taught her if a man's lips were moving, he was lying. The women in the industry were even worse. It was a sure bet whoever was smiling in your face had just gotten through calling you a skank-ho behind your back.

But eventually you had to trust someone. They had each other's back. She longed for that feeling again.

"Hey, there." Her full cheeks went into a quick smile. Jake sat down and picked up his phone out of habit. The light came up clear with no sign whatsoever she'd played with it. "What time is it?" she asked since he was looking at the screen.

"Ten forty."

He stretched and yawned. While his arms were still in the air he signaled the waiter with a scribble in the air to bring him the check.

"Guess I'm not the only insomniac."

"Yeah, I'm ready to be in my own bed. All this city hopping is for the birds. Can't get a good night's sleep."

"I thought you were having fun." Her lids dropped and she picked at her nails. Though she really did no damage. Her acrylic nails were stronger than bulletproof glass.

"You're talking to the old dude who's used to lights-out by ten, remember?"

"You used to be such fun. Most people don't get a second chance, Jay." Sirena batted her lashes before raising her eyes to him. She'd expected him to understand her meaning. When he didn't catch the bait she moved on. "I don't think you should waste it by trying to get your eight hours of sleep. Next thing you'll tell me you hate loud music."

He nodded in agreement.

"Don't even try it," she said.

He kept nodding. "I might work with music all day, but when the shop is closed, I'm all about some Coltrane, a little Maze. Slow and easy."

"You're pitiful." She turned to the waiter who was leaving the check and her Bloody Mary. "Bring this stick-in-the-mud another burned cognac."

"I haven't finished the first one."

"While I'm working on my third. There you go."

He cocked his head with a disapproving glare. "We have one more stop. You might want to slow down."

"What? I'm just trying to help you live a little. You're thirty-four. So what you're married? Doesn't mean you have to turn in your fun card."

"Actually . . ."

"Pitiful." Sirena raised a finger. "And don't let me get started on how you used to break loose, doing the moonwalk after just one drink. Now I can't get you to smile."

"I had a mean moonwalk, didn't I?" This time his perfect, smooth lips curved in a slight smile. "I hope you don't misinterpret my mild manner for being unhappy. That's one thing I can say, I love my life," Jake announced. "I love my life." He took the warmed cognac when it arrived and swirled it before taking a sip. He swirled a second time and seemed to get lost in the motion.

Jake's tastes hadn't changed. He was a sucker for sophistication. A tastefully aged cognac and the scent of a Cohiba cigar were the equivalent of a girl's all-inclusive spa day topped off with a shopping spree with someone else's credit card. Right then and there, she wished she had a specially-imported cigar to give him. She made a mental note. Call Leshawn, her cousin who worked as her assistant, tell her to order a full box of the best. Only the best.

"I didn't say you weren't happy. I just think you could be enjoying this moment. Living in the present moment and enjoying this time of success. No one has everything they want, but when you get damn close you could at least take a moment to appreciate it."

"What about you?" He leaned back in his chair, feeling lighter and more relaxed already. One sip and his wide shoulders seemed to spread like wings. "Do you appreciate the moment of having everything you've ever dreamed of? As I recall, you were determined to be right where you are right now. Is it all it's cracked up to be?"

His entrancing dark eyes pierced through her. The beauty of a confident man was only surpassed by one who was modest as well. He had no idea how fast her heart was beating, or how the heat swelled between her legs. She wanted to open wide in hope of a cool breeze.

"I'm where I want to be. Yes," she managed to say. "The last five or so years of blood, sweat, and tears guaranteed my having anything I want." She had a personal masseuse, chef, shopping sprees with no limit, but there was only one thing she was missing.

Notoriety, fame, and money didn't change the quality of men she had to choose from. The fine ones generally turned out to be dogs. If they were half decent, but had baller status, they generally turned out to be dogs. If they had no looks, and no baller status . . . they also turned out to be dogs. Once she'd embraced this truth, it only made sense to find a man with unlimited bank, who could at least spend her happy. Earl Benning knew how to do just that. He'd made his first hundred million as a record producer for teenybopper boy bands. Now he ran one of the largest recording labels in the country. Including a sprawling ocean-view mansion in Malibu. He spared no expense when it came to Sirena. She deserved the very best and he made sure she had it. So why wasn't that enough?

"Jay, there's only one thing I'm missing." She flipped her long hair over one shoulder and stroked while she yearned for the courage to tell him exactly what was on her mind.

"Let me guess, a family. A baby," Jake said almost in a sneer. Yes, the cognac was doing a fine job of relaxing him. A little too lax. He'd veered down a road she'd hoped had been roped off years ago. But he was still holding on.

Now, sitting across from Jake made her achingly sad. "I'm sorry, for the nine thousandth time—okay?"

He took another sip and swirl. "Apology accepted for the nine thousandth time."

Screw you! She wanted to scream, *Where were you?* Instead she calmly replied, "Let's stay on the subject, okay? Don't try to ignore what I'm telling you. We make a good team . . ." She paused when the waiter came to pour more ice water in the already full glasses. Nosy. Always looking to sell information. "Scratch that, we make an unstoppable team. Number-one record on *Billboard*. Movie is about to release to blockbuster status straight out the gate. We did this, me and you."

Her father had loved Jake the first time she'd brought him home, telling her he was the perfect man for her. All those years ago and she couldn't agree more. But back then she didn't appreciate his maturity and reasoning everything to death. He wasn't trying to flex. He was all about business.

It was her best attempt at flipping the ball back in her court. She didn't want to talk about the mistake she made all those years ago. Meanwhile she drank two more Marys. Jake left cash for the check then escorted her out. Times like this just made her more crazy. Any other man would've taken advantage of the opportunity. Blurry-eyed and giggling at the slightest eye contact as if everyone shared her secret. *I'm in love with this married man and he couldn't care less. But I knew him first.* She would only need him to love her up for one shining moment where she could feel worthy in his arms. Drink in his goodness and then she could walk away. She promised herself. Just once and she would walk away.

Group Hug

"Good morning," I called out when I stepped through the floral doorway. I inhaled the sweet smell of flowers and greenery.

"Well, aren't you in a cheerful mood." Trevelle spun around on the stool. She opened her hands in a magician's ta-dah to a spindly bouquet. "Look what I made. Isn't it divine?" Near the foot of her stool were the spliced remnants of her creation.

My optimistic mood was hit with a sucker punch. Trevelle had chopped up the most expensive orchids and shoved them into a short vase.

"Why are you playing around with inventory? Expensive inventory."

"I beg your pardon? Playing around."

"I mean, it's uh . . ." I stopped midway through *ugly,* but it was the only way to describe the monstrosity. I believed in karma. Maybe if I did five good deeds, starting with not insulting Trevelle, I could be on my way to a truly happy existence. Maybe I could hold on tight to the optimism I'd walked in with and not let her ruin my high hopes for good things to come my way.

"Here, add some filler." I picked up a few fern stems and shoved them into the vase. "And some of these. And here . . ." When I was finished it was picture ready. However, Trevelle's mouth had pulled into a straight line of dissatisfaction.

She was already up and moving toward my twenty-dollar-a-flower stash of imported orchids. It took everything I had not to lunge forward and protect them from her unskilled hands.

The phone began to ring. Saved by the bell. "In Bloom, where every day is a fantasy floral day. How can I help you?"

"Venus, this is Paige. Just wanted to remind you about the etiquette tea party tomorrow night."

"I will be there," I said, though I'd completely forgotten. I kept my eyes trained on Trevelle as her wedge heels stomped back to her workspace. She wiped her hands on her white denim, bedazzle-studded jeans—and this was dressing down for her. She was determined to start anew. She wasn't going to let me ruin her masterful handiwork the same way I didn't want her to destroy my mood.

"You have to be there *early*," Paige pressed on. "As the leader you need to check in at least an hour ahead and make sure everything is set up perfectly."

"I'm sure I can call ahead. The girls and I will be fine."

"I've already called." She was losing her patience, therefore her Southern politeness was being replaced by short, curt answers. I could almost feel her eyes narrowing. "Be there, early."

"Paige, not to worry. Everything will be fine." I hung up quickly. My beacon was still targeted on Trevelle. "You know, I really appreciate you being so creative. But I'd also appreciate it if you'd ask permission to use inventory."

Her bracelets spoke for her, making loud snapping noises with her movement. Though she stayed silent like a sullen child, I knew darn well she heard my every word.

"Where's Vince?" I finally asked. He would know how to turn her pouting into sweet and gooey kindness.

"On a delivery run."

"And you didn't go with him? What . . . trouble in paradise?"

"That would mean leaving the store during business hours. Seeing as how you were late as usual, I volunteered to stay behind to make it appear like you're actually running a real establishment."

"Yes. You are right. Thank you, Trevelle. I do appreciate all your help."

"Don't patronize me. I'll have you know Mrs. McMurry came in earlier to check on things and she absolutely loved my creation. She requested three for the ceremony. I was in the process of filling that order when you bombarded in here adding your two ragged cents." Trevelle wasted no time snatching out the greenery I'd added. Her bangle bracelets jangled with her every move. "You may have to admit you have an envy issue."

"Envious of you?" I faced her holding a pair of stem trimmers. She gently scooted my hand to the right.

"Really, you give me nothing but grief when all I'm trying to do is help you."

"Like you tried to help yourself to my child. Like now, how you're trying to help yourself to Vince and my business?" Breathe. Inhale. Exhale.

The back door squeaked shut before I realized Vince had caught the tail end of our tête-a-tête. I was just as grateful to see him. Surely I was backsliding downhill fast with the whole goodness-and-lightness-of-being thing. Five good deeds had been expanded to ten just to make up for this counterattack toward Trevelle and her masquerade of being *helpful*.

"Ladies." He eyed us cautiously. "I'm flattered you two are fighting over me, but please, there's enough of me to go around."

"She's jealous that Mrs. McMurry liked my beautiful arrangement." Trevelle held it up to show Vince.

He almost flinched. His lashes did a dance between us. "A thing of beauty is in the eye of the beholder," Vince said in my direction. "I think it's quite lovely."

"The mother of the bride absolutely loved it and demanded I make three more," Trevelle sang out. Her melodic voice once had the power to heal and transform sinners. In my floral boutique her voice only served to remind me there wasn't enough room for the three of us.

"An extra order, you see. It's a win-win, situation," Vince said, doing his best to mediate.

"Or here's a thought—maybe Mrs. McMurry didn't want to insult the great Trevelle Doval." I gave a patronizing grin.

Trevelle's bangles danced while she kept her monstrosity lifted for all to see. "She plans to put this right next to the guestbook to greet everyone. Two more for the bridesmaids' and groomsmen's tables. What do you think of that?"

Vince raised his muscular arms and hands for a truce. "Can't argue with that."

I could feel the karmic forces laughing at my ill attempts to turn the other cheek. "Everyone knows Trevelle on sight, at least in this town," I countered. I wasn't letting her get away with making me look like the bad guy, yet again. "She's a household name. She's a celebrity. Celebrities get treated like royalty, if you haven't heard."

"I beg your pardon. Celebrity? So receiving hundreds of hate e-mails daily makes me special?"

"I'm sure that's a pittance to the amount of love letters you get. People are enamored with fame—doesn't matter whether it's because you killed someone or starred in a movie."

"Whoa . . . hold on, now. I think we're off the grid." Vince stood up and handed me a yellow rose. "Flowers for the lady." He handed a second rose to Trevelle. She inhaled and smiled like a schoolgirl headed to prom.

"I think she's having a hard time accepting her hubby's new-found celebrity status, that's what I think." Trevelle folded her arms over her chest with her one yellow rose, like Miss America.

"That true? Talk to us, we're here for you." Vince opened his arms for a group hug. He still found time to exercise religiously even though he had taken on the full-time job of Trevelle Doval.

I pressed fingers to my lips like I was going to be sick. "No thank you."

"All right. Suit yourself, but it's obvious you need some human contact. The days ahead are going to be harder if you go on like this. And frankly, I'm not willing to be around this kind of negativity."

He was obviously making a threat. He had a subtle way of getting his messages across. I should've known better than snapping at Trevelle in front of him. The woman had a gift of twisting any situation. "Trevelle, I'm sorry for messing with your creation. Now if we could just stop talking about Jake I'd really appreciate it."

"Aha, so it is bothering you," Vince said.

"No. I'm not bothered. I'm perfectly comfortable with my husband's career. I just would rather not keep discussing it with . . ." My eyes jerked toward Trevelle.

"Fine. If that's the way you want it." Trevelle picked up her purse and keys and headed for the door.

"Whoa . . . hey, come on. Let's not fly off the handle. She apologized," Vince said, speaking up for me. For once.

"Yes, please don't go," I said deadpan as possible. I hoped like crazy she did the exact opposite.

"Well . . . if you insist," she said, instead putting her purse down.

"Great," Vince said. "Group hug."

"Great." I piled into his chest, not leaving any room for Trevelle. Her long thin arms managed to cover the circumference of us both anyway. I was pinned in the middle.

"God is good," Trevelle mumbled near my ear.

I squinted and suffered silently. Somehow I knew I was being overlooked in the goodness distribution.

I eventually made my escape. I took a long deep breath, rolled up my sleeves and got to work. I had five bridesmaids' bouquets to finish. Four flowergirl halos, two mother-of-the-brides corsages, and one bride to satisfy. The last thing I had time for was healing Trevelle's wounds, but if it brought about peace, I was all for it.

Vince gave me another squeeze for good measure and to say he was proud of me. Backing down was not my strong suit. I'd read in a magazine article that to combat negative emotion you acted positively; even if it wasn't genuine, eventually your brain would be tricked into happiness. In fact, happiness was a choice. Studies proved it time and time again.

A few hours later I waved the merry couple off as they headed out to make deliveries. The old engine sputtered before getting up to speed. I had planned to buy a new delivery van as soon as the company was up and running, with no handouts from the family account. Jake liked to point out that hobbies spent money, while businesses earned money and eventually made a profit. The time had come. I settled inside the baroque interior, feeling proud and confident. I was a business owner. Exhausted, but it felt good.

I locked the doors, flipped the sign around to CLOSED and took my shoes off for a well-deserved break. The couch was calling my name. I curled up and swore I'd only rest my eyes for a few minutes.

Before I knew it, I was in a deep abyss. Some call it sleep, I call it the devil's playground. The place where all my fears culminated in bad nasty dreams. The image of Jake and Sirena in *True Beauty*, eating each other up like they'd missed a week's worth of meals. Then came the worse part—they weren't in the movie anymore, just two silly kids in love shopping for baby clothes.

Baby clothes!

I hyperventilated before rolling off the couch, landing on the floor still struggling to realize it was only a bad dream.

Check One, Check Two

Jake signaled to the driver to stay in the car. "I got it." He opened the door for Sirena. His solid hand rested on her back, but only for a second.

She slid inside. "This limo is spinning. Or is it me? Out of control?" She giggled. "I need to call someone." She pulled out her phone. "Oh, that's right, I don't have anyone to call. 'Cause the only person I want to talk to is right here." She slapped the leather seat. "I don't bite, Jay. God, I'm so sick of this arm's-length thing you got going. Whatha—seriously?"

He shook his head and stared out the window. He remained on the other side.

She wiggled out of her boots, pushed her foot between his legs, and wiggled her toes. He grabbed her by the ankle and moved her foot to rest on the cushion.

"Big baby," she said before slapping on the door to find the button to lower the window. "I'm going to be sick."

After pulling over so Sirena could hurl her breakfast and five cocktails they were back in traffic.

The distance to the MTV studio was no more than five blocks. Jake could've run it in three minutes. Sitting in traffic, barely inching along, Sirena slept. He'd adjusted her head when it rolled forward, then stretched her out more comfortably. He couldn't help stroking her hair out of her face. That's when he saw the person she used to be, the one who'd driven him crazy with jealousy. All those many years ago, he couldn't stand it even when she talked to another man, because it was never just talking. She oozed warmth and vulnerability. On studio sets, from the artist to the camera guy, they all believed they stood a chance. Whether they were shopping in the produce aisle or stopping at a gas station, she was a magnet. It was constant, like a warm beam of light attracting every flying insect.

Never-ending battle, trying to rein her in. Protect her. Even now he could feel it starting. The enormous responsibility on his shoulders had begun to wear him down when he should feel nothing but relief that she wasn't his problem.

I don't need this shit.

I got my wife at home.

The car pulled up to the thirty-story steel and glass building. The guard and the driver exchanged hellos in what could've been construed as a foreign language. Heavy Bronx dialect was all. Jake's mother was a die-hard New Yorker. Though she'd moved to Los Angeles at the tender age of fourteen she refused to let go of her hard vowels, dragging them till they could go no further, going deeper into her New York accent whenever her sister or aunts called to say, *How you doin'?*

Times like these he could hear his mother's voice in his head, "Your stubborn ass is gonna fall into some shit you can't talk your way out of. *Mark* my words."

The gate rose and the limo pulled ahead. He'd already fallen into some shit, and then some. Homicide charges. His company embezzled to its knees. His best friend responsible for it all. Dealing with Sirena was a walk in the park. He just had to figure out where the trail was going to end. 'Cause end it shall.

"Sirena." He shook her gently. When she barely moved, he tapped her face. "Hey, MTV, ready or not." Jake had a feeling this interview would have to be canceled.

She popped up swinging. Her wild flailing arms missed him by a few inches, but the air swiping across his face made him know she meant business.

"Don't you ever put yo hands on me!" she yelled out, her eyes still closed.

He lifted his arms in truce. "Hey, hey, it's me, Jay. You all right?"

Sirena moved the hair out of her face. She quickly became alert and embarrassed at the same time. "I'm sorry. I . . . I was dreaming." She looked around, out the window, then rushed to her bag. "Shit, the interview. I'm looking like a two-dollar ho. You could've reminded me we were coming here before I downed those drinks."

"I'm not your handler." Although that's exactly what he felt like. Underpaid help.

"I didn't say you were. But you are my friend." Her head rocked side to side. "Friends have each other's back. Isn't that what you're always preaching? Little hard to practice, huh?" She flipped open her pocketbook and made an ill attempt at putting on lipstick, smudging a tiny bit between her fingers and rubbing it in her cheeks for blush. *Now* she looked like a two-dollar ho.

The door swung open. Ramona stood squarely, holding her BlackBerry like a guiding light. "You are late."

Outside I heard the doors of the van creak open and close. Trevelle's laughter and Vin's deep Jersey accent carried through the walls. I stood up from where I'd landed on the floor and still couldn't get my bearings. The store was completely dark. How long had I slept? The dream had my heart pumping erratically. Just a dream, I told myself to calm down.

I checked my watch and realized I was going to be late for the recital. I still hadn't heard back from Jake. When the phone started buzzing, I snatched it up quickly. "Hello," I answered without looking at the caller ID.

"I'm surprised you answered." Airic's steely voice could cut ice cubes. "I have a favor."

"This isn't your weekend," I started before he could finish.

"I realize that. But it's Mya's recital. I really thought I should be there."

Why?

"I thought you were really, really busy with your child bride and new baby."

He stayed silent long enough for me to feel bad about that comment. "I really don't mind if you come." I caved in pretty quickly. I could count this in the good karma column. "I'd just appreciate it if you kept a little distance. Jake will be there, and you two are like gas and a lit match."

"No problem. If I see him, I'll completely ignore him. It's he that likes to antagonize me, remember that."

"One hundred yards, how's that?" I finally found my car keys. "I'll leave a ticket at the door for you."

"Tickets? It's a six-year-old's recital."

"She's five. Her birthday is not until next month, but a father would know that." Bad Venus. Bad. "Besides, it's not my policy. The dance school is very strict about who attends these things. Don't worry about it, your ticket will be waiting."

"Actually, I'll need two."

"Ohh, nooo, you're not bringing your child bride. You're not. That's just not going to fly."

Vince finally came inside and moved past me slower than usual. He had a nasty habit of listening to my conversations. He claimed it was the only way he could get any information out of me by already knowing the first half. Trevelle was close behind him.

"I already have to deal with your last mistake," I whispered. "I'm not going to be on gal-pal terms with this one too. Do not bring her," I hissed. I faced the wall so Trevelle wouldn't overhear. "One ticket will be waiting . . . do you hear me? Not two."

"At some point, you're going to have to grow up," he announced. "The world does not revolve around your idiosyncrasies."

"One ticket. One world. Don't like it, find another one." I clicked the phone off.

"Are you headed out?"

"What gave it away?" I smartly snapped at Trevelle before letting the door slam. My adrenaline was revved high. Airic had that effect on me. We'd been engaged for two years before I realized what a jerk he was with a capital J. I thought he was the perfect man, older, wiser. I appreciated his no-nonsense approach to life. Black and white, no gray, or shades of ambiguity. He wanted a wife and I wanted a husband, the details didn't matter. It was only after meeting Jake and seeing what real love looked like up close and personal did I realize the mistake I was making. By then I was already pregnant with Mya. Jake didn't care whose baby I was carrying. He made sure I understood there was only one thing he wanted: me.

Who could ask for anything more? To be wanted and cared for was all any of us wanted. That simple.

CAN'T WAIT TO SEE YOU. Jake's text came across my screen, and not a moment too soon.

No Diggity, No Doubt

Countless times Jake had come into greenrooms of TV stations expecting the place to look like the set—plush couches and chairs, coffee, maybe a Danish or two. To the contrary. Rat traps. The couch sunk in so far, he was sure if he sat down, he'd never be able to get back up. The coffee in the Pyrex container had coagulated into a slick brown sludge.

"A little water and we're in business." He put the glass container back on the heat. "Let me see if I can find you some real coffee."

"I'm fine," Sirena slurred. "Besides, you're not my handler, remember."

Ramona must've heard her cue to show up on the scene. She stomped on the parquet floor carrying two bottles of water. "You both look like shit."

"I've been on rough duty." He uncapped the bottle and drank until it was empty. He could officially say, the thrill was gone. This was their third stop of the day, and last. He checked his watch. The flight at three P.M. would get him to Mya's recital in plenty of time.

A makeup artist came in with the energy of a paramedic sent to rescue. Her purple and black hair stuck up high and straight in a mohawk. She rolled open her black bag of tricks and got to work on Sirena.

Calmness rose around her like a blanket. Having someone pampering her was an instant salve. Sirena flipped through a fashion magazine, relaxed and contented while the makeup artist brushed her with magic. She was in her element. MTV had been kind to her. Built her up from square one. Hundreds of beautiful new talents came on the scene every day, but none had been welcomed with open arms like Sirena Lassiter. Even now they'd planned to devote the entire half hour to the movie.

Mohawk gathered her things without a thank you or you're welcome. Sirena went about business as usual, not bothering to check if the job was well done. Her eyes were bright and her skin glowed. No one would guess she'd been a drunken mess only a few minutes ago.

"I can't believe this," Sirena spoke out of the blue. "Remind me to fire Raquel as my stylist. This trick got the same dress on I wore for the *Harper's Bazaar* cover." She was talking to herself because Jake wasn't listening.

The producer breezed in with her headset over a mass of wild wavy hair. Just the sight made him wish he could call Venus and tell her he loved her. That he missed her. That he had a secret he'd been holding on to, eating him up inside. One he had a feeling he was going to pay dearly for.

"Do you guys mind performing? We have an extra three minutes we need to fill. We've got the instrumental cued up, all you guys gotta do is do what you do. Cool?"

Jake waited for Sirena to agree or disagree. It wasn't his place while in the queendom to have a say.

"Sorry, Kelly. You know I'm down for whatever but my voice is cracked. I'm not about to ruin my whole career for three minutes of live TV."

Ramona came in again, rushed. "I made sure they used the soft light and filters. It'll pick up the highlights in your hair perfectly." She stood over Sirena. "You need anything else?"

Jake wanted to say, what about him? Would the soft lights and filters do anything for him? Would it hide his fatigue? He knew anyone would trade places with him right now, but all he really wanted to do was get home. Get off this ride. Keeping Sirena at arm's distance was exhausting. He didn't know how much longer he could maintain his cool. Something was brewing inside him that he'd kept buried for so long.

"We're good. All right, then. We'll get this show on the road in ten." Kelly rushed out, already whizzing in thoughts of plan B.

"You ready?" Sirena touched his arm. "Something wrong?"

"Nah, I'm cool."

The audience was on their feet the minute the host said her name. Clapping, cheering, and whistling. So much so, it shocked Jake that they got louder when he stepped out. A chill ran through him. He took in the faces all staring directly at him.

"Welcome, JP, Sirena . . ." The host, Sonny Suarez, slapped hands with Jake. "Man, good to have you back. I'm not just talking in the studio." He shouted to the audience, "Are we feeling his hit? Yeah!" The group of mostly teenagers cheered on cue.

If Jake could bottle this moment and drink it up, he would. But he'd learned early on not to let adoration go to his head. Fan love was the worst drug of all. Highly addictive.

"Tell us what it was like being back in the studio after eleven years. Then suddenly you're back on top. Did you wake up one day with the lyrics and the beat, or was it something floating around for months, years, and now was the time?" Sonny seemed to have forgotten Sirena was in the studio. Tunnel vision.

Jake could feel her getting uncomfortable. "The writing process is scary. One day you have nothing, one minute you're empty, the next you can't shut the lyric out of your head. Just flows, man. But it helped having the right muse." He slipped an arm around Sirena to bring her into the fold.

"The two of you worked together in the past, but never in the studio. How was it for you, Sirena, putting yourself in this man's hands?"

She smiled coyly. "Being in his hands . . . absolutely amazing." She winked and the ladies in the crowd screamed.

Jake felt the grip trying to take hold and told himself the high never lasts. Don't give in.

"But seriously, JP is one of the most dedicated, talented people I know," Sirena continued. "He showed me early, back in the day, you can't get anywhere without working hard. There are no shortcuts. So we stayed in the studio for, like, five days straight." She stretched her fingers around the microphone, squeezing with both hands, putting her lips just shy of touching. "I think we got it right."

"Number one on the charts for three straight weeks, I'd say you two got it right. Then we come to the movie—not even on the screens across the whole country yet, and it's surpassed expectations in the box office. How stoked are y'all?"

"None of this was expected. I never thought about acting at all until Sirena popped up," Jake added.

"Popped up?" She frowned, quickly turning it around. "There was no popping up. I've known this man forever. It was more so convincing him he could do it. I told him he was better than those Calvin Klein ads, showing his goodies to the world when he could've been a live action hero." She pursed her lips. Blew him a kiss. Then jokingly nudged him with her elbow.

The host had to mellow the crowd with a downward push of his hand. Jake looked out to see someone holding up a poster of him in the Calvin Klein underwear ad. His chest glistening, his arms ripped. The sepia-toned photo reminded him of how good it felt working in front of the camera. Working, period. He'd been on hiatus for so long, hiding from his past. Now here he was on worldwide television, in millions of homes. He nearly smiled, but fought it off. Maybe this was what Sirena was talking about. Wondering why he wouldn't let himself enjoy the moment, bask in the adulation.

Because it never lasts.

"Speaking of knowing him forever, as you put it, there's also someone here who has known you both forever."

The music began to play an old-school favorite that half the audience should've been too young to remember, but they were all up on their feet swaying and stomping to the beat.

"A blast to the past. Please welcome, Tommy Ridley." Sonny Suarez did a quick Michael Jackson spin.

Sirena visibly flinched. Jake kept the same even expression that he'd had all along. Somehow he still hadn't gotten the message, even with the bass of the song blasting. Not until Tommy was up close and personal did it register. "Good to see you, man." He even hugged his old buddy. But his heart was pounding against his chest. *Hate* wasn't strong enough of a word.

The intro song should've been "Back Stabbers" by the O'Jays.

Sirena put out both her hands and extended her cheek for an air kiss.

Tommy had on an oversized leather jacket to hide the pounds he'd packed on. His box-cut fade was slightly too high, like in the old days. He hadn't been seen or heard in the music industry, and no one had really cared to ask. He'd run over so many and left bodies in the ruin, that no one missed him. The money he'd made off the backs of everyone else must've gone a long way for him to have remained in obscurity.

"So here's the story," Sonny Suarez said in his rehearsed tone. "You and Tommy were roommates in college, doing your thing. One of you was supposed to be a lawyer and the other . . ." He turned the microphone to Tommy.

"An English teacher," he said, dead serious.

"Not really seeing you as an English teacher."

Tommy flashed a gold-capped smile. A few chuckles followed.

"So tell us how y'all got started on the road to stardom."

"In the dorm, man. Spinning, mixing, and Jay, here, finally

reveals he's got a few rhymes. I put them to a hype beat. The rest, they say, is history."

Jake hoped he didn't expect him to put on a big silly grin and thank Tommy. More so he felt like slamming his ass to the ground.

"And you met Sirena by way of Jay, and you two made beautiful music together. A platinum album."

And here's where things got dicey.

The story had three sides. Tommy's side was that he knew Jake had written "Taste Like Honey," but took the money and ran with it anyway. But it was never about the money. The only side Jake knew was that he caught his girl with his friend. No matter how much they both claimed it was nothing more than her giving him a massage, he'd never been able to shake the image: Sirena straddled on Tommy's tatted back with her hands stretched across the dark ink scripted with the name of his label, Tommy Prince. She disappeared while the sales of the song kept rising. When she finally surfaced asking for a second chance, Jake had nothing to say. It took him ten years to forgive her, right up to the moment where they were standing.

"Do you think there's something down the pike for the three of you? That would be awesome."

Seriously?

Hell, no.

"You never know what fate has in store for us," Jake said cautiously. Hoping he was doing his part. Always the stand-up guy, the one to do what was right. Sirena's arm brushed up against him for only a second and he could feel her heat. She was nervous.

"Thanks for coming and showing your love. May I say"—Sonny took Sirena's hand—"you are indeed a true beauty. In theaters, everybody, *True Beauty*. Download the soundtrack today. It's smokin'." The closing music cued.

Jake watched the green light on the camera switch to red. He dropped the fake smile. He stuck out his hand to Sonny. "Thanks, man. Good interview."

"Anytime, Jay. Anytime."

Tommy stuck out his hand for a shake and shoulder embrace. Jake jolted forward with a fake punch, making him stumble back. Tommy landed on his ass. The microphone he was holding dropped like it had surged with an electric jolt. The clang of the speaker made everyone else jump too.

"What, Jay?" Tommy swallowed hard still on the ground. "You still beefing over some bullshit?" He got up, embarrassed. "Ain't my fault you couldn't control yo girl. That's some bullshit, Jay." He moved toward Jake with an open palm. "Squash this shit, man."

"Stay down," he warned. If he got up, Jake would have no choice but to put him down.

"Yeah, whateva. You need the facts, Jay. That's what you need, just the facts."

He felt a gentle hand on his back. "Come on. Take a breath." The producer was at his side, wondering what had just happened. "You can cool off in the greenroom."

Jake had already walked it off, moving swiftly toward the glowing red exit sign.

Sharing Is Caring

The recital was held in the cultural theater a few blocks down from the ballet school. That meant plenty of seating, and everyone should've had a good view no matter the row. Didn't stop the woman in back of me from complaining. I heard the exhaustive sigh meant for me. "Oh, great. How am I supposed to see over all this child's hair?"

There was a time when I would've spun around and cussed and spat my way into a fight, but I'd made peace with my hair a while ago and refused to spend the rest of my life apologizing for my official afro diva status. There was no retooling once the leave-in conditioner was in place. I scooted down best I could and that would have to do. Paulette came and sat next to me, leaving one seat open. I placed my purse there to save it for Jake. His flight should've already landed and he promised he would be driven straight over.

"Hey, isn't that Miriam?" My mother pointed at the woman standing a row in front of us. I shook my head without hesitation. This woman had long straight hair, whereas Miriam wore her hair short and curly.

"Mom, how would that be Miriam?"

"I'm not blind. I know what she looks like." Paulette stood up and reached out her arms. The next thing I knew she was hugging the woman. It was Miriam. The long dark wig with bangs hung in her eyes. She blinked a smile but it was obvious she was in a strange frame of mind.

"Well, what do you think?" She stroked her hair before taking the seat in front of us.

Thank goodness the pianist began to play so I didn't have to answer the question. The lights dimmed.

I checked my phone, still nothing from Jake. I put in a text and told him to let me know when he arrived. I'd come get him and show him to our seats. The pianist was a striking replica of the ballet instructor—perfect posture, elegant neck and shoulders; only her vibrant red hair was streaked with gray. I took a long cleansing breath, ready to enjoy the show.

The first set of children—including Mya—made their entrance on the stage.

The enjoyment was short-lived. I saw Airic, and with his new family in tow after I specifically threatened his life. I started to chew on the inside of my jaw. The nervous habit had followed me through childhood, teenaged angst, college, right into adulthood. It helped me take my mind off things. A nice bite-size amount of pain in exchange for focusing attention on details like my mother's breast cancer, or Jake's arrest two years ago. And now my anger at Airic. He and his young bride had found two seats together like magic. I was sick of him getting things his way.

I felt a tap on my shoulder and turned around, ready to snap at the woman who'd already huffed and puffed about my hair blocking her view. Robert Stanton's smile turned into a frown when he saw my mean mug.

"Sorry, I didn't mean to scare you."

"No. I thought you were someone else," I whispered.

"Is that seat open?" he asked, pointing to the one I was holding for Jake.

"No. Sorry. Holding it for my husband."

The audience excitedly whispered as the children began to dance.

Mya was in her bright yellow tutu and stockings. Her sweet face was framed by huge white petals made of felt and wire that I'd worried might come out and poke her. She was the cutest daisy flower. Her big round eyes and long dark lashes shined bright even under the spotlight.

"Aren't they adorable," Paulette said proudly.

"Ahuh." I kept my eyes focused straight ahead but my hand was gripped around my phone, waiting for the vibration of a text or message. It wasn't like Jake. He'd never miss the recital, at least not if he could help it. That was the part that worried me. Was he in an accident? Did something happen?

"Did you bring the camera?" my mother asked.

"I completely forgot."

Lizzie and Mya scooted around, graceful as five-year-olds could. The older girls were lighter on their feet. I pictured Mya in a few years being just as good. She had long slender limbs like a future dancer. I hoped the instructor had the video cued up like she'd told Mya, as if she could read the future and knew her daddy wouldn't be here. I craned my neck to check the door one more time.

Lizzie suddenly crashed into another daisy, sending the smaller girl skidding across the floor.

"You go, baby," Miriam called out. "You're beautiful." A few parents turned to give a nasty glare. "That's my baby, she's going places," she said, undeterred.

I put my hand on her shoulder. "She's doing wonderfully."

Without warning, the music stopped. Parents clapped while others whistled. I followed suit, realizing that just when I'd decided to stop looking for Jake and focus on the show, the entire thing was over. I'd make it up to Mya at the next one, rapt with attention, camera lens angled. I checked my phone one final time before dropping it into my purse, angry with myself as well as Jake.

Miriam's whistle was loud and distinct enough that Lizzie knew and recognized it immediately. She waved excitedly in our direction and took a bow. I'd always wanted to whistle like that and the best I could do was blow hot soundless air.

"I'll go get the girls." Miriam was already scooting out past the cheering, grinning parents with her fancy tresses flowing side to side over her shoulders. I didn't want to begin to know what was going through that head of hers.

I could see Airic navigating the sea of bodies going in the opposite direction of everyone else, coming toward me. His baby was strapped to his chest with her tiny legs extended. He waved. I shuddered.

"Mom, I'm going to the bathroom. Can you wait here for Mya?"

"Oh no . . . you're not leaving me with him." She knew me too well.

"That was great," he sang out. "Got it all on tape." He held up his video camera as exhibit A. "Paulette, I didn't know you were in town."

"I've been here for a few weeks. Guess we missed each other. And this must be the new missus and your new baby. She's just adorable."

I sneered at my mother, wondering what her angle was.

"Mommy, Mommy," Mya called out before I caught her running jump.

"Hey, princess. You were amazing."

"Yes, you were." Airic reached behind to his little woman. She handed him a small bouquet. "And these are for you."

Mya's mouth opened wide with excitement. "Thank you."

"Thank you . . . Daddy," Airic instructed.

Mya stayed silent. I rolled my eyes before beaming them into his like laser darts. The child was conflicted enough.

"Okay, are we ready to go?" I hoisted Mya off my mother's hip and onto mine.

"Mommy, Daddy didn't come." Mya wrapped her arms around my neck.

"I know, sweetpea. I'm sorry. He probably got caught in traffic."

"Caught in something, all right," my mother mocked in my ear.

The awkwardness of the moment required intervention. Robert Stanton answered the call. He appeared seemingly out of nowhere and extended his hand. "Hello, there. I'm Jory's father. I'm sure you've heard Mya talk about her best bud, Jory."

"Ah . . . no, but nice to meet you. I'm Airic Fisher, Mya's father."

I coughed and cleared my throat. If he introduced himself as Mya's father, dad, daddy, or any other loosely thrown around term describing one's ability to donate sperm and monthly checks one more time, I was sure my hair was going to catch on fire. Heat was steaming from my scalp, ears, and coming out of my eyeballs. He knew it was infuriating me. I'd asked him to stay back, out of sight and out of mind, and here he was the life of the party.

"We better get going."

Airic scooted his arm around my shoulder. I was pinned next to his cooing baby. "Too bad your husband couldn't be here to see Mya's first dance recital. Him being the good father and all. Guess he's too busy traipsing around the country with the most beautiful woman in the world."

Right then the sweet cherub hawked up her milk. White globs landed on his black shoes.

"I couldn't agree more," I said to the baby. "Let's go, Mom."

Mya reached out and touched her baby sister. "Let's have a baby, Mommy."

I didn't know how to respond. If it were only that easy. Men could procreate until their ears fell off and turned to dust, but women sadly had only a limited time slot. Along with the complications I suffered during my miscarriage, the odds had diminished. Jake and I couldn't afford to spend thousands on fertility and in vitro treatments. Maybe now it was an option. Or . . . "Sometimes it's just not in the cards," I whispered to myself. "See you all later."

"Hey, wait." Robert Stanton caught up. "Let's all go get something to eat. Come on, the kids deserve a reward for their great performance."

"I don't think so."

"Please, Mommy." Mya squirmed off my hip, which wasn't a great distance. She was gangly and long, compliments of Airic's six-three frame.

"Yeah, please," Robert mimicked.

"I'm up for a good meal I didn't have to cook myself," Pauletta added. "I've been working like a slave in that kitchen. No one's offered to take me anywhere."

"Mom, I need to get home. I don't know what's going on with Jake. I just need to get home," I said as gently as possible.

"Then I'll at least walk you ladies to your car?" Robert offered.

My mother elbowed me. "I've been in town almost three weeks and I'm just now meeting Jory's father. Why'd you keep him from me?"

"I feel the same way, Pauletta." He gently pulled her hand to his face and kissed it. "You are just as beautiful as your daughter, and your daughter's daughter."

Pauletta giggled. I hadn't heard her giggle before. My mother had always been hard around the edges. Even lately, her tolerance for bullshit had reached an all-time low. I could see her brain thinking overtime.

"Is your wife here?" I asked specifically to shut down whatever wild ideas she was rolling around.

"No, she's in D.C. attending a charity event. Standing in for me. No way was I going to miss this little guy's first big show."

Jory looked up and smiled. Pauletta reached over and patted him on his curls. "You are such a cutie, just like your dad."

Oh brother.

"We have to get going."

"Can I go too?" Lizzie's cherub face, surrounded by her daisy headpiece, was almost angelic. She'd been standing there the whole time. Only then did I realize there was no Miriam in sight.

"Sweetie, where's your mom?"

"I don't know. She said to stay with you."

I covered my face and shook my head before leading the way to the car.

Walk Like a Man

"There he is." Sirena slapped at the door handle, trying to lower the automatic window. "Unlock this fuckin' thing. Pull over."

The driver came to an abrupt stop at the curb. Strictly a no-parking zone. Cars honked. Drivers yelled.

"Manhattan during this hour is the wrong time to have a lovers' spat." Ramona sighed. "You want to tell me what this is about?"

Sirena got out of the car, ignoring her inquiry. Thank goodness Jake was held up by a corner light. "Will you please get in the car? Really, the thing with Tommy was so 1998." She was freezing. No coat. Only jeans, the white silk top that surely showed every ridge of her now frosty nipples, and barefoot.

"Go back to the car," he said, surprisingly calm.

"You're a better man than that. You can't be pissed about something that silly. Let it go, Jay. It's over."

Though it was obvious it wasn't over. Even while he stood stoically, she could see his jawline tighten and release. This was the answer she'd wanted to hear, even if it was unspoken. He still cared. Obviously, or he wouldn't have reacted to Tommy that way.

"Look at me, I'm freezing my ass off. Please. We'll talk about it in the limo." What'd she say that for?

A young girl in a pink puffy jacket faced her, then pointed and squealed. "Sirena Lassiter, ohmigod."

The minute everyone waiting at the light began to recognize them, Jake was practically hauling her back to the car, her feet barely touching the ground.

The shiny black car sat idling with humidity dripping from the tailpipe. He swung the door open and shoved her inside. He hadn't planned to get in until screaming fans started moving toward them. He jumped in and closed the door as cautiously as possible, trying not to slam any limbs in the process.

Still shivering, she tossed her jacket over the front of her like a blanket. "Thank you."

He still hadn't said a word. Brooding.

They were stuck in traffic. The airport was only a few miles away, but it would take close to an hour just to get over the bridge.

"I had no idea about Tommy. I was just as surprised as you were."

"When's the last time you spoke with your old friend?"

"I haven't spoken to him in ten years," she said calmly. "Probably, same as you."

"Really, what is the big deal?" Ramona interrupted. "The senior producer of the show called to personally thank you and Sirena. Let me tell you, whatever chemistry you three had up there came through. They had a huge ratings boost."

This seemed to silence him, but only for a minute. "Yeah, a real ménage à trois."

Ramona sighed, accepting the fact she was dealing with something bigger than what she'd witnessed. "Why don't we stop and get some dinner instead of sitting in traffic. By the time we get through eating, the bridge will be clear. It will also give you both time to cool off."

Sirena didn't respond. Jake said nothing as well.

Ramona pushed and clicked on her BlackBerry. "Fine. Airport food it is. Yummy, delicious."

Food for the Brokenhearted

I was famished. The day had taken its toll. I wrapped my robe around my exhausted body and made my way to the kitchen. Pauletta was in the kitchen throwing away McDonald's trash. I'd showered while the kids ate. Lizzie was still in my possession. Miriam had called and asked if Lizzie could stay the night. I didn't ask a single question. I had enough drama on the brain.

"I can't believe you're feeding my grandbaby that kind of mess. You'd rather feed her that than go out with the senator. Weren't you the one lecturing about the hormones and additives in the foods?"

"Yep, that would be me. Bad mother of the year."

"I'm not calling you a bad mother, but really . . ." She raised her brows to say much more than those few words ever could.

"You're right. I've just been so rushed. Seems like there's never enough time in the day."

"Why are you working this hard anyway?" Question of the week, month, and year. Her eyes squinted with no resolution. "Your husband is making plenty enough money. You should have a maid, a cook, someone to take Mya to school . . . I don't understand your need for servitude." She opened the window and tried to fan out the distinct smell of Mickey D fries.

"I have always worked hard. You taught me that."

"I didn't teach you to be an easy target."

"What's that supposed to mean?"

"You're too tired and too worn out to pay attention to what's going on around you." She walked over and turned on the television. She picked up the remote and pushed play on the DVR where she'd saved a lovely episode of *TMZ* just for me.

"Please, Mom. I can't stomach that gossip."

"You're going to stomach this."

On the television Jake was getting close into some guy's face. I covered my mouth in shock. She let it play but I couldn't hear the woman's assessment of the situation.

"So," she let it hang in the air. "Story goes, Mr. JP attacked the man who broke him and Sirena up years ago. Did you know about that? Did you know this woman and your husband used to be an item?"

"I think I may have heard something about it." I filled up the kettle with water for tea. I then opened the refrigerator and searched for leftovers that I knew were in there. I was sure my mother would point out that I was willing to feed Mya fast food, but wouldn't eat it myself.

"Taking the high road?"

"Yes, the very high road." I stuck the leftovers in the microwave and turned it on. "Are we talking about the food, or Jake and Sirena?"

"Jake."

"Whatever they had or didn't have doesn't mean a hill of beans. And if Jake punched a fool in the mouth, believe me, the guy deserved it. Obviously that's why Jake hadn't made it to the recital."

I peeled the Glad sheet back. Steam rose and my mouth began to water. I took a fork full of meatloaf and gravy. It didn't matter what she was serving, it always gave me warmth and satisfaction. I moaned a little. "This is so good, Mom."

"Only thing we agree on, is that I can cook." She went back and slammed the microwave door closed. "You need to find out the details of their past relationship. Don't sit up there and pretend you are not hurt."

"I'm not hurt." My mouth was full. I had one thing on my mind, food, and—well, two . . . going to bed with a full stomach. I'd already worried enough. I'd even missed watching Mya's dance for checking my phone every five seconds.

"Listen, you need to get to the bottom of this."

"Yes, right away." I shoved another fork of mashed potatoes and gravy into my mouth.

Pauletta leaned over the kitchen table with determination in her eyes. "I'll admit, Jake wasn't my first pick for your husband and Mya's father. Young, too pretty—those things are dangerous signals. But he's a good man. I don't want you to lose him."

"Huh?" I put my fork down. "Lose him?" I shook my head. "Do we really have to talk about this while I'm eating?"

She picked up my plate and started toward the sink.

"Mom, give me back my food."

"I thought you couldn't talk and eat at the same time." She brought it back and set it down.

This time I shoveled a buttery heap of mashed potatoes in my mouth. I wasn't letting her take my plate until it was clean. When I'd finished, just short of licking it spotless, she picked up the plate. She slapped her hands together. "Can you listen now? Are your ears working?"

"Yeah, but I wish they weren't."

"Everyone wants what they can't have. You need to put some safeguards in place. First you need to make him jealous. Create some invisible boyfriend. Make him nervous." She coughed out a laugh. "Make him think Clint is back. Dr. Clint Fairchild. Who better than the doctor who got away?" She was proud of herself. "That's it. I'm a genius."

"You're deranged."

"Did you see how you devoured that plate? You wouldn't have

eaten that food like it was your last meal if it was old hat. You see what I'm saying?"

"I don't see what you're saying. I love your food, woman. Hate to eat and run." I leaned over and kissed her on the cheek. "I'm going to bed." Her copper-brown skin was still smooth and wrinkle free. All those years of telling my father and my brother, Timothy, to go on without her; to the park, the beach, or barbecuing in our own backyard. She wanted no part of the sun. No one knew a thing about sun damage back then, but Pauletta wasn't having it.

She liked to remind me and my brother that we were lucky to have her. We wouldn't have to suffer unnecessarily with trial and error. All we had to do was ask her and skip going the long way. She already knew everything. Which made asking questions a whole lot easier.

"If that's true, if all men want is what they can't have, how have you and Dad stayed married for forty-three years? It doesn't add up. No one would stay married if that were the case."

"Play hardheaded if you want to. I'm trying to tell you plain and simple. You've got no time for playing stupid. This girl is trying to take your man. Find out the truth. If he and she already spent time together, the wanting is dead and gone." She pointed a finger and narrowed her eyes. "But if they haven't, I'd say it's time to put up some major CB."

"CB?"

"Cock blocking." She made a matter-of-fact expression. "Girl, where'd you grow up, in a fish tank?"

"Would you stop with the slang, Mom."

"CB is not slang. That's been a saying since you were in pink rollers and bell-bottoms."

"Thank you, oh great swami. Once again you've enlightened me on the ways of the world."

She'd taken care of me and Mya for the last few weeks. It was the longest she'd ever stayed away from my dad, who she'd first said was on a fishing trip with some retiree buddies. Unless he'd sailed to Alaska and back, I was sure he was back home by now. Now it dawned on me that she really hadn't talked to my father, at least not while I was within earshot.

"Mom, I think we'll be okay. You should go back to L.A."

"What? That's just plain rude. Because I make an observation, you want to kill the messenger?"

"No. I'm concerned. You always said Dad wouldn't eat unless you fed him. Is there something going on with you two?"

"Nothing's going on. After nearly half a century, sometimes you just need a break." She headed out. "See you in the morning."

As I was entering my bedroom, the phone began to ring.

"Baby," I finally exhaled. I stayed quiet, not sure what good etiquette said about asking one's husband why he'd punched someone out on national television.

"You have no idea how much I miss you." He sounded so tired. "I'm sorry I missed Mya's recital. I missed my flight."

"It's okay. There'll be more. She's quite the dancer. Are you okay? Is everything okay?"

"You saw?"

"Yeah, on TV. My mother couldn't stop rewinding and playing it over and over. The news reporter said it had something to do with Sirena. What happened?"

"I'll talk to you about it when I get home. I promise. I'll tell you everything."

"Everything?" I squeezed back the lump in my throat. "I'm just worried about you. I don't want you to get in trouble again."

He sighed. "Babe, it's over. I never hit him in the first place. It just looked that way. I promise, we'll talk when I get home."

Up and Away

"I'm just sayin', like I'm gon' take any old deal. I'm Sirena Lassiter. I earned the right to say kiss my ass."

"Miss, you're going to have to turn off your phone."

The plane was ready to take off. Seat belts buckled. Trays upright. Jake was seated beside her, staring out the window like a lost child. It was his fault they'd missed their original flight. Bottom line, she already told him she had nothing to do with Tommy on the set of their interview. She'd been just as shocked and disturbed as he. But no, Mr. Holier Than Thou always wanted to blame somebody.

He was seriously getting on her nerves. *Get over it already.*

"Ms. Lassiter, what would you like to drink? We still have a few minutes before takeoff."

"What? First you're rushing me off the phone, now we got a few minutes." Sirena huffed. "Orange juice," she said loud enough for anyone listening, and she'd come to accept someone was always listening. Then quietly, "And a Smirnoff."

"You got it. And sir, for you?"

She nudged Jake. He pulled out the iPod speaker from his left ear.

"What do you want to drink?" Sirena enunciated like he still couldn't hear.

"Water. No ice."

"Just one big bowl of fun, aren't you." But then she had to admit that was part of the attraction. He had a foundation. He didn't give in or take the easy way. He held fast and steady to what he believed to be right. Like him holding on to his marriage vows for dear life when it was obvious he could have her. At some point she was going to have to play her last card. The ace she held close and ready. She wanted to give him a chance to come peacefully.

He kept his gaze out the window onto the tarmac. What was taking so long anyway? Sirena opened her purse and took out a new script. She was behind in her reading. Her agent would be expecting an answer as soon as she was back home.

Where was home anyway? The word for normal people implied the place where she could lay her head and finally breathe a sigh of relief. There was no such place for her. Constantly on edge. Looking for the bigger better deal. If she slowed down, she feared sinking into the quicksand of irrelevancy like so many who came before her. Every blossom must fall. She'd read that someplace and understood the full meaning. No flower could last forever. It eventually would shrivel up and die, petal by petal, until there was nothing left. But while she was in bloom, she would take advantage of every ray of light, every drop of rain. Taste every bee and delight in the search for her honey.

Bottom line, she had nothing to lose and everything to gain. Because eventually, she was going to lose it anyway.

"Ladies and gentlemen, we're sorry for the delay. We've been grounded by the flight control. We're currently looking at an hour before we're cleared for takeoff, so feel free to use the restrooms or move about the cabin." As soon as the announcement was made the noise octave went up with chatter, folding newspapers, nervous babies, businessmen and -women on their cell phones.

"Shit. Great." Sirena received her drink and snapped the top off the mini vodka bottle. She took a quick sip before pouring the entire contents in the glass of orange juice.

Jake didn't budge or fidget like the rest of the plane. Maybe he really hadn't heard the announcement. The more time she got to sit next to him, the better. To smell him. Watch his every move. What she really wanted was to be in private so she could ask all the right questions. Make him admit why he was so angry. Admit that after all this time, he hadn't let go.

She tapped him on the shoulder. "We're delayed."

He pulled the earpiece out. "What?"

"We're delayed for an hour. I want to talk to you." She couldn't wait any longer. The noise would drown out her voice. Keep her secrets from carrying too far.

He simply stared straight ahead. Then pulled out the second earpiece. His forearm flexed with such a simple movement. Goose bumps rose on her skin. His hands, his touch. She didn't want it to be acting next time. They could make their own love scene.

"Life is too short to be angry over some bullshit, don't you think?"

"I couldn't agree more."

"So that's it, one little flashback down memory lane and you're going all ballistic."

He licked his bottom lip. He gave what he wanted to say a second thought, then decided to say nothing at all.

"Say it. Say what's on your mind. Let's just clear the air here and now."

"The air has never been more clear."

It was a gut reaction. She snapped her wrist and orange juice and Smirnoff flew. "I'm sorry. I . . . didn't mean . . ."

He hardly reacted, as if he expected no less. He smoothed a hand over his dripping face and pushed the earpieces back in one at a time. He did a slight bounce and nod to the beat and stared out the window.

Sirena pressed the attendant button. "I need a towel. I spilled my drink . . . on him."

The flight attendant rushed with paper towels in hand. Sirena held a handful of ice she'd already picked from his lap while he pretended she wasn't even there.

If that's how he wanted to play it.

She dived her hand in the crotch of his pants, simultaneously pulling the earpiece out with the other. She breathed heat into his ear and whispered quickly, "I will never stop wanting you. I know you feel the same about me." She backed away and gave him his space. In fact, she could do one even better.

"Is it okay if I move to that seat?" she asked the attendant after handing her the wet paper towel.

"Sure," she said with more of a questioning tone than agreement.

Ramona's eyes followed her from where she was sitting a couple of rows back. She'd missed the melee and now was dying to know what had happened.

There was no upside. No way to spin it. Sirena simply ignored the inquiring minds and took her new seat. She pulled her long hair to the top of her head and clipped it, slipped on her reading glasses and opened the script.

Fade in. She was starting from the beginning, for the tenth or so time. The story was set in the early 1920s, in Harlem. Prohibition, gun runners, and juke joints. The director wanted Sirena to play Sarah Diamond, a beautiful singer in the famed Savoy nightclub who witnessed the murder of Duke Washington, her kingpin boyfriend. She's caught between the detective who wants to solve the case and her loyalty to who she is and where she came from. After all, the police and authorities are the real enemy. What happens on the streets, stays on the streets and gets handled between them. But the city mayor and police are determined to make her testify by any means necessary, threatening her and her family. The second-in-command to the notorious Harlem rackets is Max Vondrell, who quickly takes control and offers her protection.

Sirena's eyes looked up from the script and involuntarily trailed to where she'd left Jake. He sat unmoved. Unfazed by his crotch and shirt soaking in vodka and OJ. This character reminded her of Jake. This strong character, Max Vondrell, had a weakness. When he saw someone in need, he had no choice but to protect them.

She'd done it once, she could do it again. Make him think she was helpless, useless without him. Make herself vulnerable beyond recognition. He would rescue her like a knight in shining armor. A long and hard-fought love stronger than even before.

All she had to do was start the ball rolling. The press and their insatiable need to make a story out of nothing at all would do the rest.

Then it dawned on her . . . he was married. For some reason that little fact kept slipping her mind. It was the wrong thing to do. Yet, she knew in the deepest part of her soul they were meant to be together.

"Ladies and gentlemen, unfortunately, we've been informed that no flights will be leaving LaGuardia. We have been instructed to remain on the plane for a few more hours."

Moans and angry groans fluttered over the voice of the flight attendant. "What the hell is going on?"

"There's been a bomb threat." Three more flight attendants appeared, one a male in case things got really ugly. The main one did her best to control the situation. "We have arranged for all passengers to receive a hotel voucher for one hundred dollars to be used at your choice of stay."

Sirena scowled. "A hotel voucher for a hundred dollars. Goodness. We've hit it big now." She cut her eyes to Ramona.

"I'm on it." Ramona had her BlackBerry out, locked and loaded. She was speed-dialing hotels. Apparently so was everyone else. After five solid minutes, she laid the phone down in her lap. "Booked. Every hotel in Manhattan is sold out."

"There's no such thing as booked. Okay. Did you say who the room was for?"

"Sorry, sweet britches, there's a bigger name on the line. The president is here. He's having a huge tribute with the American Symphony and African American Ballet Company. All the bigwigs have descended on the island, leaving no room for the little people."

"Who you calling a little people? Being a little person sounds like a personal issue. I don't have that problem." Sirena was fuming mad. First of all, why wasn't she invited to this . . . American Tribute? "I need to get off this plane." She dug into her purse and pulled out her own cell phone.

She was engaged to a multitasking billionaire. Surely he could finagle a private jet.

The phone rang only a couple of times before going to voice mail, which meant he'd pressed the ignore button. Her ears were burning with disgust. Earl was probably getting his dick sucked by some wannabe starlet. He could at least answer the phone.

She left a polite message explaining her predicament. She needed to escape New York and their tiny bungalows and lumpy beds. No way could she stay without the level of care and bedding she was accustomed to. Been there, done that.

Meanwhile, Jake sat silently, continuing his pretense of being unaware while she fought the obscenities from breaking from her lips.

Get me off this plane.

Blame It on the Boogie

Once the doors swung open, the passengers moved toward the fresh air like hungry cattle finding fresh pasture.

"Once again, thank you for your patience," the same attendant announced. Her hand quivered as she handed the vouchers to each customer as they exited the plane. A telling sign that she took the bomb threat seriously. The glamour of the job out the window. Her line of work had changed drastically after 9/11.

"Jake, wait." Sirena hobbled up the ramp to catch up with him. Her feet had puffed too big for her platform high-heel boots and they hadn't even left the ground. "Where do you think you're going?"

"To a hotel to wait," he answered as if they'd not spent the last few hours ignoring each other.

"Which hotel? They're all booked."

He held out his smart phone. "Confirmation for the Renaissance, one night." A smirk rose on his face. His chest rose and fell in triumph. The airport was packed with people sitting and stretched out on every available space on the icky flooring. It looked like a refugee camp. He strolled as if no one was in his way.

"Why do you hate me?"

He shook his head and kept walking.

She sidestepped and used her muscular dancing legs to keep

pace with him. "How did you get that room?" The realization hit her. "Why didn't you say something? You were staring out the window the whole time. You saw the planes not taking off. All of 'em just sittin' out there and you knew, didn't you?"

He hunched his shoulders. She followed him out to the mile-long stretch of people waiting for a taxi. The line was moving at a snail's pace. Fumes rose off the idling engines of cars parked at the curb and went directly up her nose. She had to gulp two or three times before she could talk. "You can't leave me here," she whined.

She'd wanted to pretend to be vulnerable, not really *be* vulnerable. It made her sick to need anyone. But here she was, outside LaGuardia Airport with no team, no Quincy her bodyguard, no Le-shawn her personal assistant. Ramona was inept and completely incapable of handling someone of Sirena's star quality. Her manager, Keisha, had warned her about traveling without her crew. Without someone with her best interest as first priority. But she hadn't wanted any distractions between her and Jake. It was the perfect opportunity to be alone with him.

"Please, Jay. I can't stay here."

"I've only got one room. Sorry, sweetheart," he said without even looking in her direction.

"I can't believe you're treating me this way." She talked to his wide back. "Since when did you become this cruel? If this is what marriage does for you, I'm glad I never took that plunge."

He whipped around, startling her. She bounced back, bumping into the people in the line behind her.

"Truer words have never been spoken." He still smelled of the alcohol she'd thrown on him, as if he'd been boozing it up all afternoon. But she knew different. This was a sober man telling her exactly how he felt.

"You know what . . . fuck you," she yelled.

He turned and grabbed her, squeezing her arms to her side. "All right. Chill. This shit will be posted on some gossip rag by sundown."

He knew every single person within two feet had a camera phone and they'd just given a ridiculous show of epic proportion.

She dropped her head against his chest. "I'm sorry. I will never be happy until you forgive me." In that same instant he let her go.

"Forgive you for what?"

She welled up, unable to speak.

"You can't even say it, can you? If you can't forgive yourself, what do you expect me to do?"

Once again he was right. Cameras were always watching. Except they were real pictures by real photographers who were paid handsomely to catch an opportunity such as this. Paid to make it appear to be something that it wasn't. Or maybe it was exactly as it appeared. A married man with his famous lover clutched in a tearful embrace, a final good-bye. He hated the camera-toting stalkers. He hated the lies, and falsehoods. He hated the need for a celebrity to have their whole life at everyone's instant disposal. Privacy was something he'd cherished. Now a thing of the past like cassette tapes. There was no hiding—if someone wanted to find you they could.

They hopped into a cab. Jake watched over Sirena's shoulder as she typed into her phone. Sending out a message to her endless number of fans, *Have no fear. I'm safe and in good hands.*

My hands, he assumed. *Bottom line*, he folded his arms over his chest, just more lies.

Party Favors

"Look what the cat dragged in." Trevelle lifts her eyes up over the skinny reading glasses. "We got a couple of new orders. I was looking them up to see how to arrange them, seeing as how I had to man the ship alone."

"I'm sorry. And thank you. But where's Vin?"

"Good question."

I kept looking at my watch. It was Monday, and Vince usually opened the place up at eight. "How'd you get in?"

Trevelle turned her head toward me as if I was bothering her. "Obviously I have a key."

My lips were poised for, why do you have a key? Instead I said, "Oh, good." I faced the wall and fought not to choke myself. Vince was missing and he'd given Trevelle a key. My key to my place of business.

I had a part-timer who came in three days a week. Jackie was in her eighties but you'd never know it. She could do in three hours what would take me all day. Her arrangements were what I used as displays in hotels and restaurants to get more business.

"Did Jackie call?" I asked, determined to change the subject and not to focus on something so small, even though everyone I'd come to depend on seemed to be missing.

"No." Trevelle's answer was short and to the point.

"She should've been here. I'm worried."

Her silence persisted.

"Okay, Trevelle, once again I am in your debt. I have an appointment at the Monarch Hotel." I looked at my watch again. "Do you mind continuing to man the ship?"

"I will be here," she sang. "Sitting here not because I have to, but because I enjoy it. Regardless of whether I am appreciated or not."

I rubbed my forehead. "I appreciate it, very much. I'm sure Jackie is on her way. And Vince should be here soon."

"Ahuh." She continued her refrain.

I gathered the one arrangement and my marketing materials. Three weeks of calling finally got me an appointment and all I had was a single arrangement with a number of wide-eyed chrysanthemums in warm fall colors.

The Monarch Hotel was brand-new. I'd started calling for a meeting the minute the windows went in. If not me it would be someone else, was the way I saw it.

So why not me?

The lobby smelled new. I'd worn my favorite suit. The cream wool blend was timeless. The skirt needed to be let out in the hips, a bit snug. Nothing a pair of Spanx couldn't fix. I strolled with confidence, though my heels felt uneasy on the brand-new shiny floor.

I set the arrangement on the farthest check-in counter as if it belonged. Stunning. The vibrant burgundy and orange flowers complemented the pearl color of the marble floor and counters. I made sure the In Bloom business card sat out prominently in the front.

"Hi there, I'm here for an appointment with Mr. Carter."

"Welcome to the Monarch," the young man echoed what he'd been repeating all day. "How can I help you this afternoon?"

"I have an appointment with the hotel manager, Mr. Carter."

"Yes. Your name."

"Venus Parson."

He typed on his keyboard. "Have a seat and I'll let him know you're here."

The clientele mingling in the lobby were all suit types. Men and women extending stiff handshakes reminded me why I liked having my own business. I'd spent years prancing around in corporate halls, pressed suits, pressed hair, sucking up to whomever was in control.

I inhaled my freedom and took a seat on the couch where I could have a direct view of the floral arrangement. Trevelle had made it and I hadn't said a word of thank you. I would either have to start being extra nice or put her on the payroll. Both painful choices. As far as I was concerned she still owed me for the anxiety, pain, and money I'd spent fighting the custody case for Mya. Gratitude was hard to come by when all I was thinking about was what she'd tried to take away from me.

I sat patiently, trying not to look at the time. At least twenty minutes had passed. I tried to get the attention of the young man who'd greeted me. Remind him I was waiting.

A large man came face-to-face with him before I could catch his eye. I would've guessed Mr. Carter if he hadn't been carrying a briefcase and had a woman hanging on his arm.

"Welcome to the Monarch. Are you checking in, sir?" the young man greeted.

"Checking in. Dr. Benjamin Rivera."

Tiny hairs on my arms and neck stood up. Miriam's husband? Ben Rivera. Tingling nervousness moved along the surface of my entire body. My feet suddenly felt numb, though all I could think of was to run out of there and call Miriam. Then I remembered her wig. I hadn't recognized her at the recital. Maybe it was her and Ben rekindling at the Monarch Hotel. I gave her a good once-over.

The woman was smaller than Miriam. A bit taller, but way too slim.

"We have you here with us for one night. Will Mrs. Rivera be needing a key also?"

"One is fine." He leaned his large brown head into the lady with dark straight hair slightly flipped up on the end. They nuzzled nose to nose. I'd only seen him once or twice in passing. Had his name not been announced, I'd never have recognized him . . . but here he was like a big red target with a lighted arrow pointed at his indiscretion. Why now, why me? I didn't want to be a witness to this crime.

"Venus, hello. I'm Will Carter."

Midswallow, "Hello." He offered his hand. My grip was weak and unsteady. *Poor Miriam.* "Thank you . . . I brought flowers."

"Yes. Good." His brow raised, sensing I was off balance. "I saw them. They're wonderful. Let me get you some water, or juice. Something you prefer?" He was gone before I could answer. His short squatty legs moved fast. He came back with a sweating bottle of orange juice with a napkin that was already soaked through. "I'm sorry I made you wait."

"No. I've just been fighting something." I used the napkin to pat my forehead and nose. "Nothing to do with this beautiful place." I gulped the juice and fought from turning my head toward Ben. "If you've got to wait, here is the place to do it. Monarch is just breathtaking."

"You don't have to be nervous. It's just three hundred million dollars and a work in progress."

"I can see every penny of it." I looked overhead at the enormous chandeliers. Old-world style at the current prices. "I know you were expecting more of a sampling."

"I'm impressed, trust me. The wife of JP holding down her own business—that's to be commended."

"Oh . . . yes . . ." I blinked back the recognition. "Let me assure you, In Bloom is a bona fide full-service floral center. We put effort and pride into each arrangement. Your deliveries are guaranteed to last seven days. No limp willies."

He grinned. "You have the contract."

I was relieved. "Enough said, then. Thank you."

"Come, let me show you the areas we need to fill."

I took a chance and glanced in the direction where Ben and his mistress were last standing. All clear. I followed behind the manager. The place was massive. I was listening and writing while he talked.

"We have twenty floors."

"So you'll need an arrangement at each elevator."

"Absolutely."

I was calculating the bounty in my head. Multiply that by fifty-two weeks. *I'm rich, rich, I tell you, filthy rich.*

"I'm assuming you will attend our grand opening."

"Oh yes. Wouldn't miss it."

"And your husband. I'm sure he's a busy man, but it would be great attention for the hotel if he and Sirena arrived. We do this whole red-carpet thing. Make sure the media is on the case." His knees butted together when he stood still.

"When, exactly? The date. I'd have to clear it with his publicist."

He relaxed his hands in his pockets. His stance said we weren't taking another step until this part of the offer was noted and accepted.

"I'm sure it won't be a problem," I added.

"We'd need Sirena there too."

"I really can't speak for Sirena," I said lightly as possible.

"I'll make sure you get *two* formal invitations." He held up his fingers so there was no mistaking his terms. All or none. He was back in stride. His short legs sure could move.

Ring the Alarm

How would he explain this to Venus? She'd understood everything else—missing the recital, not calling—but not this. No way she understood this, even if the story was about as predictable as humanly possible. A bomb threat was about as plausible as "the dog ate my homework." Excuses. The same way he hadn't believed her story the night he'd found her ex-boyfriend, Clint Fairchild, in her hotel room. After flying cross-country he swung first and asked questions later. There was nothing Venus said or could've said that was enough. No matter how many times she explained how their room keys got mixed up, he couldn't hear her because he hated Clint Fairchild from the beginning. Didn't trust him.

But it was all about trust, his wife had said. "If you trusted me, none of this would've happened." He mocked her voice in his head. Still angry when he thought about it. Now it would be her turn. The shoe was on the other foot. *She simply had to trust him.*

He'd start by explaining with the fact he couldn't bear to see a woman cry. Any woman, for that matter. He'd watched and listened to his mother's sobbing over one man or another. Going through men like they were Kleenex tissue. As a child, he never understood why he and his brother weren't enough to make his mother happy. He took it personal. Very personal. There were other things, plenty to be grateful for. Living, breathing, seeing a sunset.

Regardless of what he understood now as a grown man, a woman's tears meant he was at fault. Crying over a man was the worst offense; even if the tears were over him, somehow he'd failed.

"Let's go." He held the taxi door open for Sirena to get in as she sobbed.

As they pulled away, they passed Ramona, who was obviously looking for them. His phone started buzzing.

He held up a hand to silence Sirena. "Yeah, Ramona."

"Where are you two?"

"We're on our way to the Renaissance," he said nonchalantly as if it were a practice run for his own situation. "One room. At the Renaissance," he repeated. "That's all they had left and I snagged it. Let me know when the airport clears us for departure. I want to be on the first thing smoking."

When he hung up, Sirena had inched her way under his arm. He had to lift and slide over her just to snap his phone back on his belt.

"I'm sorry about throwing the drink on you. I'm sorry about Tommy. All the old emotions coming out. It was hard for me too. If I could change time, I would."

He nodded. "It's squashed. Like you said, the past is the past." He cracked the window, grateful for the sooty air versus inhaling her perfume. Her mascara was streaked and smudged around her eyes. Her vulnerability scared him as it always did.

He adjusted himself in the backseat of the cab, desperate for his own space. They were moving in the opposite direction of traffic. He felt like he was going backward, traveling down a road he had no control of, toward a bullet aimed directly at his head.

"So only one room. Who gets the bed?" She grinned. Her apple cheeks glowed with color when only moments ago, she was a sobbing mess. She slung her hair over one shoulder, grazing his face.

"We'll work it out," he said calmly, though underneath, his hurried heartbeat was a sign of things to come. He hadn't had an asthma attack in some years. The last time was when Venus had caught Beverly, his designer from JP Wear, giving him a very personal fitting.

Now here he was again, walking a very fine tightrope.

He kept his eye on his phone, waiting for information about the airport reopening. He sent a text to Venus letting her know there was another flight delay, but not a word more.

"You're awake." Sirena was wrapped with a towel that barely closed. Fully aware that the towel conveniently showed her V-spot, smooth except for the little stash of hair trimmed like a little old man's beard.

He closed his eyes, but only after a few seconds too long. "Yeah, wide-awake. I can't believe Ramona never called. The airport can't still be shut down." It was hours later and Jake had awakened in the bed where he wasn't supposed to be. As lavish as the hotel room appeared, with satin drapes and scrolled arms on the high-backed chairs, there was barely enough room to walk around the king-size bed. He'd stretched out blankets and pillows on the floor, but that hadn't lasted long.

"I ordered something for us to eat."

Jake rolled over and looked for his phone, which was never more than an arm's reach away. Lately he'd gotten sloppy—in more ways than one. Instead his eyes landed on the condom wrapper.

"Looking for this?" Sirena held up the black case. She walked it over to him. "It was on the floor so I put it out of harm's way." She leaned over him. "My earring." She picked up the gold hoop of charms and jangled it. "Guess things got a little crazy."

"Sirena, this stays between you and me, you understand."

"Of course. I have as much to lose as you. In fact, more."

"What's that supposed to mean?"

"My reputation," she exclaimed. "I'm supposed to be all about girl power and I'm setting myself up for failure with a married man." Her voice softened. "Circumstances. What do you do?"

He could've corrected her. In fact his mind was shouting how wrong she was. He could've made it clear right then and there. There were no circumstances, only the fact that he would never leave Venus, plain and simple.

He grabbed Sirena's face and called her by the name he'd used so long ago. "Cee Cee, listen . . ." Instead she pecked him on the lips. He let out an exhausted breath. "Promise me this will go no further. Not to your girlfriends, your manager, not even into one of those journals you like to keep."

"I promise. I understand. I'm not pushing. I have a fiancé, you have a wife. What's between us, stays between us."

He stuck out his pinkie the way Mya always made him. "Pinkie swear."

Sirena linked her finger around his. "I'm not the one you have to worry about. You were always too honest for your own good, Jay." She rose, letting her towel fall. "Gotta get dressed. Ordered you a stack of pancakes and an omelet."

It began with a pillow fight. The way they used to play. She always started it, taking the first swing. When he wouldn't respond, then a second and a third until he was so mad he had to fight back. Pillow warfare.

He'd clobbered her over the head, no holding back, just to teach her a lesson. That only made her teeth clench, growl, and attack. That was the fun part, watching her try to defend against his blows.

"You never learn, do you?" he said, nearly out of breath. It was a workout. Swinging, dodging, springing to the other side of the bed while she chased for revenge like a madwoman. He thought the hotel management would be sent up. Surely they were making too much noise, stomping on somebody's heads below.

"You're the one who never learns," she huffed, crouched with her arms out, her long hair splayed covering half her face. She was wearing nothing but a T-shirt and panties. It struck him then how she hadn't really changed. The same person, even after fame and millions, she carried nothing but a T-shirt and a change of underwear on trips.

"All right, I'm warning you. Next connect, you're going down."

She took a leaping hike, using the mattress as her launchpad. Up and over like something out of *The Matrix*. Landing on top of him. He felt his knees buckle. She straddled him and swung with all her might.

"I give, I give."

"Yeah. Who's your momma?"

He shook his head, no. She popped him hard with the square pillow. "Who's your momma?"

If he won, he got to be the daddy, the boss. He got to tell her what to do, and how. But that's not where the game was supposed to go. Not anymore. He was married. *He was married*. He'd repeated it over and over. Thank God those words would keep him alive.

"I said, who's your mamma?" By then she was already gyrating against his pelvis. He could feel his body betraying him. She pulled the T-shirt over her head, exposing the pierced nipple with a small gold ring. She leaned over the length of his torso, then slid down. He thought he would cry when her warm wet mouth engulfed him.

"Shitttt," he gasped. "Cee Cee . . ." He swallowed the rest of what he wanted to say. *No. Stop. Damn it, girl, you gon' get me killed.*

"When was the last time . . . huh, Jay?" she asked, taking her tongue in a full circle at the top. She remembered. "Tell me, pretty boy. I bet nobody does it like me." She squeezed him to the brink, then let go. She was up on her feet, moving fast. Before he knew it she was back, unwrapping the condom. Tasting and kissing him all at the same time.

"I bet she can't do it like me."

And that's when it happened. Like pulling the plug on his chug boat. He deflated slowly, leaving his once all-powerful organ without a pulse. She sucked, poked, grabbed, and squeezed, and nothing happened. Embarrassment shrouded them both.

"Oh, it's like that." She grabbed her T-shirt and threw it on. Jake lay on the floor with his arms across his face. He thought about telling her it wasn't personal. It seemed she needed consoling more than he did. A blow to her very large ego. What man would pass up this opportunity?

"Sorry about that?" was all he could muster, because he was indeed sorry, more like pitiful. He'd probably have gone through with it like a poor little lamb to slaughter had his mind not intervened. Mind over matter. Just the mention of "she," meaning his wife. *I bet she can't do it like me.* Sirena may as well have invited Venus into the room to watch.

Even now, first thing in the morning, his usual greeting and salute was limp and uninterested in starting the day. He could hardly feel his own hand as if he was being punished with numbness. If God were listening, or even watching, *He* had to know Jake was innocent. Not deserving of this kind of punishment. *Nothing happened.* That was his story and he was sticking to it. Once he realized there was no chance of his dick accidentally slipping into Sirena, he'd hopped in the bed and told her to scooch over.

She'd slept angry. He'd slept scared. Barely grazing each other in the middle of the night and jumping to the other side if they did. He couldn't wait to get into his own bed.

Leaning over the edge of the bed now, he picked up the open condom package that still held the silicone. Unused. "You see, God? Innocent."

Who was he kidding? There was no free pass for his manhood failing on him, even if it was the result of having a conscience. Like stealing a candy bar, taking a bite, then trying to return it to the store. The damage was already done.

Sirena's shower ran. He knew she'd be out quick, never one for long contemplative waterworks. He threw on his pants and shirt. He found one shoe. The other, he assumed, was buried under the sheets and blankets on the floor where he was supposed to have slept.

The shower turned off right when he'd found his black Bruno loafer. He bolted to the door, easing it open with as little sound as possible, then closing it tight behind him.

Stealth-mission escapes from hotel rooms had been his past life. When he was on the road back in his early music days, waking up with someone he hardly knew was part of the job. Groupies who'd promised him the best night of his life only to be just another silly bump and grind, were a requirement not a privilege. If you didn't partake in the bevy of offerings, suspicion would arise. Was he gay? Did he have the package, the disease? So many times Jake had faked the funk. He only pretended to swallow the little blue pill the road manager passed out like vitamins. One-a-day. Fuck-all-night. He could've used one last night. Save his reputation but destroy it as well, all in one fell swoop.

The elevator opened at the lobby. Bright light streamed, hitting him square in the eyes. He had to squint but at least he knew to follow the sun.

"Sir, can I help you?" The bellman stood straight and unaffected by the fact he was wearing a silly hat and suit like a chimp that played the accordion.

"I need a cab to the airport."

"Absolutely, sir." He put a whistle to his mouth and blew. "Do you need help with your bags, sir?"

Bags? He'd left his one bag in the room. There was no way he was going back to get it. "Nah, that's it," he said. He meant it. He was sick of the back-and-forth game with Sirena, because in his heart, he knew eventually he'd slip up.

Picture Worth a Thousand Words

"I know someone who can fix that." Trevelle pointed to her own forehead, but her frown was directed toward me. "Those lines right there. Instant removal."

"What lines?" I rushed to the bathroom. I had my mother's genes. There should be no lines.

But there they were. Three little dashes in the center of my forehead. I rubbed and stretched where only a few days ago they hadn't been. Even the senator had pointed them out.

Eyes red. Skin in need of hydration. Stomach in a knot. I hadn't slept more than a couple of hours, and even then it was on high alert. As if the boogey man were lurking in the closet or under the bed. My cell phone had five messages from Jake. I hadn't listened to a single one and it was eating me up inside.

"I feel your pain, Venus. If anyone understands infidelity, it is me." Trevelle stood right outside the bathroom door with her long arms outstretched. "I saw Jake and Sirena in their loving embrace. I know I should leave those sleazy gossip sites alone, but it's a guilty habit. Especially after they spent so much time talking about me."

I put up both my hands. "Stop right there. I don't want to hear any gossip. I really don't."

"Sometimes, most of the time, more often than not, there is a grain of truth to their stories. I lived through it. Remember when the story broke about Airic being charged with statutory rape? The sex tape was indeed date stamped three days shy of her seventeenth birthday." She nodded her head to rest her case.

Vince opened the door and pushed his way in backward carrying a box. He put the box down when he saw me and rubbed his hands on black jeans that always looked brand-new. "There's my girl. How you doin', sweetheart?"

"Well, look who decided to show up." I knocked his hand away before he could give my shoulder a solace squeeze. "Why weren't you here this morning?"

"Hey, no need to pretend. Trevelle showed me those pictures of your hubby lip-locking that Sirena broad. Tell me if you want me to teach him a lesson. I'll have him fixed like that." He snapped his finger.

"There's nothing to fix."

"Sweetheart, they weren't actually kissing," Trevelle corrected him. "Now you're worse than these gossip blogs, adding your own details."

My eyes darted side to side between them. Trevelle already knew where I was going. *Sweetheart.*

Her bony shoulders were erect, along with her noble chin. "Excuse you for your nasty thoughts. Vince is my friend. He is someone I cherish. Does not mean we engage in fornication. That's the problem with these relationships. They're all based on fornication and lies. You can't have a blessed union without God's approval. You and Jake need to come to Jesus." She came over and slapped the stack of new orders in front of me. "I will pray for you."

"Pray for yourself," I snapped.

Vince disappeared.

I'd driven without the radio on, specifically not to hear some lame gossip. I'd ignored Jake's messages to not hear the truth. Heaven forbid I thought In Bloom was a safe haven. I'd walked right into the devil's playground and Mother Teresa was the ringleader.

"Trevelle, in the future, I would appreciate you keeping rumors, gossip, anything of that nature to yourself."

"Fine," she said, going into her silence that drove me crazy. Her modus operandi was from one extreme to another.

"Don't start with the one-word answers. Please. I'm not in the mood."

"Fine. You want to hear the rest of what's on my mind?"

Not really.

"Vince and I are very concerned for you. We have discussed your situation and think you should take some time off—you know, to get yourself together."

Vince came in carrying another box. "Now don't get your thong too tangled. This was mostly my idea."

"Take some time off? Hmm, and that would mean leaving you two crazy kids all alone here."

"Three of us. Don't forget about Jackie. When she does show up, she's very efficient. After you left, she filled nineteen orders in a record three hours."

"Just because I have a couple of creases on my forehead doesn't mean I'm bushed. Everyone has a bad night."

"What you need is to take this opportunity to be by your significant other's side." Trevelle blinked her synthetic lashes slowly so I'd get her meaning. "And speaking of bushed, sweetie, you're going to have to do something with that hair of yours. That is just not sexy." She raised her arms in a circle. "So 1970. You're not going to win this hair war, okay? Accept it and move on."

"I'll tell you like I told my mother, there's no contest. I don't need to get in the ring and fly like a butterfly and sting like a bee. Who I am, is who I am. Jake married me, not Sirena, or her character on the big screen. Me." I picked up the box cutter and began opening the fresh shipment of flowers. I was doing my best impression of not giving a damn. Pretending the two of them ganging up on me didn't hurt my feelings.

"It's float like a butterfly . . . not fly," Trevelle corrected.

"What?"

"She's holding a sharp object," Vince announced, slightly out of breath. At fifty-five or so he had the body of an athletic thirty-year-old, thanks to all the hours he'd spent in the gym, but the simple task of carrying boxes made him winded. I wanted to point and say, *"Ha, that's what you get for all those late nights sitting at the Wicked Witch's house watching* TMZ *and searching gossip sites till wee hours in the morning."* But instead I put the box cutter down and went to the mini refrigerator and got him a bottle of water.

"You should take a break."

He gulped, then recapped the bottle. "I'm a man of steel."

"I can see that. When's the last time you had a man-check?"

"Been a while."

"And I'm supposed to leave my precious baby in your hands. Trust you and the—" His eyes narrowed, daring me to say what I called her when no one was around: the Wicked Witch of the South. "How are you supposed to take over the business when you're probably more tired than I've ever seen you?"

"Teamwork," Trevelle said. "Vince and I know how to work as a team. Something not everyone understands. My ministry was a multimillion-dollar business before your ex destroyed my life."

"*My* ex?" I shook my head. "Unbelievable." I rubbed my temple. "Trevelle, I never made it down the aisle with Airic. *You're* the only one who married him."

"Okay, you two. Let's not get off on tangents. First order of business, just know we're here for you. All we're saying is, if you need to take some time off to get your affairs in order, we got your back." Vince stood up and stretched, then yawned. His eyes even watered a bit.

Trevelle, on the other hand, was bright eyed and full of energy. "Exactly, we're here for you."

"I appreciate it," I said, finally glad to bring mom and dad's lecture to a close. The bell rang, announcing a customer. I peeked best I could past the wide glossy leaf palms and ficus trees. I was grateful to have the Monarch Hotel contract. Now I could clear out some of the inventory that was crowding the store. I hadn't got a chance to tell Vince the good news, too busy dodging the knife he'd tried to stick in my back. Whatever spell that woman had over him was quickly pulling him to the dark side.

I clapped my hands together when I got close enough to see a friendly face, even if she was shrouded in her new wig. "Miriam . . . oh my goodness, what a surprise." While I hugged her and blew the flyaway hairs out of my face, Ben came through the door behind her.

"I'm the one with the surprise," Miriam said, beaming. "Guess what . . . we've decided to renew our vows. We're going to have a ceremony, big and beautiful."

"But, I . . ." My heart was racing. It was only hours earlier I'd seen him with the other woman. "Congratulations."

"Ben, you've met Venus before, right? She's the one I tell you about, the wife of JP."

He only had to lean to reach me with his extended hand. "Nice to meet you." I'd only seen a second or two of his profile when he was kissing the other woman. Head on, he was a tall, imposing man. His gleaming brown skin was hairless except for his stark black eyebrows. He wore glasses like a mild-mannered good guy wearing a suit, but I knew better and tried to contain my disgust.

"Renewal vows. Isn't that just lovely."

Miriam leaned on his arm. "Ben wants to have the ceremony at the Monarch. Have you been there? It's absolutely beautiful. Their courtyard looks like springtime in Italy."

"As a matter of fact, I was there recently. Like around ten in the morning. In the lobby." I had to stop myself. No sense in ruining someone else's happiness just because mine was on the skids.

Ben didn't seem to be fazed. Temperament control was a

requirement for liars. "Does that mean you can get us a good price?" He grinned. "Even better, can you have Sirena Lassiter sing at our ceremony?"

If I had a dollar for every time someone mentioned Sirena's name . . . "I don't think she does weddings."

"We're shooting for Valentine's weekend."

"Miriam, that's the busiest time. Not to mention the most expensive time for weddings. Nearly everyone doubles their price."

"It's your blessed day, you make it anytime you want," Trevelle sang out from the back.

"Who was that?"

"My bad dream."

"I can hear you."

"Good."

Trevelle made her appearance. Her Dolce & Gabbana jeans and Jimmy Choo high heels were considered dressing down. Her jacket was studded with rhinestones. Her casual look would cost most people a week's salary. "Is this the lovely couple?"

"Miriam," she said, offering her hand. "And this is my husband Ben."

"Pleasure to meet you. I'm Trevelle Doval, floral designer and event concierge . . . at your service. I know everyone who is anyone."

"Trevelle, I'm going to handle Miriam's ceremony. She's my friend and I'd like to give her that personal touch."

The woman was gobbling up my life.

Miriam's eyes widened with surprise. "You're the famous Trevelle Doval. Oh my!" she reached out and hugged Trevelle with all her might. "What in the world are you doing here, working here?"

"I ask that question every day," I interceded. "But here she is."

"Yes, here I am. And as I was saying, you are in the best hands."

"Absolutely, mine."

"And as we were discussing before Miriam arrived, you really need some time off," Trevelle added with a flail of her long wrist.

Her nails were the only thing natural about her, and she'd only taken the acrylic off because handling wet flower stems all day was a recipe for fungus disaster.

"Well, I'm free now."

"Keep in mind, we're both here for you." I felt Trevelle's heavy eyes all over me.

"Everything is going to be perfect." Miriam could've been eighteen again the way she bopped up and down, her smile wide as all outside. Her skin glowed with happiness. No one had whiter teeth than Miriam, I was absolutely sure. I had to admit she was glowing. She soft-punched Ben in the arm. "First things first, we need to get the Monarch penciled in. Valentine's Day," she ordered. "Go big or go home." She pursed her lips and they kissed.

Money, obviously, was no longer an issue. Lights, water, gas, food, shelter, and girlfriend all for one low, low, price. Her dignity. May I announce Dr. Benjamin and Mrs. Rivera.

"Let's get started, then."

"Anything you need, I'm still at your service." Trevelle did a defeated wave before clicking her rhinestone Wicked Witch heels and dashing off.

I rubbed the lines in the center of my forehead, scared I was beginning to look like a Shar-Pei puppy. Age and wisdom were supposed to make life easier, not harder. But as I got older, the only thing I'd really learned was not to say the first thing on my mind; in fact, I'd learned to voice the opposite since most of the times I got it wrong.

"She's so helpful," I said with a grimace that could pass for a smile.

The day had left me spent, which was really no different from the one before that, and the one before that. And surely the one to come. It was time for the tea party that I'd taken on. I'd crawled into my car with the intention of sitting still for a moment. My phone

began to sing the ring tone of Jake's song—although the seven seconds mostly featured Sirena's hook. It was a great idea at the time.
I'd tried several times to change it back to the standard ring only to
hear her melodic screech even louder.

"Hey, you," I answered coolly as if the last twenty-four hours
hadn't happened.

"Hey, baby. I miss you," he said practically whispering.

"Where are you?" I whispered back. "Did you find a flight out?"

"Yeah, finally. It's been a circus. People everywhere trying to
leave New York. Worse, they keep dropping off more people who
can't get their connecting flights." He paused. "I just wanted to tell
you how much I love you, baby."

"I love you too," I said, still maintaining a degree of distance.

"I have to tell you something," he said shakily. "*We* had to stay at
a hotel—"

"No, you don't have to tell me anything. I love you and I trust
you. Okay. Let's leave it at that."

He was bursting with his story already rehearsed and ready to go,
emphasizing the *we* so I'd be prepared for the worse. I stayed silent.
Not taking the bait. Knowing Jake, it was killing him that I wasn't following the plan. Ignoring the script. No big deal. They'd been in
many hotels, in many cities, why would now be any different?

"I'll see you when you get home," I sang out in a pitch too high,
quickly pressing the END button. Worse yet, I powered the phone
down entirely. Whatever his story, I couldn't stomach it right now.

If he'd planned to lie, it would now become the truth. If he'd
planned the truth, maybe he'd have to reconsider a new one. Change
directions, change course.

Good-girl Rules

I was late.

Not just a few minutes late. Not a quarter-past late. I was seriously-greeted-with-sneers kind of late.

"I'm so sorry," I announced after traveling up the flight of stairs into the private party area of the Chelsea Tea Room. The girls sat around the white linen-covered tables dressed properly for a tea party, their hands resting in their laps, all ready to burst but under strict instructions to sit still. Before I could tell them all how pretty they looked, I was intercepted by the tea lady.

"You must be who we've been waiting for—for the last forty minutes," she added with a hard glance at her delicate gold watch.

"Ms. Parrot, right? I do apologize." I waved a magic hand. "Now we can get started."

"Perot, the T is silent. I'm not a bird," the stern woman enunciated. "This is more than a tea party. This is an etiquette class and being late . . ." she emphasized loudly, letting it hang in the air, ". . . is rude and rather disrespectful behavior."

I probably could've made it on time if I hadn't changed clothes five times. I was standing there in a yellow dress reminiscent of *Breakfast at Tiffany's* with silly white gloves and my hair gelled in a pristine bun. Obviously I knew the value of a good old-fashioned tea party. "I . . . I'm sorry, again, I apologize, to all of you," I said in my most professional voice.

"Apology accepted, and now we can move forward," Jan Perot sang out to end the lesson.

"But don't let it happen again," Miriam chided near my ear. It was a relief to see her, even masked in her wig. I hugged her tight. Her linen bolero jacket scratched my chin. All the other mothers were dressed casually, which meant they'd all planned to vacate the premises. Miriam and I were the only ones dressed properly for a tea party. The rest of the mother sneerers were obviously planning to escape. They were angry because I'd cut into their happy-to-be-free time. Hair, nail, spa appointments, martinis, and shopping were put in jeopardy because of my tardiness.

Ms. Perot snapped her fingers for attention. "I'd also like to welcome someone from *Life 'N' Style* magazine who's doing a story on children's etiquette. Who actually was on time. I've never read this periodical, but I'm told they're very reputable."

I spun around to see Melba Dubois. Our eyes met and she winked. She was accompanied by a photographer. I put out my hand to block his first attempted shot. "Wait a minute. They're not here for a story on etiquette."

Jan Perot peeked past me. "I beg your pardon."

"They're here to focus on my daughter, and me." I faced Melba, "How did you know I'd be here?"

"I didn't," she said smirking. "But you're welcome to remove your daughter from any photographs."

The clicking of the camera had already begun. Jan Perot opened her palms. "Why would they be here for you?"

"My husband is Jake Parson."

A wry smile rose on Melba's smug face. "Her husband is an actor." The words left her mouth as if it were a dirty profession. "I don't think one parent should decide whether or not the rest of the girls get a chance to be famous, featured in a very popular magazine. Right girls?"

The group let out a chorus of, "No, that's not fair." All the while giving Mya the evil eye.

Her breathy husky voice rose. "So smile for the camera."

"Mothers are excused." Ms. Perot seemed to be targeting me specifically. However the whole group filed out fast, tramping down the stairs with hushed snickers. They were obviously pleased with their prompt dismissal, and my punishment.

"I think I'll stay," Miriam said, taking a seat at one of the tables, fanning out her white linen skirt. I felt like kissing her.

I sat patiently, ignoring Miriam's pokes and frowns every time Ms. Perot listed another good-girl rule. Sitting up straight. Making eye contact. Talking should never take precedence over listening. Congeniality attracted friendship. Respect was the Golden Rule. If you didn't respect yourself no one else would. Then it was proper placement of the napkin. Sipping, not slurping. Place settings were a roadmap. The outer silverware was used first, working toward the plate. All this was before the tea and pie were even served.

In the corner, Melba Dubois sat quietly jotting notes. I'd bet any amount of money she was drawing smiley faces with devil horns coming out of their heads. One would be her firstborn since she'd obviously sold her soul. What kind of person uses children out of spite? Since I hadn't cooperated, this was her way of getting under my skin. It wasn't working. Her cameraman was fiddling with parts. So far he'd taken only one picture for their imaginary story.

The cavalry arrived with pie. Three waitstaff dressed in white tuxedo shirts, bow ties, and black trousers each carried a tray on his shoulder. I wanted to clap at the sight of them.

"Key lime or pumpkin?"

I was starving. All I could do was point for fear I'd dribble at the mouthwatering glaze. The pie was set down in front of me. I picked up the thick slice of pumpkin and bit first and asked questions later. My white gloves were now orange at the fingertips. I slipped them off, then continued until my jaws were full. I felt the hand land on my shoulder.

"This is a classic example of what not to do. Flatware is for civilized eating. Hand-to-mouth feedings are for bread only. The exception, a slice of pizza," Ms. Perot offered. "Possibly a cookie, which is part of the bread group. No other exceptions. And you, my dear . . ." She pointed to Mya. "Remember to dab the corners of your mouth. Don't swipe."

I could feel my momma-bear claws come out. Picking on Mya was unnecessary.

"More important, wait for your tea to be served," she said sternly. Forks dropped, hands fell to laps. The girls breathed a sigh of relief when the waitstaff returned with kettles of steaming water. "As I was saying, eating with your hands is a no-no, especially if it requires both of them to do the damage."

"What about a fat juicy cheeseburger?" Miriam whispered, but not quietly enough.

"Exactly," Jan Perot chimed. "I recommend you remove cheeseburgers from your menu or you will be fat and, dare I say . . . juicy." She eyed Miriam's lower torso spread comfortably under her skirt. "They're filled with by-products and unhealthy calories. Say no to burgers, young ladies. You'll thank me in the future."

Miriam cut her eyes. "This woman is way too pent-up."

Lizzie raised her hand. "What about tacos? My mommy makes tacos and I have to eat them with two hands or all the stuff falls out."

Ms. Perot eyed Lizzie's roundness. She had her mother's apple cheeks but they no way reflected her actual size. "You would be a perfect example of what I've just stated."

"Oh, I've had it." Miriam stood up. "Lizzie, let's go. Up," she ordered.

"Mommy, I want to stay. I'm having fun."

"I'll bring her home," I said to Miriam.

"That's not the point. Did you notice there are no Hansels here? Why is it only our daughters are being brainwashed with this non-sense? Why aren't little boys growing up with good manners? All the good manners in the world won't stop your husband from cheating on you," Miriam nearly whispered.

So she did know. She must've known everything.

Little girl gasps and then giggles followed. Melba Dubois perked up. The evening just got interesting. Maybe there was a story here after all.

Miriam went on, her accent sharpened. "Listen up, princesses, the only thing good-girl rules are going to get you is a sink full of dishes and an empty bed."

Ms. Perot was beyond shocked. Speechless. Meanwhile Melba Dubois seemed to be in her element. Her pen was waving across her notepad at the speed of light. The camera rose and followed Miriam's every step.

Lizzie walked slowly to Mya and gave her a hug, then made her exit, waving to the rest of the girls, who felt sorry for their fellow Gretel. Lizzie's short six-year-old legs could barely keep up with her mother's stride. "Mommy, wait."

"Let that be an example of how not to behave," Ms. Perot announced.

"No, she's right, Ms. Perot. Girls have a hard enough time loving themselves. You crossed the line talking about what Lizzie's mother was feeding her. Talking about a child's weight in that manner was just wrong. I think you're the one who needs an etiquette lesson." I faced the girls. "Don't ever let anyone tell you who to be. Be yourself and love yourself."

I rushed out to catch up with Miriam. She'd parked on the far-thest side. A lamppost hung over the area but flickered, barely giving off light. Miriam fought with the car keys, wiping the moistness from her eyes and pressing the wrong button until the alarm went off. Flashing headlights and a blaring horn only made her more flustered.

I took them from her and pressed the button for silence, unlocking the doors. I helped Lizzie in the backseat, strapping her in. "Guess what, I'm going to take you and Mya to the movies next weekend. We'll see the new Disney movie and eat loads of popcorn." She smiled big and wide. Children were so easy to let go of the past, even if the past was five minutes ago.

Adults were another story. "Okay, now you . . . you're scaring me." I closed the car door. Miriam was still shaking. How long had she been holding on, ready to bust with the information she had about her husband?

"I'm scaring me. I can tell you, I've never been more angry in my life. All that talk about being proper and good. Please . . . good girls lose. Plain and simple."

"So you saw him with someone?" I knew it was dangerous territory I was treading. "What happened?"

"Of course. I saw enough. I want to kill him. I swear if I could get away with it . . . Do you understand me? I want to see his lifeless body laying out in the street. That's what I want."

The other moms were beginning to return. I searched around, over my shoulder, praying no one was within earshot. I thought I saw a shadow but wasn't sure.

"Miriam, don't ever say that again. Nothing even close. You can't talk like that, not in this day and age. People take a threat like that seriously."

More important, we both turned our attention to the backseat of her SUV. We both knew Lizzie had heard and understood every word.

"I don't want to feel this way." She shook her head. "I love him." She dabbed her eyes with her sleeve. "I've got to keep it together. But I tell you, back in Cuba, women had a remedy for men like this."

"You're not alone. I know it feels that way, but I'm here and I'll do whatever I can for you. I'm sure we can get your deposit back from the Monarch."

"Why would I need my deposit?"

"You're not going to go through with the renewal ceremony, are you?"

"Of course. What . . . you expect me to end up like that crazy old bat in there preaching about what to eat and what not to eat? How to be a lady. I bet she hasn't been laid in twenty years. Why should I hand my husband over to another woman just like that?"

Our hug was brief. My phone began to vibrate and ring all at the same time. I saw that it was Paige and let it go to voice mail.

"Your husband?"

"No. Paige. She's looking for good news about the success of the tea party." This made Miriam burst out in a laugh that was good enough for me. The mood instantly lightened. "Call me if you need me, okay?"

"I will." Another hug. Her distinct brown-sugar-and-spice scent was strong. I preferred airy natural perfumes. I walked away, still smelling like her and probably would for the next couple of days even after a hard shower.

Along with her scent, I was carrying Miriam's pain. I knew the heartache and rage caused by rejection. I knew what it felt like when someone else was chosen over you. When it felt like no one loved you all because *one man* didn't have the good sense to know your worth. We knew how to deal with death and taxes, but rejection . . . never went down easy.

For me it was Dr. Clint Fairchild, whom I supported for four years while he went to medical school. After Clint graduated, I assumed he would rush to the nearest jewelry counter and buy my engagement ring. Instead, he bought me a puppy, then turned around and married someone else within the year.

Nearly seven years later and the emotional memory was still as raw as if it were yesterday. Clint broke my heart. Jake healed it. Only problem was, the scar never went away.

At this point all I wanted to do was end this day and find myself in my husband's arms. I was overloaded with too much information.

"Great little speech in there." Melba Dubois popped out of the darkness. "You're the kind of friend I'd love to have. So supportive," Melba said before letting me pass back inside.

"Is your friend all right?" Ms. Perot put out a genuine hand.

"She's fine."

"The magazine staff left as soon as you did, so I'm concerned our presentation may have been ruined by her outburst."

I let out an exhausted sigh. I didn't have the energy to tell her no need to worry. That she'd never see her name or the Chelsea Tea Room in print, at least not in *Life 'N' Style* magazine. Melba Dubois was after one thing and it wasn't tips on etiquette.

"Yoo-hooo," the voice sang out.

I'd seen Paige coming and did my best to punch the gas, only to hear the engine sputter. *This car.*

"I wanted to tell you what a fine job you did at the tea party." Her pink lips curved in a hard smile.

My face scrunched up. "Really?"

"Yes, absolutely. The girls raved about what a good time they had. That's why I have to ask, do you mind taking over the meeting this Sunday? The Hansel and Gretels are scheduled for a culinary field trip."

"You mean food tasting?"

"Yes, absolutely. It's essential that our children learn good nutrition while enjoying the possibilities. More to life than hot dogs and hamburgers."

"I can't, I'm sorry."

"Why not?" she asked pointedly. "The handbook specifically stated the requirements of membership. Volunteering is one of the requirements."

"Yeah, but it will be two weekends in a row. What about the other fifty or so parents?" I did the math in my head. Fifty-two weeks in a year, fifty mom and dads. I shook my head, no. "Not to mention, Mya won't be attending the field trip because it's her . . ." I trailed off. It wasn't public knowledge that she had visitation issues. It was Airic's weekend. He never missed a date and would threaten me with a sheriff visit if I even thought of not honoring the judge's order. Like clockwork he'd be pressing my doorbell with his stupid sweater tied around his neck and his pleated trousers tailored to perfection, armed with treats and a good time to be had by all. "I'm sorry, not this weekend."

"Really, Venus, I hadn't expected all this notoriety to go to your head so soon." Paige raised her eyebrow. She dug in her oversized Dooney & Bourke and pulled out a computer printout. She let it fall inside my open window. "Keep in mind your daughter will need a stable environment, real friends she can count on. You may want to consider her needs while you and your husband are enjoying his fifteen minutes of fame."

"Paige . . . really, it's not that serious. Of course Mya will remain in the Hansel and Gretels, we're just not going to be there this weekend . . . okay? Simple as that." I eased off the brake, this time with a small prayer to get me out of there. The car pulled out smoothly. I waved when I felt like flipping the middle finger.

When I was a safe distance away I stopped the car and looked at the paper. Jake and Sirena, a photo of them together face-to-face. Actually it was four pictures, each one as emotionally drawn as the next. I tore it up in small pieces and smashed it into the old paper cup that held my morning coffee.

I beat the steering wheel until my palm hurt. When I turned to apologize to Mya, I saw the seat empty. I burst into tears. I'd forgotten my baby. I'd gone to the school to pick her up, got chased off by Paige, and left my little girl. What was wrong with me?

How to Lose Friends and Win Enemies

"You look like you've seen the devil himself. What's wrong with you?" Pauletta smashed the turkey burger cooking in the skillet. She shook a little salt, then came and sat at the table.

"It's kind of a long story. I saw Miriam's husband at the Monarch Hotel checking in with . . ." I couldn't mouth the words. "Anyway, Miriam seems to know all about it and still wants to go through with her ceremony. Wow," was all I could finish with.

"Ahuh." Pauletta made sure to raise her skinny eyebrow. Not that she'd plucked them to death. The tiny hairs had thinned from her chemo. In fact, she was thin all over. It took some time getting used to. I came from a family of bountiful ass—aunts, cousins, and nieces, properly pear shaped and proud of it.

"What?" she asked.

"What, what?" I would not win the what battle. I got up. "Never mind. I need a shower. I feel so dirty. I should've told Miriam and I didn't."

"She don't want to hear nothing you have to say about her husband . . . kind of like somebody else I know."

"Got that right. Thank you, Mother. Makes perfect sense to me. Because I'd be a whole lot happier not hearing another word about Sirena Lassiter."

She stuck her tongue into the side of her cheek. "Well, unless you have magic skills to make somebody disappear, she's your reality. Deal with it."

I lay in bed staring at the ceiling with my cell phone placed in the center of my chest. If I died now, it would be waiting for Jake's call. Seemed that's all I did these days, wait for Jake's call.

I stopped watching TV weeks ago. The trailer for *True Beauty* played on just about every commercial break of all my favorite shows. I could read if my eyes weren't tight and blurry from my earlier breakdown. Surely sleep would come to save me.

I felt a brush across my lips and imagined I was Sleeping Beauty. Those damn fairy tales were the bane of every little girl's future existence. Waiting for the prince to arrive and save her.

"Baby?"

Oh God, why couldn't we ever stop waiting for *him* to save us?

I opened my eyes and threw my arms around Jake.

He kissed me deep and wide, then held my face in his hands. "You have no idea how happy I am to be home."

The next morning, I woke up to voices vibrating through the house. Voices and footsteps. I thought I was dreaming that Jake actually came home. He did. I arrived downstairs in time to see Mya reenacting her recital dance for him. She was excited to show off her new shiny yellow ballet slippers. She'd grown out of the first pair. The child was cursed with long narrow feet.

Jake clapped and cheered. When she was finished she leaped into his arms.

"You are the best ballerina I've ever seen." He kissed the top of Mya's head where it was parted down the center. My mother had taken on the duty of combing her hair. She'd parted it down the middle and put it in two country plaits, claiming she wasn't used to plantation hair.

"This child needs a perm. It's too thick. I don't have the arm strength to wrestle with this stuff," she exclaimed every morning.

"Would you not say things like that over my baby's head? I'm not getting her a relaxer. If she wants to straighten her hair, it will be when she's grown and on her own."

"Lord, have mercy," Pauletta had wailed. "Where did I go wrong?"

Miriam would've seen the lunacy of the situation. She would've listened to me and made me laugh about the whole plantation-plaits thing. Now I was so afraid our relationship was built on a lie. Me pretending to be happy for her, smiling in her face when I should've been trying to talk sense into her.

I tiptoed back to bed, not wanting to interrupt Jake and Mya's father-daughter time.

Not long after, the bedroom door opened and closed. I lay still and tried to steady my breathing. We still hadn't talked.

"You awake?" he asked.

I had been contemplating how to escape this nightmare unscathed. How to protect myself from being hurt. How not to hear whatever he wanted to talk about.

"I'm awake," I confessed to the back of his head. He scooted back and laid down.

He pulled my arm around his waist. "You are the best thing that's ever happened to me."

"You're just trying to get into my nightie again," I said.

"Is it working?" His hand was groping, making direct contact. I hated to admit it, but it was. Sex seemed to be the panacea for all that ailed us in our relationship. The one time we couldn't feel the heat for each other was right after I'd lost the baby. Months and months it took for us to find each other again, both so lost and hurt.

He turned around and faced me. He slipped below the sheets and ducked underneath my nightie. He licked, nibbled, and sucked until I couldn't hear the doubt and fear in my head. The chatter stopped, replaced by the guttural moan in the back of my throat. Finally, I'd found my voice. I climaxed into tears.

When he tried to hold me I scooted, pushing him back. His eyes glistened with worry. "What's wrong?"

"Now I'm ready to listen."

"Are you? I've been trying to tell you the truth and you haven't wanted to hear it. Are you ready to listen?"

"Yes, but I'm going to do the asking. You're not going to fit your words nice and neat into my head like some brainwashing session." This almost made him smile. He fought it back.

"Brainwash you? Impossible. You're the most stubborn woman I know . . . well, not including your mother. But you got it honestly." He stroked my hair spread in a halo against the pillow. He kissed me between the eyes. "Ask me anything."

"A journalist came to my floral shop. She said Sirena and you were in love; in fact she claimed she was your first love. I'm trying to figure out why this fact was omitted from our countless conversations." It took every muscle in my body to sit up. I was still shivering from the orgasm. I really should've been in a euphoric state. Instead it was like some superorgasm that gave me superhero strength. A heightened sense of awareness. My skin tingled and my head was spinning with too much information.

"I still didn't hear a question."

"Did you sleep with her . . . in the past?"

"Yes."

I inhaled and smiled, but there was a steady stream of tears moving down my cheeks.

"Did you sleep with her—"

"There's nothing between me and Sirena. What we had was a long time ago. So long ago, I didn't feel the need to talk about it. I'm sorry. I should've told you. But I knew you'd be nervous. I didn't want to give you a reason to be concerned."

He looked me directly in the eye and slid the moistness away with his thumb. "I'm sorry, baby. Sorry I didn't tell you. There's nothing between Sirena and me, do you understand?"

My brows knitted together. "You're doing it again."

"Doing what?"

I sniffed. "That brainwashing thing." I covered my eyes with my hand.

I could tell he was smiling. "Okay, listen without your eyes. I love you. You and Mya are my life. I wouldn't jeopardize what we have. Whatever questions you have, I will answer."

I dropped my hand. "Aha. That means you won't volunteer anything. I've fallen for that trick before."

"How is it a trick when you said you were going to do the questioning? I'm telling you . . . I will submit to your polygraph or whatever masterful skills you have for getting the truth." He leaned forward. "I do know of one fail-proof way to get me to talk."

"Oh really."

He slid his soft cool hand up my thigh. "Timeless, tried and true. The oldest method on the books. Mata Hari, all the great female spies knew exactly how to get the information they wanted."

"You mean like this." I pulled my nightgown up, crawled on his lap and straddled him. I yanked his head back and trailed with slow wet kisses. I squeezed my thighs together and ground against him until he moaned.

"Yeah, oh yeah. I'll tell you anything you want to know." He flipped me back on the bed and landed on top.

"Oh yeah, I can see I have complete control of the situation."

"Yes, I'm all yours. Do with me what you will." Only it was he sinking his mouth around my nipples. His hands pressing into my waist, pulling me down closer for easy reach.

The bed started shaking like one of those quarter machine rides in front of the grocery store. "Either Mr. Happy grew a motor, or your phone is vibrating."

He flipped the phone out of his pocket, tossing it. The sound buzzed near my ear where it landed. I grabbed the little monster. "It's Ramona."

His tongue was in my belly button. The vibrating stopped. He kept going. The vibrating started up again. I picked it up and tapped him lightly on the head . . . with the phone. "It's Sirena."

He lifted up his face, let out an exhaustive sigh. "Tell her I'm busy." He put his face back between my thighs.

"Hello. How you doin', Sirena? This is Venus."

Jake tried to grab the phone. "I was just . . . kidding," he desperately whispered.

I swung my legs over the edge of the bed. "That's good to hear. Yes . . . yes, we're just happy to have him home. He's in the shower but I'll tell him to call you back as soon as he's out. It's an emergency, right?" I was up walking by now, Jake's eyes following me with each paced step. "I mean, you just spent the last thirty-six hours together, nonstop, so I figure it must be an emergency."

Jake put his head down and shook it.

"Oh, oh, I see. Yeah. No, yeah, I'd say that was an emergency. I'm sorry to hear about that. I'll let him know." I pushed the END button. "Her father had a heart attack. She said you and he were close and thought you should know."

Jake stood up. He took the phone out of my hand, then kissed my forehead. He tilted his head, seeing a new picture altogether. He rubbed a hand across my face to try to wipe away my quivering lip of guilt. "Baby, how were you supposed to know?"

"Have you ever felt like nothing you say or do is right?"

He nodded. "All the time."

"Give her my best," I said before slipping on my robe. I'd let him console her in private. I couldn't bear to listen.

He reached out and grabbed me. "Where do you think you're going?"

"I thought you'd want to call her back. Her father . . ."

He interrupted with a kiss. "I'll call and check on her, but there's really not much I can do. It's okay. I just want to spend some time with you. Sirena's got an arsenal of hand-holders. Today we're going to do whatever you want. Just me and you." He powered down his phone, then went back to lock the bedroom door. "Now where were we?"

Collector's Item

Outside Sirena's bedroom door Leshawn knocked for the third time. "Seriously, you have to eat something."

"Come in," Sirena yelled with her face still smashed between the down pillows. Her bed was overflowing with multiple layers of fluff. Fit for a queen. So large she felt lost and all alone most nights. "If that means you gon' stop talking, bring your ass in here."

Leshawn carried a tray on her hip and wrangled one side of the double door. "You are so wrong. People can't be nice to you. People get their feelings hurt when they're nice to you."

"The sound of your voice—"

"Irritates you . . . right. I know. I think it's a damn hangover, that's what I think." She popped the top of the V8 juice bottle, then poured it over ice. "Try it without the vodka, it might make you feel better."

"Get out."

"I'm going. But I'm taking this dang phone with me. You sitting up here thinking that man is gon' leave his wife for you, or some craziness. Unh-unh, I can't let you go down this road."

Sirena nearly knocked over the tray raising up to try and grab the phone before Leshawn could take it. Too late. "Give it back."

"Oh no, cousin dearest. You need an intervention."

"I have important calls coming. I'm not sitting here waiting to hear from Jay."

"Yes, you are. That's why you concocted that craziness about Uncle Larry having a heart attack. Who lies like that on their own parent's health? And guess what . . ." She looked at the phone. "He still ain't called."

"Get out!" Sirena yelled and winced at the same time. The bottle of aspirin was nearly empty. She poured two in her hand and used the tomato juice to wash them down. Her head felt like someone was playing the drums in the center of her brain.

"This is how you treat your cousin." Leshawn headed out. "What if Earl calls—remember him? The man you're engaged to be married to."

"Tell him I'm asleep. Tell him I'm in Egypt, I don't really care. But if Jay calls, bring me that damn phone or you gon' be looking for a job," Sirena screamed before the door closed, leaving her to her misery. The frustration was what gave her the headache, not the drinks she'd consumed the night before, partying with her girls, Dawn and Gayle. They were celebrating Gayle's part in a new movie. The girl hadn't seen no parts of a camera for the past three years. Roles for sistas were far and few between. The very reason no one could understand her tamed mood, laughing and smiling when cued by everyone else, though she was hardly paying attention to the world around her.

She had everything. If being fabulous had its own Wikipedia page, her mug would be sitting front and center.

But no matter how much she shopped and filled her world with the latest bling, she still felt null and void.

Her opportunities were running out. Getting Jake alone in a hotel room was like *Mission: Impossible*. Getting him in the bed right beside her had been a miracle. And still she couldn't close the deal.

Sirena was convinced it was more about punishing her than

him actually being happily married. She wasn't falling for that. She'd been in the room with those two—they had no chemistry, no heat.

"There she is." Earl barged into her room without so much as a knock. "Give me some, right here." He pushed his large face into hers. His black horn-rimmed glasses gave him a bookish charm, but anyone who knew him was afraid, very afraid. One phone call, or at tops two, he could make you or break you.

"Long time no see." Sirena scooted fast out of the bed. She wasn't in the mood for his three-minute bip-bap-boom.

"Come on, you're still mad?" He loosened his tie. Ever since *Esquire* magazine had voted him one of the best-dressed men, he felt the need to always don a suit. This one was Cavalli. She'd been with him at the fitting and begged him not to taper too close at the waistline. Especially if he refused to lay off the steaks and buttered bread.

"Worse than mad, I'm embarrassed. I was stuck in New York watching everybody and their momma be invited to this presidential soiree except me. Why? That's what I want to know. Here I'm engaged to one of the richest men in the world, I'm an international star, and I'm on the bottom of the list. Whatthahell good are you?" She slammed the bathroom door. She was hoping he'd be gone when she came out. He never knew how to handle her black mood, as he called it. She simply wanted him to leave.

She peeked out. So why was he still here?

She padded across the Persian rug. Her closet was the room next door converted to look like a high-priced boutique. Her shoe collection was ridiculously large and had been featured in at least ten magazines and television shows.

"Can I help you?" she asked, walking past him in his thinking-man pose.

"I've apologized for not being available. I am sorry for not having the jet sent to pick you up. I explained, I was in the winery fields. There is no reception there."

"Please, you and your li'l winery can kiss my ass. You're supposed to be looking after me, my career. You're supposed to be such a big hot honcho and we can't even be invited to a damn ballet."

"I know something that will make you feel better." He stood up and slipped his hand into his suit lapel. He pulled out a slim jewelry case—unrecognizable, even to the trained eye. Earl Benning didn't do the cliché of Tiffany's, or even Cartier.

He slowly pulled open the top to reveal a choker necklace with one blue stone in the center.

Sirena was no dummy. The blue diamond was all the talk in her circle. Not the Gayle and Dawn circle; no, she was referring to the old-money families who'd taken a liking to her authenticity, her ethnicity without having to get their hands dirty. This particular piece was from the Sotheby's in London. Rare, exclusive, probably one of its kind. His other hobby besides winemaking was buying up anything of substantial value.

"It's stunning." She liked that word. Earl liked it too. His small teeth revealed a smile of satisfaction. What good was spending nearly three million dollars if it wasn't appreciated?

"Just promise me," he said quietly in her ear. "The night you're awarded your first Oscar, you'll be wearing this necklace."

"Stop." She blushed underneath the weight of his compliment. She turned and faced him. "You think that much of me, that I could win an Academy Award."

"I do. I think that much of you." His spindly fingers pushed her long wavy hair past her shoulders for a better look at his investment. He then traveled down her back to the firm thickness he'd wanted to get his hands on from the first time he saw her in the magazine. The only reason he knew she existed was because she was featured three pages after him. She was voted the sexiest woman alive, and he was in the ridiculous running for best dressed. Within hours he'd picked up the phone and made one call, and she was sitting across from him at Stavio's.

"Knock, knock." Leshawn came in holding Sirena's phone like it was as precious as the stone around her neck. "Um . . . that important call you were waiting for, on line one."

Sirena blinked hard. "Can you take a message?"

"Well, yes I can, but you fa-siphically said to bring you the phone so you could take this call personally."

"Take the call, darling. It's fine." Earl took the phone from Leshawn. He looked briefly at the screen but showed no acknowledgment of her pet name, J-Baby. She'd renamed everyone. Even Earl's name came up as DaddyWarbucks.

"Thank you." Sirena took the phone and wondered how she was going to answer questions about her "ill father." How she was going to feign distress when she was wearing a three-million-dollar choker around her neck.

"Hello, Jay. I'm glad you called, but I'm kind of busy right now."

"Can I get you anything, Mr. Benning?" Leshawn asked far too loudly. Jake probably heard. Certainly her intention.

"Yes, I'm fine. Thanks for checking. Exhaustion. Long day. You're too sweet." She glanced over her shoulder. Both Earl and Leshawn were staring dead in her face. "Kiss Mya for me. Tell Venus I said hello. Thank you, again. Yes. Yes. Okay, bye now." She hung up.

"Jake's nervous about the worldwide release of *True Beauty*. He thought I was too." Her face felt hot, moisture popping up on her newly slimmed nose. The surgery was the last, she'd promised herself. No more going under the knife even if Dr. Bailey was a brilliant surgeon and had done a wondrous job. Surely her luck would run out like the rest of the cut-and-paste faces gone wrong.

"What's he worried about, not like he's got anywhere to go but up." Earl chuckled. "I mean seriously, he's lucky he got the role in the first place. Trust me, this was a one-time thing. He will disappear into obscurity where we found him."

"A one time thing?"

"If not for me being the executive producer on the project, he'd remain on the D-list. Come on, sweetie, surely you're not banking on the two of you becoming the next Bogart and Bacall, or Spencer Tracy and Kate Hepburn."

Sirena shook her head. "Who? I don't know what you're talking about. All I know is JP played the hell out of that role. I think he'd be good for this too." Sirena dug in the Prada bag she'd traded Gayle for. It was worth less than half the price of the Jean Paul Gaultier she'd given up, but Gayle needed a high-profile bag, now that her star was about to shine. She couldn't let her friend go out with frayed edges and peeled snakeskin.

She handed the script about Sarah Diamond and Max Vondrell to Earl.

"Please," he scoffed before even reading the title.

Leshawn already saw the direction this was going. "If either one of you need anything, I'll be right down the hall." She backed out and closed the door.

"I finished reading it on the long-ass plane ride home. Thanks to you I had plenty of time on my hands."

He cocked his head. "What am I supposed to do with this?"

"Read it. I'd get involved if I were you. You just said you thought I could win an Oscar. Well, that one right there might be the one."

One of Earl's many faults was his inability to keep his mouth shut. Crassness came with his checkbook. "I'm not going to produce this movie so you can spend more time with your washed-up rapper."

Sirena snatched the script from his hand. "Nice."

He caught her by the wrist, pulled her down, and planted a sizable kiss on her always-wanting mouth.

"I don't want to talk about work," he said. "I came here to make love to my fiancée. You know how much I hate Atlanta and all these wannabe celebrities in this town. Come home with me."

"I'm not moving in with you until we're married. Don't start with me."

He kissed the blue diamond on her neck. "I would think this was a large enough deposit. And this . . ." He held up her ring finger to indicate the eight-karat princess cut. "And this . . ." He slipped his fingers inside her with ease. "Now we're speaking the same language." She was juicy wet, but not because of him. The choker around her neck had almost given her an orgasm the minute she saw it. He went in for a second helping of her full moist lips.

She put up her hands. "I'm going to pop in the shower, then you're going to take me to lunch."

He hesitated, thinking what he'd rather eat was right in front of him. "Hurry." His penetrating eyes scanned her body up and down.

"Be out in a minute."

The minute turned into half an hour. She came out of her bathroom, hardly remembering she had a headache, until she saw Earl holding her phone.

"Quite a little photo album." He held up the screen to face her. "And here I thought it was all good harmless promotion. Nothing like rumor and innuendo to get people's attention. But this . . . this looks a bit too real."

"Give me that." Sirena snatched at the phone but came up empty. "Do I go through your shit? Then don't go through mine."

"So where are the others? His phone holding pics of you naked as well?"

"There are no others."

"So it was only you, the enamored photographer?" He tossed it to her. She tapped the CLOSE button. She should've hit delete, but couldn't bear the thought of removing the pictures of Jake from her phone. She'd taken them while he was sleeping, his bare perfect torso with the sheet hung low covering the edges of his pubic line. He didn't know she had snapped all night. No one knew, except now Earl.

Sirena shook off his question. "Really, this is so third grade. You got a question, ask it."

"You two fucking?"

"Not lately. Anything else?"

"Do I need to destroy him now, or later, because he's about to disappear."

"What's there to destroy? Remember? He's a washed-up rapper. Why in the world would you be jealous of him?"

"Jealousy and envy are for the weak and powerless. I don't have that problem."

"Good. Conversation over and out." Yet she knew it was hardly over. Earl had power. He had friends in high places and in low dark corners that you wouldn't want to be caught dead in. When and if Jake finally did come around, she didn't want Earl's interference.

Her thick thighs straddled him. "Baby, I was just having a little fun. We were stranded in the hotel together, but nothing happened." She raised her right hand. "Give me a stack of Bibles and I'll swear. Nothing, nothing happened. He's married and I'm one hundred and fifty percent committed to you."

Lunch would have to wait. She pulled the strap of his belt, then his zipper. She reached inside and decided to take matters into her own hands. Put his mind at ease. "Let's eat in."

Keep It Rolling

The park was nearly empty. Shaded tree benches were open and available for Jake's choosing.

"Right there," he said, pointing. "That one's perfect." He dragged his wife by the hand. She had fought tooth and nail, not wanting to picnic on a Wednesday. She had work to do, a business to run. He wouldn't take no for an answer. He had his life back and wasn't about to sit on the bench as it passed him by.

She held the blanket. They spread it out together. The shade would last for hours under the full tree. That's what he wanted, a few hours alone, no phones, no hotel rooms, no Sirena.

He dropped the deli bag, and the skates they'd bought when they lived in California and had yet to use since their move to Atlanta. If he thought about it, they never really skated there either. Both always so busy chasing their careers. "Let's skate first, eat later. Work up an appetite." He was already peeling off his shoes.

"Whatever happened to good old-fashioned wheels? I'm scared of Rollerblades."

"Technically, they're still wheels, it's just four of them."

He stood up and helped her on her feet, or wheels. The sight of her cut-off jean shorts and light zip-up jacket were enough to make him want to take her back home and throw her into the sack, but she'd probably try to escape. Ivy Park was nice and empty while all the kids were in school and parents hadn't yet made time for the younger children to hit the playgrounds. He would know, he'd spent a good amount of time here with Mya before all this movie business.

"I am so out of shape," she huffed, taking short glides.

"Just relax, we got all day."

"No, we don't have all day. Honey, I told you, I have a new contract with the Monarch Hotel. The deliveries start tomorrow. This place is huge, twenty floors. I thought you would be proud of me—this business is finally paying for itself, and you got me out here skating." She finally took a breath. "What do you have to say for yourself?"

Jake had stopped and she was gliding by herself. When she realized he wasn't at her side she began to stumble. "Oh . . ."

He rushed to catch up, but she was already down on her butt. "What happened to you, you were doing so good?"

She poked him in the chest. "You knew I was going to fall the minute you left my side."

Jake nodded. "Let that be a lesson to you, Miss Independence. You need me . . . by your side. Everything else is an illusion." He opened his hands like the Grand Swami. She always accused him of trying to hypnotize or brainwash her; he may as well take advantage. "The only thing you need to do is be my wife."

She squealed. "Sprinklers." The water shot out from every angle. He scooped her up and they raced like Roller Derby pros. Suddenly she could move pretty good.

The shade spot with their blanket was still dry. The water hadn't come on in their picnic area yet. Jake dived first, then she landed nearly on top of him. Both working hard to catch their breath, he turned her face toward him and kissed her deep but gentle. The exhilaration must've made her forget she was angry. "Having fun yet?"

"I am." Her smile, he loved her smile. He couldn't recall the last time he'd seen her relax. The last time, yes . . . he remembered.

When she held Mya in her arms right after she was born. He walked into the hospital room and saw the tears pooling in her eyes and knew what love was supposed to look and feel like. Though they hadn't even discussed marriage at the time, he knew right then and there he was going to make her his wife, and Mya would be *his* child, regardless of what the biological facts held.

"I'm glad you made me come."

"Finally, an admission."

"You always make everything look easy. It's not like that for me." She rose up on her elbows. Her high cheekbones glistened from the quick sweat they'd worked up. "I'm always on guard because I'm so used to everything falling apart. The floral shop is going well, really well. But in the back of my mind I'm anticipating the wheels, or at least one of them, falling off." She finished with a sneeze, then brushed a flying bug off the blanket.

"You have me, so you don't ever have to worry about the wheel, 'cause I'll fix it."

"That's the thing, I don't want you to always feel like you have to fix everything. Don't you sometimes feel burdened, a little, having to pick up all the pieces all the time?"

"No, I don't. I want you to need me." He went to kiss her again. She sprayed him with a sneeze.

"Oh God, allergies."

He dropped his head on his forearms. "Guess we better leave."

"I'm sorry, baby. It was fun. I mean, even for a little while, right?"

"Yeah, fun. But I wanted to ask you something first, before we go."

She braced herself. "What?"

"Why have you been so cautious around me? Seems like you're holding back. And we both know that's not you. I depend on you to tell me what's on your mind."

"I . . . I've been cautious? That might be a good word for it. Just mostly trying not to get in your way. I haven't wanted my insecurities to stop you from going all the way . . . that's probably what you're seeing."

"What insecurities?"

"You and Sirena, being together." She took a deep breath. "I already told you all of this and you already answered my questions, so that's the end of it."

"There's nothing else, nothing you want to tell me."

She dropped her head, as if she'd been found out. A breakthrough, he was thinking. Finally.

The sprinklers gave a warning spurt before she could carefully organize her words. Again, the cautiousness. They moved fast, gathering up the blanket and picnic basket. This wasn't the end of it. He could sense there was something eating away at her. Treading lightly, afraid to leave a footprint everywhere she went, instead letting others walk all over her. This was not the Venus he knew. In the old days she would've busted him out hard . . . the whole Sirena thing, finding out about their past. She'd let it go too easy, and it m ade him nervous.

While he drove them back home he reached out and took ahold of her hand.

"There is one thing, I guess, I was afraid to ask."

"Okay," he anticipated. "Go ahead, baby, you know you can ask me anything."

"Well . . . the manager at the Monarch Hotel wanted to have you and Sirena as guests for the grand opening. More like, demanded. I hate to ask, but I think my floral contract may depend on it."

Jake shook his head, frustrated. "That's it?"

"Yeah, that's it. I told him I wasn't in charge of your schedule, or Sirena's, but he pretty much made it clear, no show, no contract."

"Fine. When is it?"

"Sunday."

"Yeah, I'll tell Sirena. I'm sure she wouldn't mind." His annoyance was hard to mask.

"I'm sorry."

"Stop that . . . just stop it. You see? That's what I'm talking about."

"What?"

"What're you *sorry* about? You don't need to be sorry about anything."

"Damned if I do, damned if I don't," she said coolly.

"We're a family. Me and you, I got your back, you got mine. I'm the same person I always was. I'm your husband." He squeezed her hand. "You got me?"

She nodded but he could tell she was on the verge of tears. He wouldn't press any further. He'd already made his assumption. After those men had snatched her at the gas station last year, she'd spent a good amount of time talking about karma, ordering books on the subject. Wondering if somehow she'd deserved what happened, though the attack had not been centered on her in the first place.

The loss of their baby, the custody battle they'd had to fight to keep Mya, and now Sirena showing up with the threat of reclaiming lost love. Tragedy seemed to strike even if it was aimed in the opposite direction. She still managed to get hit. He could see it all from her point of view, and he had to admit, it didn't look good. But he couldn't keep telling her everything was going to be all right. He had to prove it.

"We're a team, baby," he said and left it at that. *Everything is going to be all right.*

Breathing Underwater

The bathwater was lukewarm. Mya didn't seem to mind. She'd been playing in the tub for nearly an hour while I sat beside her with my hands patiently clasped on the towel draped over my knees, ready to close the party out. Jake left around six in the evening. He promised to be back in time to read Mya a bedtime story.

"Okay, sweetie, time to get out."

Mya rose dripping wet and shivering, knowing there was no use in arguing for a few minutes more. Her little fingers and toes were shriveled and pale. I wrapped the towel around her body and kissed her nose. Water trailed the center of her face from dunking her head even after I'd warned her there was no way I was spending an hour combing out the twists and tangles. She'd simply have a matted mess to contend with.

I slathered her up, not giving the lotion a chance to settle into her skin before pushing the nightgown over her head. It stuck to parts of her body. I pulled the wet hair trapped underneath the collar and squeezed her spongy tresses to get the rest of the water.

"You have the most beautiful hair in the world." I repeated this truth at least once a week. I already knew the angst she inevitably faced when she started to believe her textured hair was a curse, not a gift.

I grabbed the comb, brush, and more of the same lotion I'd used on her little body. "Come on," I said in the middle of an exhausted yawn. "To the bat cave."

"Can I stay up till Daddy comes?"

"No, sweetie. I'm not sure what time that will be. You have school tomorrow. When you wake up, we'll make sure he fixes banana pancakes, your favorite."

"No, they're *your* favorite," she retorted. "I like apple."

"Oh, right."

The bedroom door pushed open slowly. Mya and I both stared, wondering if we should scream, run, or just sit still.

"A puppy," Mya announced. "Daddy, you got me a puppy." She jumped up and greeted the tiny powder puff. It stuck its tongue out and gave her a quick lick on the nose.

"What in the world?"

"Actually, it's for Mommy, sweetie. But I'm sure she'll need help taking care of . . ." He put the dog in my lap. "It's a boy. You have to name him."

"Why in the world did you buy a dog? As if I don't have enough to do." It was a fluffy bichon frise with dark inquisitive eyes staring up at me.

"Mommy, name him Toby."

I still held the comb in one hand; the other I used to keep Toby from jumping into my face for a doggy kiss. He was cute and cuddly. I could see it was too late. The puppy had curled up in my lap while Mya gently stroked. Jake stood, proud of his plan.

I finally conceded. "You're paper-training him, and cleaning up all little black lumps of coal for at least the first thirty days."

"Will do," Jake said, giving me a salute.

I picked up Toby and held him close. "You are such a cutie." His raspy bark in return sounded like, "Thank you. I promise to be no trouble at all."

I heard my mother coming before she entered the room. "Did I just hear a dog bark?"

I kissed Toby on the head. "Yep."

She scanned the room, landing on Jake. "Nice."

"I thought so," Jake said with no apology, before sliding out with Mya's hand in his. "Hey babygirl, let's go raid the fridge."

"You're going to read me a story," she confirmed as part of the deal. One side of her hair was in a nice long braid; the other was raw bushel of coils and puffiness.

They disappeared down the hallway. When he was out of earshot, my mother sat with me on the white leather bench at the foot of Mya's princess bed.

"You know this is nothing more than a distraction, right?"

"Absolutely." I smiled.

She sighed. "What am I going to do with you? I'm not cleaning up dog poop. I'm here to help, but that's where I draw the line."

"Mom, about that . . . I think everything's going to be okay. I know I've kept you away from Dad long enough. It's okay if you go home. Jake is back to pick up the slack. So we're good." I waited for her response. She folded her thin arms across her chest. Toby sniffed her before tapping her with his small paw.

"Mom, why don't you want to go home? Something happen—I mean, something more than usual?" My mother had been bossing my father all forty-plus years they'd been married. I'd watched Henry nod, shake his head, and hunch his shoulders, all to avoid an argument.

"He's met someone," she blurted out. "He denies everything, of course, but I'm no dummy."

"Another woman? Please, Mom." My father was afraid of Pauletta Johnston. The notion of him crossing her was way too farfetched.

"Yes, another woman. She was my nurse when I was going through that second bout of cancer. I laid up in that hospital room barely conscious, but I could hear them, their voices. He and that woman got close, bonded, and right over my listless body. I'll never forgive him."

"Well, what did you see, or hear?"

"I heard his laugh. I heard the way he deepened his tone, trying to get all manly for her. And her light happy-just-to-be-here phoniness. Women know. You can pretend not to know. But a woman knows."

"But so what, Mom? Really. So what he relaxed and enjoyed another woman's company? Big deal. He's been your husband, supporting you, taking care of you for like a hundred years, but this you can't forgive."

"I think these little spikes growing out of your head have entered your brain," Pauletta said with a hard thumb to my temple. "Men are like dogs. They escape outta the yard, they will be trying to get free every time you turn your back. Well, he can just be free, roam the land like some little stray mutt. I don't care."

Toby barked as if he took offense to the reference.

"So then, what's your plan?"

"Haven't got one yet."

"So what sense does it make, after all these years to disappear on the man?"

"You have to put your foot down. The sooner you learn that, the less trouble he'll be. Bringing home a dog, nothing but a distraction to keep you too busy to notice his tracks."

"Are we talking about Dad, or Jake?"

"Ahuh, I think you know." She got up and scooted away in her house slippers.

First thing in the morning, I was calling my father. No way Pauletta Johnston was staying in Atlanta with me and Jake. Somebody had better fix this mess, and fast.

Who Let the Dogs Out

The three of us met at the Monarch Hotel. Miriam skipped around, picturing the beautiful ceremony reuniting her and Ben as man and wife. Ben never once mentioned that he'd been there before, acting in wonder at the lavish entrance and parlor. I'd spent the afternoon holding my emotions and tongue.

"Can't you picture all our guests seated and watching us renew our vows?" Miriam snuggled against Ben's suit-covered arm. He loosened his striped tie and nodded in conciliation.

I was sure there were more important things to worry about in the world than the fidelity of one's partner, yet I kept being pulled into the insanity. It was all around me—Jake and Sirena, Ben and Miriam, and now the unfolding drama of my father and mother. My dad hadn't picked up the phone so I left him a rather long message, begging, pleading for him to make things right.

"And over here, I want a harpist. I've always wanted a harpist, a woman dressed elegantly with long flowing hair over one shoulder while she plays something achingly romantic."

"Hold that thought, Miriam." I grabbed my phone, hoping that the vibration was my father calling back.

"Mrs. Parson, this is Mary Stone, the principal at Whitherspoon Academy."

I faced the large mantel in the large but intimate ballroom of the hotel. "Yes?"

"I have Mya in my office. There was an incident between her and a couple of other girls here at the school."

I faced the happy couple. "Miriam, I have to go. There is an emergency at Mya's school."

I had only been in the Whitherspoon main office twice—once to ask for the golden key of entrance, and once to write out a fat check for enrollment. "What happened?" I was standing in front of the reception desk where Principal Stone's office door was open. I could see Mya's little legs sitting in a chair off to the side.

The receptionist waved me inside.

Principal Stone was on the phone, looked up and said a few more words before hanging up. I had a full view of Mya now, disheveled. She rushed to my side. "Mommy." She sniffed. "I want to go home." A shiny pearl of skin showed through her scalp. I pushed it gently side to side. To my horror I found an even bigger spot with red specks where the roots had been ripped.

"Mya was in an altercation with two of our second-grade girls."

"Altercation? This is an assault, the kind where someone should be in handcuffs. I don't care how old they are." I swallowed and fought hard not to get loud. "Who did this?"

"The other girls are in Vice Principal Garret's office, awaiting their parents. This sort of thing has never happened at our school before. In this unusual circumstance, I'm trying to keep everyone separate. Parents especially."

"Queenie said Daddy was bad," Mya said.

Goose bumps rose on my arms. "Queenie . . . ?"

"She had a picture of Daddy naked and showed everybody. She called me bad names, so I called her bad names right back," Mya announced in between sniffs. "They said I thought I was important. She said no one liked me and Daddy was going to *divort* us."

"Divort . . . divorce? Oh, sweetie." I picked her up, which was almost impossible these days. She was long and gangly. Her feet banged against my knees while I adjusted her on my hip. "Everything's going to be all right. Nobody's getting a divorce."

"Now I'm ugly, Mommy."

Principal Stone stood up and handed me a tissue. So much for my attempt at keeping my emotions under control. This morning I'd watched Mya walk into the large oak entrance of Whitherspoon Academy, happy and excited. She'd been proud of her cascading waves. After last night getting it wet, she'd slept with braids. When I undid them, it was too pretty to pull back. I couldn't resist letting her feel free and beautiful. If not now, when? It ended so quickly. This much I remembered—growing up, suddenly not liking anything about yourself. Body, hair, freckles, nose, feet. Head to toe, an endless list of flaws. Not until we were near forty, reclaiming ourselves on our own terms, did the self-doubt subside. But did it ever go away? And what a waste of all those years in between.

"I want to talk to Queenie. I know her, and her mother. This picture she's talking about, where is it?"

Principal Stone's hand shook when she lifted the wrangled piece of paper from her desk. Obviously taped back together for evidence.

Through my tear-stained eyes, the grainy printout was hard to see at first. When my focus came, I saw Jake in a bed, arms spread on the back of his head. A sheet barely covered the essentials, leaving his bare chest and narrow waist as the main attraction. I read the printout at the bottom out loud. "Looks like the *True Beauty* star gets his beauty sleep."

My hand shook more than Principal Stone's when I folded it and tucked it into my purse.

"I'm sorry, but I'm going to need that to show the other girls' parents. This is a big offense. There may be suspensions involved."

"Suspensions. I'm not bringing my daughter back into this school until Queenie Lawson and the other girl are removed." I had no choice but to set Mya down. Her weight, along with the heaviness in my heart, was too much to bear. "Expelled. Not a two- or three-day vacation." I licked back the tears and fought hard to keep it together. The one tissue she'd given me was already soaked and tattered.

She stood up and handed me another. "Mrs. Parson, girls have altercations. I admit one of this magnitude is unusual, but I'm sure by next week the girls will forget it ever happened. Usually the parents are the ones who overreact."

"I bet if the hair was ripped from your head, you'd have something to react about—what do you think?" I wiped my nose, dried my tears, and took Mya's hand. "Either they're out of this school or you can expect to hear from my lawyer." With Mya in tow, I stomped out through the grand foyer and down the manicured cobblestone path, fuming.

I didn't have a lawyer. I was hoping the mere threat was enough. Having to enter a courtroom for any reason ever again in my life made me queasy. Between the custody case for Mya, and my own minor brush with the law, nothing had ever gone in my favor under the roof of justice.

"Venus, yoo-hoo?" Paige called out. I spun around to see her swinging her solid hips toward me. "Venus, I'm so sorry about the mishap. Mya, sweetie, are you all right?" She bent slightly and gave a soft pat on Mya's head. Mya let out a soft yelp from the stinging contact.

"Mishap? Your daughter and her friend attacked Mya. She's not *all right*."

She put her hands to her face and gave an oh-my expression. "I'm only just hearing about this. Believe me, LaQueena will be punished, if she's in the wrong."

"She showed Mya a picture off the Internet. Guess you don't know anything about that either?"

"I certainly do not." Her eyes darted around to make sure there weren't any witnesses to her lies. "I assure you, I had nothing to do with any pictures. I only showed you the first one out of concern. You know how kids are online—she could've gotten a picture of your husband anywhere."

My eyes narrowed, letting her know she'd just been busted. "I never told you who or what was in the picture, Paige."

"Principal Stone told me," she recovered quickly.

"Yeah, right. Stay away from me. You keep your little wild daughter away from Mya."

"Children fight, it's not the end of the world."

"Look at my baby's head. Look at it." I tried to be as gentle as possible, separating the hair where it was torn. "Let me know if Queenie has scratches, bruises, anything at all." I tried to keep my voice from shaking. "For God's sake, how could your child be so vicious?"

"You're doing a lot of finger-pointing to not have any facts."

"The only facts I need are what Mya told me, and what she told Principal Stone."

The clouds began to pull together and thunder clattered overhead. Living in Georgia wasn't like Los Angeles where I grew up. There, clouds rolled away as quickly as they came, leaving the desert by the sea continually starving for water, no matter how much the weatherman promised sweet relief from the dry air, it was only a threat.

Here, the threat was real. It would rain any minute and I knew Paige wasn't about to let her freshly straightened coif get wet.

"I am going inside to get to the bottom of this." She turned and started walking toward the entrance.

"Yeah, I bet." I followed her a few steps and jumped in front of her. My finger was almost up her nose. "You know damn well you started this mess. Just admit it. You printed out that picture and filled your baby's head with nonsense. And for what? I've never done anything to you. Why would you be so mean?"

She sputtered and insisted, "Honestly, you and your celebrity-chasing husband are not the topic of conversation in my home."

"You see, that right there . . . *celebrity-chasing husband.* That's what I'm talking about. You need to stop dreaming about me and my husband."

Now it was she following me. I'd said my piece. The alarm twirped, unlocking the car only a few steps away. Her swinging hips made it around to the driver's side after I'd strapped Mya in the backseat.

"My husband is an established executive with a big oil company. I'll tell you this much, Jeremy would never have me driving this old raggedy car and working my fingers to the bone while he skips from party to party with another woman on his arm. Me and my child are well taken care of. Sorry I can't say the same for you. Some of us can afford a visit to the hair salon once a week," she added, hoping to throw a little more salt on my wounds.

I slammed my door, almost grazing her arm. "Obviously once a week isn't enough." I watched as the rain drizzled and flattened her bangs.

She was gunning up for a response but I beat her by stepping on the gas.

"Mommy, I'm not ever going to be Queenie's friend again." Mya offering solidarity. "She's mean, like her mommy."

"Sometimes we can't help who we are, sweetie. We just can't help it."

And like my mother, I wouldn't be made a fool of, at least not twice. Three times was actually my limit if we were counting from the beginning . . . okay, four. But I wasn't counting from the beginning.

I was starting from the day Sirena came into our lives pretending to be the good Samaritan.

"Who took this picture?" I pushed the printout in front of him. Jake had been reading a new script and was supposed to have it read before sundown. He finished the page he was on before directing his attention to the sheet of paper.

"Where'd you get this?" He looked genuinely confused, turning it side to side, as if the angle could've been better.

"Who took it, Jake, and when? That's all I want to know."

"Apparently, I was sleeping. So I don't know."

"Are you going to sit there and tell me Sirena didn't take that picture?"

"No. I'm going to tell you the truth, which is, I don't know who took it."

"Well, I do. I do know who took it. And you know what, Mya just got the living daylights beat out of her over this. Defending Daddy's honor."

"Where's Mya?"

"Upstairs with my mother."

He rose from his chair. He didn't waste another minute with my interrogation. The sound of his footsteps told me he was headed to Mya's room. I picked up the script and read the note attached.

> *Jay, this part is perfect for you. We're so perfect together.*
> *Sirena XXOO*

I tore the note off and balled it up, tossing it in the trash. I knew she'd taken the picture and leaked it for gossip or attention—interchangeable, if you asked me. Or worse, it was never her intention for it to get out. A private moment was no longer just between them. The thought made a lump swell in my throat.

I sat at Jake's computer and went online. So many pictures of them together, you would've thought they were a real couple. And finally, an exclusive feature on *Life 'N' Style*'s Web site with the pictures of Jake sprawled in sheets. The last one showing a pair of smooth cocoa-brown thighs straddled over his torso. I'd know those legs anywhere.

Guess he'd slept through that too.

How much was I expected to understand? All for the sake of his career.

The computer light glowed and pulsed, daring me to do something about it. I pushed the PRINT button. When the clicking and gurgling was done, I neatly stacked all the images on Jake's desk where he'd find them. I tore off a sticky and wrote: *You look so peaceful. Wish I knew the feeling.*

Sitting there feeling sorry for myself, and for Mya, an innocent victim, I couldn't even wrestle up a tear. I was too tired to cry. Numbness was a danger sign. A precursor to not giving a damn.

What I could feel was the tickling at my ankle. There was a creature crawling at my feet. I jumped and screamed. "Toby!" I reached down and picked up the new addition to the family. I'd forgotten about the new baby. His short tail moved briskly back and forth. "At least somebody is happy in this house." I put him on top of the desk. He must've been afraid of heights. Toby let out a fast hard stream of wee-wee all over Jake's script.

"Oh no, Toby." I tried to shake off the puppy piss and the ink went with it. Even the pictures I'd just printed had black drip streaks. "What have you been drinking, Toby? A forty-ounce?"

I rushed off to get paper towels, then changed my mind. On second thought, I couldn't care less about his script. I'd had it with the entire nightmare and it was time to wake up.

⟡

Vince was locking up when I arrived at In Bloom. I hadn't seen him in so long without his wing woman, Trevelle, at his side I actually hugged him.

"Whoa, what's going on? You all right?" He grabbed me by both shoulders to get a good look. "You've been crying." He pushed the door back open and escorted me in. He flicked the lights on. The fresh air of living, breathing flowers always soothed me.

"I just came to get an arrangement. I'm fine, really."

"An arrangement?" He followed me to the back. There was a challenged bouquet with drooping petals. It was tempting, but I knew dead roses would never get me past the front door at Sirena's house. She had bodyguards, assistants, and a maid or two.

"These will do perfectly." I grabbed the blue glass vase with a modest white peony bouquet. Understated, yet classy. Far more than the jezebel deserved.

"That's supposed to go out in the morning," Vince said with an authoritative tone. One that also said, *You need to find another choice.*

"I really need to take this one. Don't we have more peonies?"

"Actually, no. This was the last batch and the order specifically requires . . ." His dark eyes zeroed in on my blotchy red cheeks and pouting lips. "What's the emergency? Did someone die? What's going on?"

"I need a fake peace offering to get in Sirena Lassiter's house so I can get past her entourage and threaten her life."

Vince didn't know whether to bust out laughing or do a backhand to snap me out of crazy mode. "If you make a threat, you better be willing to carry it out."

"God . . . would you stop with the mob-boss talk. You're a flower arranger."

He took a long, deep breath. "You're too good for whatever you're planning."

"No, I'm not. I want to push these flowers in Sirena's face and tell her to stay away from my husband. Mya got beat up in school because of her selfishness. I'm sick of it. And it's all her doing." I plopped down on the stool at the work desk. "You know what I realized about these so-called celebrities? They live and breathe scandal. They need to be front and center or they don't exist."

I leaned in. "Trevelle is no exception. She's basically the epitome of what I'm talking about. No cameras, no focus on her and she's a figment of our imagination. Poof, she's disappeared."

"I assure you, she's real," Vince said, suddenly interested in what I had to say. "She's dealing with a fall from grace. That's not easy."

"Would you stop feeling sorry for her? She's a user. She's a vampire of energy. She'll suck you dry and leave your body in a heap of dust."

"Don't talk about Trevelle like that, Venus." He folded his solid arms over his chest. "As a matter of fact, let's stick with the subject of you."

"Sorry I brought her up. Okay. I'm just crying out for help and no one can hear me." I let my head fall into my hands. Vince touched my shoulder, then squeezed.

"I hear you, kiddo. All I'm saying is, you're barking up the wrong tree. A man knows what he wants and will go after it with full gusto. If he's too stupid to know, then he's roadkill, and any scavenger can have 'em. You get me?"

"Yes, but I know plenty of women who feel the same way. They'll go after a man with reckless abandon, not caring who they hurt. I think Sirena might be one of those women."

"Takes two to tango."

"What if she can dance good enough for the both of them?" I didn't wait for his grand pooh-bah knowledge. "Still his decision," I answered, knowing he was absolutely right.

He nodded and said quietly, "Sirena's not your problem." The caring in his voice reminded me of my father. My father, who still hadn't called me back. I was starting to fear something had happened to him. Or worse, he really wanted out of the forty-year marriage with my mother. If there was no hope for them, no one stood a chance.

"I got a date," Vince abruptly remembered out loud. "You go home. Take a hot bath, relax. Let this day end."

"Lady Trevelle awaits?"

"No. She won't go out with me in public, yet."

I nearly choked on my disgust. "What do you mean, she won't go out with you in public? Who does she think she is? Are you serious?"

"Listen, no. It's not like that."

"Well, how is it?"

"We're friends. She doesn't want any rumors started that could hurt her return to the ministry. That's all."

"And you fell for that."

"Look, until I get on bended knee and offer her a ring, she's not playing the dating game. I respect that. I understand what she's saying. I'm an old dog, and she's right. A man knows what his intentions are."

I snapped my fingers in front of Vince's face. "Vin, you in there?"

"A man knows what his intentions are," he repeated so I would get the message loud and clear. "See you tomorrow, li'l lady."

"Yeah, heading straight home," I said, still not so sure my plan was completely thwarted.

What a great plan it was. Walking up to Sirena's door, pretending to deliver flowers, then pushing them in her face with a warning. *Stay away from my husband.*

I gave the lively fresh bouquet one last glance. Someone was going to have a beautiful delivery in the morning. Why waste them on Sirena Lassiter anyway?

Mayday

Music played loudly through the door of Jake's studio that he'd had built in the back of the house. I didn't bother knocking.

Pushing the heavy wood door open I pictured him with Sirena by his side, collaborating, the way I'd found them last year about this time, laughing nearly nose-to-nose. I remember the way my heart skipped, landing in a puddle of doubt. He'd explained, made me understand there was no other way to get Sirena to buckle down. She needed attention, admiration, and constant compliments.

"You working?" Those were the only words I'd spoken to him in the past twenty-four hours. My silence, not speaking to him, seemed to hurt only me.

In his studio, he was alone. Absolutely no one in his ear or by his side to bounce ideas off. Ironically, he looked quite comfortable that way, working alone, focusing on what he wanted to focus on without coddling or babysitting.

"Look at you." He nodded with admiration. He flicked a couple of switches and the music went to a low decibel. "Where do you think you're going dressed like that?"

"Oh, this old thing." I smoothed a hand down the fifty percent Lycra, thirty percent cotton, and twenty percent other stuff I couldn't name. Definitely fitting in all the right places. "Miriam's bachelorette party. I'm obligated. I have to go."

"That dress is quite an obligation." Raised eyebrows and then a sly smile.

"What?" I stroked my wild hair, then did a small pose balancing on one full hip. I knew I'd picked up some pounds since wearing the dress last. That's what the Lycra was for. "Miriam wants to have a good time. I can't show up in a nightclub looking like Mary Poppins. I'll see you later." I bent over, giving him a bird's-eye view of my smooth cleavage. I kissed him on the lips. He grabbed me and didn't stop, moving his tongue gently around my mouth. My head swam. My body warmed—as well as my resolve to stay mad at him.

"Don't wait up," I said when I was finally free.

"Oh, you best believe I'll be up waiting." He leaned back in his chair. "I can think of other obligations you have." His left hand dropped slightly to his chest, then down, down, disappearing behind the workstation.

"See you later," I said, making my mad dash to the door. A few more seconds and Jake would've had me on top of the grid, making me forget my plan to make him jealous. He needed a dose of his own medicine. This time my mother's advice was on target.

Like It's 1999

Getting my club groove on and wishing someone would ask me to dance were distant but painful memories. Obviously people didn't dance anymore. I was sandwiched at the crowded bar in the upscale Davinci's nightspot waiting for the wedding girl and her party. It was nine thirty-five and I could've been home in bed fretting over my laundry list of woes. To send Mya back to Whitherspoon or not. To find a way to confront Sirena, or ask Jake not to take the next film project with her.

"Hey, sexy-can-I." The medium-height—almost cute if not for his crooked teeth—guy smiled at me. "How you doin'?"

"Great." I would've turned my body in the other direction if there were room. My crossed legs and high heels were pinned forward. I kept checking my phone for a message from Miriam.

"I like your hair. Sexy, kind of wild, like the jungle." He bumped his pelvis against me, surely by accident.

"Oh . . . I think I see my friend. Excuse me." I really did see Miriam. I'd gotten used to her wig making an appearance before her. I waved as best I could over the crowd. "Oh . . . thank goodness . . . you're here."

"Of course I'm here. It's my party." She raised her arms like Diana Ross. "I'm the guest of honor." She did a sexy wiggle in her pink tasseled minidress, showing off a mountain of thigh. The equivalent of throwing red meat into an ocean of sharks.

"So where is everyone?"

"We've got a VIP section. Come on, I'll introduce you to everyone."

The first person I laid eyes on was Robert Stanton, the only male in a group full of women in sexy party dresses. He was happier than a pig in . . . well, let's just say he was in his element.

"Everyone, this is my good friend Venus, who I'm forever grateful for talking sense into me. I wanted her to be my maid of honor but she's busy being the wife of JP," Miriam sang out. "JP, the sexy hot actor." She clapped her hands in giddy fashion. "Now of course you know our HHF, hot hubby friend, Senator Stanton."

"Please, here I'm just hot hubby Rob. You can leave off the 'friend.'"

I rolled my eyes. "Who let you out of the house?"

He winked and sipped on his martini, glaring over his drink. "One more of these, I'm going to show you my moves."

"Yeah right." I rolled my eyes. His precious reputation would be at stake. I wasn't going to miss it though if he did let loose. Maybe pictures and a threat of blackmail would keep him in his place.

"And this is my cousin, Jeanette . . ."

I noticed her right away, even in the moody lighting of the nightclub. The hair, the face, the resemblance to Miriam, only younger, sleeker. The new version, the very woman I'd seen at the hotel with Ben.

Maybe I'd seen it all wrong. My mind playing tricks on me. The way she held his hand at the check-in desk. The way he'd let his hand trail her back. Surely I could've been seeing things. But hadn't Miriam said she'd seen him, too, with another woman?

"Miriam . . . I . . . Can I talk to you?" I held on to my clutch bag and tilted my head like a confused puppy. Smile for everyone, though my teeth were clenched.

"You most certainly cannot. This is a party. No talking, only dancing." Again with the raised arms and shimmy-shimmy of her tassels.

"That's right. No talking, time to dance." Robert stood up and did a little twist.

I covered my face, refusing to be a witness. As much as I needed blackmail photos, I couldn't watch. "Someone is going to get you on tape, Senator."

"Good, that means I'll be president someday. All the great prezes know how to dance."

Jeanette came between Miriam and me. She bounced up to Robert Stanton and started snapping her fingers.

"Miriam, I really need to talk to you. I won't feel right the rest of the night until I do."

"Venus, life is way too short to worry about—"

"I know, things we have no control of." I eyed Jeanette and tossed the idea around of saying something to her instead, but I could hear Vince's voice in my head. I was once again going after the wrong person. "You're right, let's have a good time."

Miriam caught me eyeing her cousin. "Jeanette planned the bachelorette party. She's also my maid of honor. Don't worry, she's just playful. I promise she won't go after your man, hot Rob."

"She can have him." *It's your man I'm worried about.*

Jeanette squinted. "Have we met before?" It dawned on her we were staring. She had left Robert to dance alone.

"I don't think so. I'm a florist and event planner. What do you do?"

"Event planning," she excitedly reported. "I've only lived here for the last few months. I graduated from the University of Miami. I was staying with Ben and Miriam until I got on my feet. Still no job, but I have my own place now."

"I bet you do," I said under my breath.

"Do you need any help in your establishment? I'd be happy to give you my résumé."

"Oh, that won't be necessary. I can see what you're qualified for."

The music was too loud. "What?" She squinted and tossed her hair back to hear better.

"I said, I know you're qualified. But I'm not in a position to do any hiring right now." I searched for relief over my shoulder. "I need a drink."

The music was thumping through the floor. To my surprise it was even louder in the bathroom where I'd gone to cool off. The transparency of Miriam's cousin . . . of all the two-timing, cheating, backstabbing, gold-digging, man-stealing—

I stood at the mirror and watched as Sirena went flying past me. Speak of the she-devil, or at least the leader of the group.

I waited with folded arms against the granite counter. She looked me in the face and saw no recognition.

"Sirena, how are you?"

"I'm fine, thank you." She washed her hands and fluffed her ever-growing length of hair. "Oh, my goodness, Venus. I didn't recognize you. Is Jay here?" The question took a life-or-death tone.

"No, I'm out and about all by my lonesome."

She laughed smartly. "So you're a party momma. Wifey likes to get her groove on occasionally. I heard that." She threw the paper towel in the trash and dug for lipstick.

"Peacock, how you doin'?" The man's voice pushed past the small distance after he'd opened the door to the ladies' room.

"I'm cool," she yelled out. "My bodyguard. Can't leave home without him."

"Really? Was he in the hotel room with you and my husband when you took half-naked pictures of him?" I raised my hands, al-ready regretting what I'd said. "You know what? I'm sorry. That was inappropriate. Jake is the one married. It's his responsibility to act like it."

Sirena smacked her lips, making sure the color was even. She dropped the black case back in her purse, then pulled out her phone.

"These little things are just so convenient. Sometimes you can't resist." She pointed it at me, then squeezed the trigger. "You ever been followed around, somebody taking your picture all damn day long? Don't matter where you go, what you do . . . someone's always taking your picture."

She snapped again. I flinched. "You get used to it," she continued. "Becomes a way of life. Doesn't steal your soul like tribal taboo. You just live with it." She snapped my picture again.

I could only imagine each shot with me more angry than the last, then another, and another. "Okay, that's enough," I ordered in my mature voice. The one that said, I'm bigger than this. I'm better than this.

"My point is, it's not against the law." She put the phone back in her purse. "Besides, he wasn't naked. He had on those sexy silky boxers he likes to wear. Old-school BVDs with plenty of the black-on-white writing."

The first thing I felt was a thick wirelike tube. I'd completely skipped the length of her hair and my hands had dug into her scalp with clawlike precision. Her scream echoed loud enough to hurt my ears, but I wouldn't let go.

"Get your hands off me, bitch." Sirena dug her nails into my arms. I wouldn't let go. The scuffle lasted mere seconds, and then I felt the air leave my chest. I was being squeezed to death.

"You all right, Peacock?"

"Quincy, I'm fine. Put her down."

"Nah, who is this trick putting her hands on you?"

A woman came in and screamed. She ran out just as fast. If I could've moved my lips I would've screamed for help. It felt like my head was going to pop. His hard thick arms pushed against my neck.

Suddenly he dropped me like a sack of potatoes. My knees hit the hard bathroom tile. Quincy crashed to the floor, right next to me.

"The little boys' room is next door. Think you made a wrong turn," said a familiar male voice.

"He's my bodyguard," Sirena yelled in defense. "And this woman was attacking me. You need to call the police."

I felt an arm loop around my waist, pulling me up, and I cried out in pain. "It's okay. I got you," he said.

"Vin . . . what're you doing here?"

"My job."

"She attacked me," Sirena yelled. "You need to call the police. I want her arrested."

At the same time Quincy was getting to his feet, rubbing the growing knot on the back of his head. He lunged toward both me and Vince, still unsteady. I'd never seen Vince move so fast. He threw elbows and the bodyguard was facedown; this time not a budge. The solid weight flattened in retreat.

Sirena leaned over him and tapped his face. "Quincy, get up."

"I'd let him stay down if I were you."

"Oh my God . . . Venus, are you all right?" Miriam was at my other side. The crowd in and around the bathroom door was hard to push through. I got jostled, making the pain around my chest hurt worse. Vince wouldn't let go.

"He's inside the ladies' bathroom," Vince told two other bouncers scrambling to get through the chaos. I could hear Sirena still screaming she wanted someone to call the police.

Miriam hugged me when I got to the nearly empty lounge seating. Everyone else had run to see the commotion. "Are you all right? What happened in there?"

"Sirena Lassiter."

"You and her. Fighting in the woman's room. No."

"More like two against one. Her bodyguard almost squeezed the life out of me."

"Let's go. Come on. We need to get you home."

Vince came back with a glass of water and a wet towel he placed on my knees. I hadn't even realized they were scratched up from falling to the floor.

"Since when are you a bouncer here, at Davinci's?" I asked Vince.

"Need the extra money . . . if I want to buy that ring."

"Vin." I shook my head in pity. There was no winning. In the past twenty-four hours every married couple I knew had proven faulty. And here he was ready to take the plunge.

The wedding party began to trickle back. "I ruined your bachelorette party. I'm sorry, Miriam."

"You didn't ruin anything. I'm just glad you're okay."

"Do you need me to take you home?" Vince stood firm.

"No. I think I'll stay. Let her go home." We all turned to watch the sea part as Sirena made her way out of the club.

"I'm taking you home. You shouldn't drive." This time it was hot hubby Rob. The senator stood by my side, and the determined look on his face said he wasn't taking no for an answer.

◎◡◎

We drove in silence. The highway was clear and dark. His elbow grazed against me for an instant, then he made sure it didn't happen again. I stared out the window and hoped he didn't ask me any questions.

"So what happened back there?"

I pushed my seat back and closed my eyes. "I lost my temper. She's probably going to sue me or something."

"A lot of hostility going around these days. Jory told me what happened to Mya at school. Is there anything I can do?"

"No. I wouldn't want to get you involved. I know you have a lot of clout at Whitherspoon, but this is something I have to deal with."

We exited, then came to a stoplight. "Were you fighting over your husband?" Robert stared straight ahead. But when the light turned green he still stayed put.

"It's green," I said. "And yes, I guess you could say we were fighting over my husband. I'm a complete fool."

"Complete," he said before stepping slowly on the gas. "But it's every man's fantasy."

"Really?"

"It's true."

"In the last few days I've learned more about men than I really wanted to know. Please spare me any more special information."

"Just one more thing . . . I wish it was me you were fighting over."

"Got news for you, I'd go into a ring with Hulk Hogan before I put on the gloves with your wife, Holly."

He laughed before reaching out and taking my hand. "Stay out of the ring, period. These little hands weren't meant for boxing."

By the time we pulled up to my house, we were singing to Marvin Gaye's greatest hits. Robert sang his part to "Ain't Nothing Like the Real Thing." I clapped before joining in as Tammy Terrell. He did a slight bow. That's when I saw Jake, his face enraged in the window. When Robert's head came up he saw my look of shock and turned to see Jake too.

"What the hell . . . you scared me." Robert let the window down. "How ya doing, Jake?"

Jake completely ignored him. "Get out of the car."

"Thank you for the ride home," I said graciously.

"Anytime."

"No. See, that's where you're wrong. Not anytime. Not ever," Jake announced.

I jumped out and ran to the other side. "What do you think you're doing? Ohmigod, this is Jory's dad."

"I know who he is."

I leaned into the window. "I'm so sorry. I'm . . . please," I said, hoping Robert knew it was best he left quickly.

He straightened his collar and started his engine. "Take care," he said to me before driving off.

"I can't believe you just did that to Jory's dad."

"Don't play that mess with me," Jake said. "I look out the window and all I see is teeth and gums. You leave here dressed like that, then roll up with that dude. I'm sick of him sniffing around you like I don't have a clue. I'm not stupid."

"What you are is a hypocrite. I'm tired," I said unequivocally. "Tired." I started walking to the front door.

"How is this about me?"

"Robert drove me home because I had a bathroom brawl with your girlfriend. I'm not even going to say her name because you know damn well who I'm talking about. And if you say her name, I'm going to take this shoe I'm wearing and clock you over the head with it. Tired. Through. Kaput. Finished. We are done doing the blame game. No more accusations. You make some choices and they better be the right ones."

Jake stood in front of me with an incredulous look on his face. Only when he saw my mouth quiver and scanned the rest of me, did he soften up and pull me in for a gentle hug. "Baby, damn. Damn. Are you all right?"

"I'm tired, you hear me?" I blubbered into his shoulder.

He held me tighter.

I moaned.

"We need to get you to a hospital. You might have a broken rib."

"No, it's not. It just feels sore."

"Baby, I'm sorry."

"Me too," I said, making my way into the house and up the stairs slowly. The pain was only beginning. By morning I wouldn't be able to get out of bed. He scooped me up and carried me. I rested my head on his chest, and wished I'd been better than this. The embarrassment all came rushing back. I wept into my pillow.

The next morning Jake brought me two Advil tablets and water. "Your mom is getting Mya ready for school."

The sunlight was already bright in the bedroom. I squinted and winced from both the daylight and the pain. "No. I don't want her going to school today." I rose up slowly on my elbows. He tucked the pillows underneath me for support. "I'm waiting to hear back from the principal at the school."

"This is all my fault."

"No, what those girls did to Mya is not your fault. It's theirs. Then I'm no better, wrestling in the ladies' bathroom."

"What'd she say to make you go off like that?"

"It doesn't matter. I shouldn't have reacted that way. I think that guy, that bodyguard, would've killed me if Vin hadn't come in. He's a bouncer there, moonlighting." I knew I was babbling. Nervous chatter. My karma checks and balances were weighing heavily on the negative side. I'd never get ahead. The cloud of doom hovering over me refused to go away.

"I guess he was just doing his job." I was welling up again. "Look at us. What are we, Bobby and Whitney?" I shook my head. "I feel like we sold our souls to the devil. So we have to put up with her for your film career, and the next movie, and the next? It's not worth it. In Bloom is doing well. We don't need—"

"We're supposed to begin shooting on the new film in a few months. But if you want me to pull out, you know I will. I just have to give back the money."

"How much . . . I mean, what are our souls worth these days?" I sniffed and patted my wet eyes.

"Two mil. Plus they want me to produce another track. That's what I was working on yesterday in the studio."

"Two million dollars?" I folded my arms over my chest, which probably still had the big bodyguard's imprint. "Who needs a soul when you gotta eat, right?"

"So you'd give me up for a couple of mil, is that what you're saying?"

I tilted my head and hunched my shoulders. Seriously, his eyes asked.

"I'd never give you up. Not for all the money in the world."

"Ahuh," he said before kissing my forehead. "But you have to roll with the punches. You can't let every little thing printed or caught through a lens make you believe any of that mess is true."

"The lens caught you nearly butt naked, Jake."

"Nothing happened. You have to trust me." He kissed my hand like the deal was done. "So two mil, that's all I'm worth?"

I shook my head. "You're priceless." When he left the room I folded myself back into the fluffy sheets and wished I could start the entire week over. But I knew there was nothing I could do except start right where I was. Move forward. Somehow, get through the next film with Sirena. Somehow, swallow my pride and keep my head high all at the same time. Lofty goals. But I'd have to make it through. It wasn't about the money. I didn't want my insecurities to come between Jake and his career.

Tell It to the Mountain

"Hi, Daddy."

"Hey, you all right?"

"I'm fine." Sirena gave her standard answer. But Larry could've guessed she was hardly fine, because she rarely called him daddy. And even if she did, it was to manipulate him. Either way, he didn't mind, as long as she called. "I think it's time I told the truth."

"Did someone find out?" he asked, assuming that was the only way she'd ever open the door to her past.

"No one found out."

"Then why? Why now? You've gone this long."

"Jake. He deserves to know."

"So you're doing this for him. Nothing to do with you, or what you want?" Why did he bother to pose it as a question when it was obviously an accusation? He knew one thing about his daughter: Her need to be famous, to rise to the top, took priority over everything and everyone else. Putting someone else first would be an anomaly, not likely to happen, and if it did, it was by accident.

"I've always cared about Jay. I thought he hated me for so long, I stayed out of his life. I never tried to contact him. But last year, seeing him face-to-face, and spending all this time with him, I see he could never hate me. No matter what, there'll always be the connection between us."

"I don't know." Larry Lassiter exhaled sharply. "I don't know if this is smart."

"Well, now who's the selfish one?" Sirena asked. "You're always telling me I'm just like my mother, that I don't do nothing that doesn't satisfy me first, and now when I want to do the right thing, you're thinking about your damn self," she huffed.

"I have always done what you wanted."

"Because I've paid you to do what I wanted. You wouldn't be taking care of Christopher if I wasn't paying you."

"I took that boy as my own from the day he was born. Don't you tell me I wouldn't be there for him, money or no money. He knows me as his pop, period. I'm his father."

"No . . . Dad. He's my son."

"But is he JP's son? You still don't know. And now you want to risk him the heartache, coming forward as his mother, and disrupting his life."

"You have never cared nothing about me. I hate you." Sirena hung up before he could say more to try and change her mind. She knew what she had to do.

"Leshawn," she yelled at the top of her lungs.

"Where's the fire?" Leshawn stood wide-legged at the foot of Sirena's bed.

"I need a flight to Detroit."

"You going to see your dad?" she asked, not believing what she was hearing. "Wow, he didn't really have a heart attack for real this time, did he?"

"No. The man is healthy, too healthy. He's never going anywhere." Only then did Sirena realize the truthfulness behind that statement. Her father would never give Christopher up. He'd fight her, and use her own money to do it. "Get me a first-class ticket for tomorrow morning."

Leshawn still hadn't moved, waiting for the answer as to why she was going.

"Mind your damn business and get me a flight out of here."

"But you have the interview tomorrow with *Life 'N' Style* magazine."

"Whatthahell, didn't I just do an interview with them? Cancel it."

Leshawn flapped her arms. "You're in need of some serious anger management."

"Get out." She had planning to do. First step was to get Christopher. Second, she'd show that little wifey who held the winning card. Coming after her like some banshee from hell. Miss Venus was in for a real awakening. Jay would see Christopher and know instantly he was their son. Know instantly where he belonged, and to whom.

"So now you're going to be known for scrapping in the women's bathroom with ex-lovers' wives." Earl stopped short of calling her a few choice names. The embarrassment of the situation made his eyes hurt. He took off his glasses and rubbed the dry itchiness.

"She put her hands on me, first." Sirena was out of breath, moving through the airport. Nervous about missing her flight to Detroit. The five-inch ankle boots didn't help. "She is one crazy nutcase. I don't know how JP puts up with her."

Earl was thinking the same about his own situation—how much longer he could put up with Sirena. They'd been together for eight months. Men didn't usually count, but for some reason he'd been marking a calendar, day by day.

"What do you want to do about it?" That's all he wanted to know. He didn't have time for the emotional rant. "Now would be a good time to get him off the film we just signed. No harm, no foul."

"I don't want him off the film." She calmed instantly. "That's not what I want at all."

"I bet," Earl sarcastically teased. "What you want is obvious." He was bitter and not ashamed to show it.

"Oh please, I am telling you, this has nothing to do with me.

She's crazy. She just attached her fingers to my head like some kind of bat out of hell. She's jealous of me, pure and simple. I tried to explain we were friends, just friends."

And I'm the tooth fairy, Earl thought.

"Ah sir, you can only go through with two carry-ons." The security guard had put a hand up to stop Quincy.

"He's carrying my bags, and his." Sirena was close behind, nearly bumping into her bodyguard. She turned her attention back to her phone call. "Earl, baby, isn't there something we can do?"

"Walk away, now. This kind of thing can hurt your career, your reputation. Your fanbase won't take kindly to you breaking up a marriage."

"How am I breaking up a marriage? Huh? What do I have to do with their marriage?" She knew she was getting loud. Quincy put up a hand to try and warn her to keep it down.

"I'm looking out for you. I'm just telling you," Earl said into the phone.

"You're telling me what, exactly?"

"Leave her alone. Walk away. The box-office numbers are rising every weekend for *True Beauty,* which is unheard of. You don't want to bring that crashing down by being the 'other woman.'"

"How am I the other woman when I'm engaged to you?"

"Good question," he said, and left it at that. He had nothing else to say on the subject. The phone line went dead.

Forty Acres and a Child

Sirena tossed her phone in the tray and waited in line for her pat down. The airport security recognized her as always and would make sure to find an excuse to pull her to the side anyway. Cheap thrills. *Female assist, my ass.*

The metal detector beeped. "You might want to take off your bracelet," the wavy-haired man offered. He gave her an approving up-and-down glance.

She rolled her eyes. "Sure, whatever." She went back through. This time, no beep.

"Bag check," one of the others yelled from the belt, holding up her brand-new Fendi.

"I'm sick of you nosy people," she growled. "You want to rummage through my stuff just to say you did."

Quincy stood by her side. "Calm down, Peacock." His demeanor was less on edge. He was used to the harassment.

The blue gloves came over carrying her bag. "May I?" he asked as if she had a right to say no. He shoved both hands in and came up with prescription bottles. He held them up one at a time and shook them. "You've got quite an arsenal," the smart-mouthed security guard quipped.

"Is it your damn business? Hurry up before I miss my flight." She felt a camera or two pointed at her back. Somewhere there'd be a picture, zeroed in on the yellow bottles. Names printed out clear as a bell. Oxycontin, a high-dose pain medication. Vicodin, slightly useless, at least for her system. And Prozac, which she refused to take though it had been prescribed to her on many occasions.

He zipped her purse back up and handed it to her. "Enjoy your flight."

"Screw you."

"Peacock, they're just doing their job."

"Yeah, but they only want to do their job when they think it's going to garner a little bit of attention. You know how many people got prescriptions in their purse, everybody. But they want to put all my business in the street."

"Why do you have all that stuff anyway? You don't use it." Quincy's attitude had been adjusted after that old dude nearly broke his head in the ladies' bathroom. He had calmed down and become a bit more cautious. She hadn't prepared for him to ask her about the medications.

"My back has been bothering me," she answered quickly. "Ever since I got back from New York, you know when I had to sit on the tarmac for four hours . . . now just the thought of sitting up straight for a three-hour flight makes my back hurt."

Quincy seemed satisfied. She wasn't concerned if he believed her or not. He was loyal and would never turn on her. Besides, she hadn't planned on hurting her father, just giving herself enough time to get Christopher out of school and on a plane. Her father would wake up and have to accept the fact the boy was gone. She was his mother, regardless of what the sealed adoption record said. She would always be his mother.

On the Other Foot

Sirena and JP's on-screen chemistry was hot. Real hot. Almost too good. Earl could understand how JP's wife may have lost her cool. Sirena could punch every button, leave fingerprints, and swear it wasn't her. But Earl never really cared about Sirena's true personality, only the one on-screen.

"I want her out of the way so JP and I can work together. Isn't there something you can do?" Sirena had whined when he first answered the phone. "I've got to keep her out of my hair." She paused and waited. "What the hell is so funny?"

Earl Benning normally didn't laugh. There were few things funny in this world. Here he was still wiping the remnants from his eyes. He'd laughed so hard it brought him to tears. "Keeping her out of your hair . . ." he sputtered. "That video circulating with you getting your ass whooped . . . did you see the last seconds where the camera panned down on the weave left behind?" Earl had to straighten himself out. "You need to take care of that."

"Can you write it in his contract," she asked, refusing to be swayed from why she'd called in the first place, "saying his wife has to stay clear of me, and him, while he's working?"

Unheard of. "Sirena. Listen, don't get involved with him and his wife, or I promise you it's going to backfire."

"I'm not . . . look, fine, but if she makes one derogatory statement about me, or even looks my way, I will have Quincy finish what he started."

Unbelievable. The part she didn't understand was that people always rooted for the underdog. "Just leave her alone, do you understand? No instigating, no phone calls, no more pictures being leaked." He rubbed the thick folds around his jowl. "And don't even pretend it wasn't you."

Silence was enough of an answer; she'd hung up. Well, he'd had enough kids' play. All he wanted was to slip off on a private flight to Saint-Tropez and see her in that eeny teeny yellow bikini. The thought of all her assets shoved into that bathing suit was enough to make him remember why he put up with her in the first place.

Leaning back in his chair, thinking about her perfect body, beautiful face and hair, a tight smile came across his face and just as quickly disappeared. None of it mattered if she was a has-been. He only wanted the best, and right now the best was Sirena. He had to keep it that way, at least until he was done with her.

"Mr. Benning, your lawyer is still holding on line two," his assistant announced on the intercom.

"Put him through." He waited until he heard the assistant hang up. "Coop—what's shakin', man?"

"Got your prenup finished. I added the final addendum. Both of you are set up to leave with what you came with. Her net worth is pretty substantial so that shouldn't stop her from signing."

"Good. I have a feeling that prenup will be put in use pretty early."

"That's no way to enter into marriage, man." Coop was one of Earl's most trusted friends. He was a lawyer and CEO of his partners' law firm.

"Hey, I'm a realist. We've got some trust issues."

Coop stayed quiet, knowing the rules. Never speak ill of a friend's woman even in agreement.

"When's the big day?"

"Sorry, Coop. I can't tell you. The word gets out through the airways and we've got helicopters and paps sneaking in trees."

"Too bad. I'd love to be there."

"Nah, I'll get you by my side for the next one."

Coop laughed. "Already got the next missus lined up, do you?"

"Hey, there's always a newer, better model rolling off the assembly line."

"Yeah, but eventually you realize the comfort of the model you can rely on. You know the sound of the engine, the quality matters."

"And I wish you and Val continued longevity in your marriage. But me, I get bored."

"Then why . . . why are you bothering with formalities?" Coop asked.

"Exclusivity. You put a ring on a woman's finger, she's less likely to fuck around. Simple as that. While she's mine, I want her to be all mine," Earl stated honestly. There was no mention of the L-O-V-E word. In fact, neither he nor Sirena had ever used it once in their relationship and it suited him just fine.

"I wish you and Sirena the best, regardless. Who knows, you two might be a match made in heaven. A couple of kids, and you'll be on your way."

"Don't even say 'kid.' Children are not in my vocab."

Coop sighed from exhaustion. "All right, man. But that reminds me of something else you two need to discuss. Prenups lose a lot of ground in court once children are involved. Call me if you need anything else."

"I got everything I need. Thank you for covering my ass," Earl said before hanging up. Children. He shook his head. Not even a worry. Sirena would never want a child. She was all about Sirena. Risking her figure or taking time out of her skyrocketing career would never happen, not in this lifetime.

Deal or No Deal

I was already dressed for the grand opening of the Monarch. For once I was ready before Jake. He used to be ready in a flash; now he spent extra time in the mirror checking all sides and angles, never knowing which shot a camera would capture.

The doorbell rang and I figured it was the driver. I swung open the door and couldn't believe it.

"Dad!" I leaped into his arms, forgetting about my expensive dress.

"Hey, Precious."

I gave up on my perfect makeup since my face was pressed against his cheek. "You came," I said quietly. "Does Mom know?"

"Well, look who's here," Pauletta said from the top of the stairs.

"She does now." Henry stepped all the way inside. "I guess I caught you heading out."

"Jake and I have a party to go to. That'll give you and Mom some time alone," I hinted with a wink.

"Oh please," Pauletta said. "You may as well turn yourself right around and get back on that plane."

I faced my father with fear and pleading. "Don't leave . . . please."

"It'll be fine. I'll be here when you get back," he said.

⊙〜⊚

The hotel grounds were lit up like an Italian villa. If not for the limos and town cars lined at the entrance you wouldn't know it was the twenty-first century.

Jake squeezed my hand. "If I see another red carpet, I think I'm going to hurl."

"Oh, the hard-knock life of a movie star." I leaned against his shoulder.

"Did I tell you how beautiful you look tonight?"

"Yes, but I don't mind you telling me again." The deep V-cut dress in the back in shimmering cobalt blue was one I'd picked after trying on about twenty of them at the Purple Door. The boutique was small and catered to a select clientele. I'd received a special invitation to shop . . . a perk of being JP's wife. Told to pick out anything I liked, free of charge. In exchange for mentioning where I'd gotten it, of course.

The familiar sound of the electric lens focusing, and then the shutter, made me flinch. Still traumatized after the nightmare run-in with Sirena, but this time I was obligated to join in on the photo party. I took my trained step backward to let them take pictures of Jake first without the wifey on his arm. Then I'd have to move forward and somehow mention the Purple Door. Making deals, selling off pieces of yourself was something I was going to have to get used to. The exchange of one thing for another was part of the business. Jake and his career in exchange for putting up with Sirena. Someone's camera caught me smiling painfully with the thought.

I quickly noticed all of the cameras directly pointed at me, no matter how much I backed up and tried to get out of the way.

"What are they doing?" I called to Jake. "Is it time?"

"Maybe they like your dress too." He grinned. He put out his hand. "Come here, baby. Come on."

I came to Jake's side. We made a dashing couple, him in his black suit, me in cobalt blue and the bronzer on my skin shimmering under the warm lighting.

"You look amazing. Who are you wearing?" The first question caught me by surprise, not believing how easy this was.

"Bertrand Gund, from the Purple Door." I smiled and tilted my chin down with eyes up as I'd been told by—of all people—Trevelle. She'd spent the entire day making me practice smiling and posing.

"Venus, did you and Sirena kiss and make up?" The second question was from the same direction. "Who won the fight? Was it over JP and their affair?"

Trevelle hadn't made me practice for that. My face fell flat.

Jake grabbed me by the elbow and rushed us inside.

"Oouch." I rubbed my arm, snatching it back.

"Sorry. It's one of their tricks. First they say something nice, then hit you with something embarrassing just to get a reaction. Never talk to them. You can smile and pose, but don't ever respond."

"Thank you, 'Ramona.'" I was flustered and already embarrassed. The entire intrusion made me uncomfortable. "I can't stand this." I was about to go into my diatribe.

"Mr. JP, it is a pleasure. William Carter, manager of the Monarch." He shook Jake's hand. "Thank you so much for coming."

"My pleasure. I wouldn't have missed it," Jake said politely, though he knew the man had basically extorted him into being there.

"And where's our other half?" Mr. Carter turned around. "No offense," he said to me.

"Sirena can't make it." I kept a bland expression, one that didn't say *eat poo and die.*

"You mind?" Mr. Carter turned around and posed with Jake by his side for a picture. There were three or four cameras going off in succession. The difference was these guys were wearing suits and name tags, legitimately hired for the event. The chandeliers brightly glittered from the high painted ceilings like the Sistine Chapel. The room was filled with well-dressed people holding champagne glasses.

"If you'll excuse me." I backed away, determined not to find myself caught in another lens.

Inside, past the lobby I took a deep breath, feeling safe. In the display corners and on every table sat beautiful floral arrangements in buttercream colored vases, all courtesy of In Bloom. Proud and feeling accomplished I was greeted by a serving tray of oil-brushed tomatoes with goat cheese. I took one and shoved it into my mouth, remembering Ms. Perot chastising me for eating with fingers. Guess she forgot about cocktail parties. There was no other way. I washed it down with the champagne, which was never my favorite. It tasted either too bitter or too sweet, no in-between. But it was the drink of champions.

I sipped with my pinkie extended to blend in. The Atlanta society climbers were out in force, already in their various cliques, pretending to be better than each other, as if only one person could be on top. I noticed I was one of a few with a short dress on. Everyone else wore long gowns.

I cringed with the fear I might bump into Paige, or one of the other Hansel and Gretel mothers, anyone who might know of Jake's pictures on the Internet, and of course my bathroom brawl. Word traveled with a click of the enter button.

"My, my, don't you look stunning."

I turned around to see hot hubby Rob transformed back into Senator Stanton. His expensively tailored suit and gold cuff links were something out of a magazine. His strong chin still had fine stubble, as if he was too much of a man to fully shave.

Relieved to see a friendly face, I couldn't help but smile. "You clean up pretty good yourself."

"So is everything okay?" He nudged his eyes in the direction of where Jake stood having his picture taken.

"You're sweet, yes. Everything is fine. We kissed and made up."

"Good. I wouldn't want to be the cause of any turmoil in your life."

"Trust me, that's my job. I'd say you're even risking your reputation right now just talking with me."

"What . . . no. You were defending your man. I think that's rather honorable, and damn well sexy," he whispered a little too close for comfort.

"Where's Mrs. Stanton?"

"She's here, somewhere," he answered nonchalantly. "I think our secret undercover lovefest is more of a concern for your husband than my wife."

"Yeah, I think we've been found out. It was nice seeing you."

"Just nice?" He raised a playful brow. "We should have you two over for dinner," he spoke pointedly. "Let the kids play and we'll eat and be merry."

"Yeah." I waved a timid good-bye, cutting the conversation even shorter. My escape was interrupted by Holly Stanton.

"That's a wonderful idea," she chimed in. He must've seen her coming, that whole gear switch. Inviting Jake and me over for dinner was for her benefit, and thank goodness mine too.

She slipped a long slender arm around me and gave an air kiss. She stood model height, six feet tall, and that was without high heels. She still had the muscle tone from her years as a celebrated female basketball player in the late nineties. Her shimmering dark skin and perfectly arched cheekbones were recognizable from the Nike fashion ads back then.

Her twenties bob and regal neckline went perfectly with her ruffled yellow gown. Her cordial tone was surprising. Normally, she spoke to me like I was the help and could do nothing for her. "We should all get together. Robert and I are having a fund-raiser in a few months. It would be great to have you on the committee."

"Really? On the committee?" I had to catch myself from saying more. Like, *seriously, get outta here, you gotta be kidding.* But now it made sense. Jake had made the leap into the substantial income bracket, plus a nice source of notoriety. Naked pictures on the Internet and bathroom brawls be damned. Who cared about respectability?

Long as a nice check with plenty of zeros could be written Holly was Miss Hospitality.

She flipped a huge diamond-covered hand with stark white-painted nail tips. "Of course we'd love to have you." She slipped an arm under her husband's. "We have space that needs to be filled on a couple of boards as well. When you come over for dinner we'll talk about it."

"That would be lovely," I said. "But if you'll excuse me, I see a friend." *Catch me if you can 'cause I'm the gingerbread man.*

"I'll call you," Holly said.

The last time I went to Holly Stanton's house, she'd taught my child how to straighten her hair with a flat iron. Burns on her neck and ear took weeks to heal. I swore I'd never let Mya go back over there. Which really hadn't been fair to Mya or Jory since they still considered themselves best friends, and here I was still holding a grudge. Maybe the principal at Whitherspoon had a point. It was the parents who held on to foolishness. The kids rolled with the punches.

I roamed with no direction. I kept sipping and checking the door for Jake to make his entrance. Mr. Carter was probably using Jake like a cardboard popup for photos. Perhaps I should go and rescue him. I marched, albeit a bit wobbly from the champagne on an empty stomach. I pushed past the incoming crowd. First I saw Jake, then I saw Melba Dubois, the gossip journalist who'd cornered me in my floral shop and then at Mya's tea party.

"What are you doing here?" I asked.

"Oh my, you're quite the fireball. Are you going to bludgeon me too?" She scratched at the air with a cat growl.

I was five, four, three . . . *Don't talk to this woman* . . . two . . . one second from losing more karma points.

"Excuse me." Jake took my hand and led me a few feet away. "What's wrong with you?"

"What's wrong with me? That was the lady I told you about. She's the one came to my place of business with one goal, to let me know you and Sirena were bosom buddies in another lifetime. Then she was at Mya's tea party taking pictures of our daughter . . . and for what? Why would someone want to write a story just to drag someone through the mud? I don't understand it."

"I thought you agreed. You're going to hear a lot of rumors with me in this industry. You're going to have to learn to deal with it and move on."

"The word 'rumor' usually implies something untrue." I smacked my lips and turned away before I made a bigger fool of myself.

"You said you were going to be all right with all of this. Remember, we made a deal." He followed me out to the valet. I was ready to go home and I knew how to make it happen fast.

"Maybe Senator Stanton can give me a lift home." I peered around as if I were really looking for him.

"I think you better watch yourself," he said. "Calm down and get it together."

The Pretenders

Our house was still a good distance. There was no easy way to get to the Hadley Estates. No back shortcuts. The suburban gated community was one of hundreds housing mini mansions just big enough to pretend all was right in the world. Pretend that marriages weren't falling apart and children weren't losing their identity each day they went to school.

"How was it?" Pauletta peered over her reading glasses where she'd relaxed on the couch.

"Nice." I held my shoes in my hand. "We had a great time. Where's Dad?"

"He's lying down. He had a long flight." She left it at that and turned back to the novel she was reading.

"Okay, I'll see you in the morning." It was as good a face as I could put on.

Jake didn't bother. He'd gone up the stairs without a word. He'd never been a good pretender. There was no ability to smile when his heart was aching. That was for clowns, he'd tell me. Or for the camera, I wanted to add. He seemed to always smile for the camera.

"Venus," my mother called before my feet were completely out of view, so I couldn't pretend I didn't hear her.

"Yes." I peeped past the ascending ceiling.

"I'll be up a little while longer if you need anything. There's some beef tips in gravy, mashed potatoes, and salad, if you're hungry."

My stomach groaned and shifted uncomfortably. My mouth watered. For a minute I didn't say anything, trying to figure out how I could get to the buttery mashed potatoes and tender gravy-smothered steak without having to eat it in front of her. My mother's food may as well have been truth serum. When she needed answers she'd separate my brother and me like prisoners. Bring us in one at a time to the dinner table, set a delicious meal down, and wait for us to start tattling on the other. Squawking like ducks getting a bag full of bread crumbs. When there was nothing left on the plate, we'd know we'd just betrayed the other.

"No, thank you, I ate way too many finger foods. See you in the morning." I hiked two steps at a time, delirious with hunger pains.

"Mommy, is that you?" Mya was in bed. Darkness except for the nightlight coming from the corner of her room.

"Hi, sweetie." I leaned over her and planted a soft kiss between the eyes. "I missed you today."

"I missed you too." She held her stuffed brown bear close to her chest. "Is Daddy home too?"

"Yes, he's home."

She turned Brown Bear toward me. "He wants to know if we can go to school tomorrow." She always used Brown Bear to ask her difficult questions.

I secretly hated the stuffed little troublemaker. Airic had won it for her on one of their many trips to the amusement park. I suppose answering Brown Bear felt like I was answering Airic. I'd even checked it once to make sure it wasn't bugged, or wired for sound.

"Mya, it's going to be a few more days before you can go back to school."

"But why?" she whined. "It wasn't my fault. I'm not in suspense."

"Suspension. And I know it's not your fault. You did nothing wrong. But we have to wait until Principal Stone expels Queenie. She did a very bad thing."

"She's bad. Not me." Pouted lips on Mya looked like she was awaiting a kiss. I couldn't resist.

"Go to sleep. I promise to call the school tomorrow."

"Mommy, I miss school and my friends," Mya gave her final pitch.

Short Order

Lately, Jake had been thinking of what his life would've been like had he not met Venus. He wondered about the intersection of crossroads and how one change of events could realign your entire life. He was wondering if there was such a thing as fate, or did choices move the arrow to say, This Way.

He'd gotten exactly what he'd asked for, like the best off the menu. It happened sitting at a conference table while he was drumming his fingers on the glass top as she gave her presentation. Venus, Legend, and William—the marketing dream team had arrived to save his fledgling hip-hop clothing line. She was the leader of the tribe. She swished around in her tight skirt and her blouse tucked in to show a tiny waistline and flat stomach. He could hardly listen for watching her move around the room.

"Do you mind?" She leaned over him like a teacher in a classroom. He flattened his hand to stop the nervous habit. "As I was saying," she continued. "You need to create a new brand, a new line, and gradually step out of the urban clothing box. It's time to move on to bigger and better."

"So you're saying I basically need to recreate the wheel."

"You do if you want to keep rolling," she'd said, one hand on her glorious hip. She was all work and no play. A far cry from the women he'd surrounded himself with in his past.

"Let's face it, these little baggy-pant–wearing boys eventually grow up. Let's assume some of you actually grow up," she'd said toward Legend. Their love/hate relationship was obvious from the start. "When they do, you want to be there to catch them."

By the end of the meeting, Jake had made up his mind. He didn't care about the rock she was wearing on her ring finger. She was smart, sexy, and business savvy. It was a list he'd narrowed down over the years. Three out of three, hitting the bull's-eye.

"Would you have dinner with me?" he'd asked after they'd finished their meeting.

"No. I'm sure whatever we need to discuss can be done here, tomorrow morning." She packed up her briefcase and marched out of his conference room. He watched her walk away. She turned back around and he could see she was glad he was still there, staring.

Rare to have a woman say no to him. There was pleasure in the chase. Nothing worth having ever came easy. Pursuing Venus Johnston became a vital part of enjoying his workday. As soon as Legend learned of his intentions he threw back his head and opened his white teeth for a boisterous laugh.

"That's like taking a badger home as a pet because it looks like a rabbit." He stopped smiling. "Badgers are one of the most vicious animals in the world. Carnivores. Don't let her petite frame and smooth skin fool you."

Jake never saw that side of Venus. She soon learned of her mother's breast cancer and fell apart before his very eyes. She couldn't make it through the day without battling tears. Her fiancé was two thousand miles away in Virginia. Vulnerability was hardly a level playing field. Jake hadn't meant to take advantage of the situation. Could he help it if she needed a soft place to land? He ran a bath. Gave her a massage. Helped her get through the day, and she still said no.

He thought about the first night they'd slept together. When she finally came to him, ready, he'd wanted to be tender and caring because that's what she needed. But once he held her and was deep inside, he lost all control. He made love to her like a man who'd been stranded on an island for too long. She was water for his tired, parched heart. After all, he'd sworn he'd never get caught up, lose the upper hand in a relationship again.

Yet she held his heart in his hand and there was nothing he could do about it. Now, six years later, he wondered if he'd made different choices, changed course, where he would be.

He slid into the covers of their bed. She was already on her side, pretending to be asleep. His shower must've lasted a lot longer than he realized.

"Good night," he whispered to her back, afraid to touch her.

"Good night." Her stoic reply confirmed the fact she was still mad.

He thought about telling her a story, one that would set the record straight so she'd know why Sirena would never be an issue between them. The story would be brief and quick and to the point. But then there would be questions. The kind he didn't like to answer.

He closed his eyes and hoped maybe tomorrow would wipe the slate clean. He didn't want to be right, that maybe he'd made a mistake in his choice. He didn't want to be the unlucky one who had to start over, find a new place for his heart to be safe. But the one thing he knew, he would never let himself be broken and hurt again. If she wanted out, he would clear the way.

Cash and Prizes

"Cee Cee, are we going to bring Pop anything back from Chick-fil-A? He likes the double piece with corn on the cob for a side."

Sirena wrapped an arm around Christopher. "No, sweetie. I think Pop will be asleep by the time we get home. The movie let out pretty late." They walked out of the theater in the mall and were greeted by a crowd of waiting fans.

She slipped on her Dolce sunglasses and prepared for the camera flashes. Even the local yokels had paparazzi, though here they were just guys who ran home to get their cameras. The word traveled fast that Sirena Lassiter and her little brother were watching *Transformers* at the Metroplex.

Christopher put up both hands, giving the peace sign. He enjoyed the attention, offering up his cheesiest smile.

"Slow down, little man," Quincy ordered. He stepped in front of the boy to clear a path. Outside, the driver waited with the door open to the limousine.

"Are we going to go through the drive-through?"

"Sure, if you want. Anything you want," Sirena offered.

"I don't think we should. 'Cause the car's so long. We might get stuck, or worse, knock over the ordering sign. Then they'll charge us a million dollars." He cracked himself up. "A million dollars for a Chick-fil-A double with sides."

Sirena smiled and gritted her teeth. The boy was so corny. Larry was raising him in the same house she'd lived in, but the neighborhood had changed for the worse. To keep Christopher from being exposed he hardly let him go anywhere or do anything without an adult, namely himself. On his Wednesday Indian Bingo trips he left Christopher at the neighbor's, Mrs. Winston's house, which conveniently was her Bible study night.

"Can I open the sunroof?"

"Sure."

"It's like it's my birthday or something." He stood up and poked his head through the opening and screamed, "Yahooooo."

"Your pops is going to be pissed when he hears about this," Quincy chided. "Is it his birthday?" he asked after giving it a few seconds of thought.

"Can't I do something nice for my baby brother? He's cooped up with that crazy old man. They don't even have cable. Who doesn't have cable in the 2G's?" She shook her head. "That's why he's coming to live with me for a while."

Quincy stuttered, "You kidding?"

"I'm happy you have such high expectations of me."

"No, it's just that . . . who's going to watch him? You're gone all the time. I know you ain't trying to leave him with Leshawn. She'll have that boy doing shots and counting dominoes like a seasoned con."

"I haven't really planned that far ahead, and excuse me if I don't feel the need to discuss this with you further."

"My bad." Quincy lifted his meaty arms and grasped Christopher by the waist. "Come on down, boy. You 'bout to climb up outta here and be roadkill."

"Aww, that felt good. Fresh air," Christopher exclaimed. His ears and cheeks were red. His skin tone had always been fairer than Sirena's. She had only two choices of who his father was, Jake or Tommy, and both men were her complexion. Maybe if her father let him out of the house once in a while, he would've darkened up. She just wished she could be one hundred percent sure. Her wish was that Jake would take one look at Christopher and see a distant relative—an uncle, his father, or brother. That Christopher looked like someone on his side and was undeniably his son. It would be too risky to take a DNA test. The book would be opened and shut before Christopher showed what a great kid he could be, a great son.

"We're here, we're here."

"Why don't you run inside and order whatever you like." She handed him a fifty.

"Whoa . . . fifty dollars." He pulled on the door handle and shot out like a rocket.

Quincy sucked in his cheek and tried not to appear too disgusted. "I'll go. He shouldn't be running around at night flashing dough. You see what kind of neighborhood we're in?"

"If you'd stopped talking three sentences ago, you could already be in there with him."

"So now I'm the babysitter, already."

"Four sentences ago."

Sirena watched his large massive self walk into the fast-food place and get beside Christopher while he ordered. She hadn't planned for day care. The boy was nine years old; he could watch himself. At that age, she was already cooking dinner and doing laundry. By ten she was plotting her escape from dullsville, by eleven she'd let the teenaged boy who lived across the street sample her goodies, giving her the first and most unforgettable orgasm.

Everyone had to grow up sometime.

Larry wouldn't be there to follow him around and take care of his every need. The same as he hadn't been around for her. She turned out all right.

When they arrived back at the house, both the ambulance and a huge red fire truck were blocking Paramour Drive.

"Wow, what happened?" Christopher rolled the window down, taking in the excitement. Smoky air wafted into the limo. Sirena leaned past him to roll the window back up. The smell of someone's pitiful dwelling up in smoke.

She wouldn't be surprised if a neighborhood crack house caught fire. The entire area had gone to the dogs. As much money as she was giving her father, he could've moved, but refused. His house was paid for. If and when her career took a dive, he'd still have his home, he'd said, planning for her failure.

"What would you like me to do, Miss Lassiter?" The driver sat patiently with the car engine running.

"We can walk, I guess." Their flight wasn't till the morning, planned for after Larry had his first cup of coffee. She'd poured the contents of five capsules in his sugar bowl. His idea of a good cup was three parts sugar, one part cream, and a drop of java. By the time he finished drinking it, he'd be too numb to stop her from packing Christopher up and out the door. He might even be ready to listen to reason.

They got out and started the trek past the other run-down houses. Seeing the area now, Sirena couldn't believe it was legal to plant so many boxes on one square block.

"Sirena, oh child, there you two are." Mrs. Winston came toward them. Her rolled hair was tied underneath a scarf. She pushed her robe tight around her neck. "Your father . . . they're taking him to the hospital."

"Where's Pop?" Christopher started running. Quincy latched on to his collar before he could gain any distance.

"Son, he's in the ambulance." Mrs. Winston's voice shook. "I smelled the smoke before I saw it. Came outside and couldn't believe your father's place on fire. This is his evening tea and cigar time. I told him about smoking those old nasty cigars." She crossed her hand over her heart. "They got him out in time, I think. God willing. Bless him, Lord, bless him."

Sirena watched as the paramedics shut the doors on the ambulance. Larry had used the sugar prematurely. This wasn't her fault. Who knew about evening tea hour? The windows were all that was left in the front. The door had been knocked down by the firefighters. She shook her head in disgust.

"Come on, we'll follow the ambulance," she said to Christopher, hoping it wasn't too late. She only had wanted to put him out of commission for a minute or two, not kill him.

Satin, Bows, and Fairy Tales

"You don't think it's too young for me, do you?" Miriam twirled around in the cloud of fluffy tulle. The bodice was fairy-tale white with a heart-shaped neckline.

"You're beautiful." I helped her with the matching veil.

She faced the mirror. "I really love it. Ben's going to love it too. I feel like this is all new. I have butterflies in my stomach. I'm excited and nervous." She wrung out her hands. "A brand-new start."

"We could all use one of those," I agreed wholeheartedly.

"Thank you for coming with me today. Jeanette had to go on a job interview. I couldn't be mad at her for that."

"No," I blurted out. "But I could think of other things."

"What?" Miriam turned around and faced me. "What're you talking about?"

"Nothing. I just meant there are worse things to be mad at."

"You're still having a hard time with Jake? And here I am about to renew my vows. Trust me, I understand your frustration." Miriam pushed back her long tresses.

I was sick to death of that wig and the lies that went with it. "Thanks for understanding."

"Okay, unzip me and let's go to lunch. I'll starve myself tomorrow."

Miriam and I had an outdoor café seat at Salvo's uptown. It was her favorite restaurant. They served Cuban cuisine and tall mojitos with fresh mint and real sugarcane.

"You're going to love the black bean soup. It's just like my mother used to make."

"Beans, beans, good for your heart, the more you eat, the more you—" I rolled my eyes. "You know the rest."

"What's with you today? You're usually so optimistic about everything. Seeing the brighter side, the big picture." Miriam looked concerned. She pushed back the corners of her long strands of hair.

I sucked the last of the rum from the bottom of the glass. I crunched loudly on the homemade tortilla chips and salsa. Learning to keep my mouth shut had made me look impossibly glum.

Miriam eyeballed me. She blinked suspicion. "Tell me what is really going on."

"You're just like my mother. She feeds me, then asks me a million questions. Everything is fine. Please, let's celebrate the way we should have before I so rudely ruined your bachelorette party."

The waiter saw the empty glass and rushed over. "May I get you another?" He was authentically Cuban. Miriam said something to him in Spanish and he went away.

"Does that mean I don't get my second drink?"

"Yes, exactly. I told him you were unstable, right now was not a good time for liquor. But for me, I ordered another."

I busted out in laughter. "Good one."

She didn't break a smile.

"It's nothing, I'm just dealing with tons of issues. You know about Mya and the school. They haven't agreed to take Queenie out. And I'm not about to let Mya return until they do. She misses school."

"Then let her go. She's a tough, smart cookie, like her mommy. She's going to be fine."

I bowed my head, knowing it was the truth. Standing on my resolution was only harming my own child.

"One down. Next."

"I'm worried about my mother, my dad, my husband, my good friend . . . Vince. Shall I go on?"

"You have your health, your family intact, and your friend will have to fend for himself." She opened her hands. "And for my next trick, I will make your stress disappear." The waiter left one mojito. She slid it in front of me. "Drink up."

"I once believed that finding the man of my dreams would solve all my problems. Having a friend, lover, and spouse all rolled into one would be the elixir for life's ever-changing dilemmas. I once believed no harm could come to me once I was safe in a good honest relationship. A woman believes this even when she sees signs. Great big arrows with sharp points coming your way. And yet we still believe."

"Whoa, okay." Miriam wasn't expecting this when she'd asked me to start talking.

"I have to go."

"What do you mean you have to go?" Miriam stood up as I did. She couldn't believe I'd just walked away. I stood at the edge of the café, staring out.

Walking on the opposite side of the street were Sirena and a boy. So distracted, I nearly knocked over a waitress. She gave me the evil eye. Sirena's attention trailed in my direction as if she felt my energy all over her. As if she knew someone was watching. But someone's always watching—she knows that too.

They actually stopped and posed while a man took their picture. Another passerby stopped her; this time he asked the boy to take the photo using his camera phone. Sirena grinned as if the day had infinite possibility—not just this day, but all the ones ahead. The boy handed the camera back and pulled out something from his front jeans pocket.

An inhaler.

"Venus, what in the world is goin' on?" Miriam caught up with me, out of breath and disturbed. "You're goin' to have to tell me, right now. Are you on medication?"

I pointed like I'd seen a ghost.

Her eyes followed. "Sirena."

"She's got a boy with her."

"So what, it's her baby brother. What's the big deal?" She realized I had no clue of what she was talking about. "She has a little brother. They've been together in pictures before." She pulled down her sunglasses and gave a hard stare. "Yep, that's him. Just a little guy. Innocent. Can we go back and finish our lunch?"

"Miriam, I have to go." I gave her an air kiss since it was impossible to get past her wig. "I'll be at the rehearsal."

"Stay out of trouble," she yelled.

Shred of Truth

Sirena opened her cell phone and saw there was still no word from Jake. She'd left four messages, asking him to call her back. She'd told him about her father, the fire, his hospitalization. Maybe he didn't believe her this time, after she'd lied about the heart attack. Still, he could at least have called her back.

"Cee Cee, I'm tired. I'm ready to go." Christopher puffed on his inhaler. The plastic contraption was odd and embarrassing. If she was going to take care of him, she had to manage his asthma. She would work it out. Now that Larry was in the hospital, she couldn't go back on her plan. In fact, it was the ideal situation. She had plenty of time to work up to her goal without any interference whatsoever.

Letting Jake know Christopher was his son. *Could be his son.* She wasn't sure how she was going to word it. All she knew was that he would be grateful, especially after she'd learned Mya wasn't his biological daughter and Venus had miscarried their son. That Melba Dubois was very useful. Her exchange of information was minor compared to what she'd gained.

Jay was ripe for the picking.

"Finish your ice cream."

"Dairy products aren't that good for me."

"Who doesn't like ice cream? Eat," she scolded, all the while checking her phone every five seconds.

"Pop says ice cream makes my asthma worse."

"Does he, now?"

"He says it creates mucus in the lungs. Mucus is the cause of asthma."

"Bad luck is the cause of asthma. Eat."

She could use a massage, a pedicure, and a good romp in the sack. She was already tired of Christopher whining about every damn thing.

"Excuse me, Sirena, can I take a picture with you?"

The woman blocked the sunlight when she looked up. That was a good thing. "Of course. My ss . . . brother will take the picture," she said, nearly making a mistake. She'd practiced so long and hard explaining everything to Jake she was starting to see Christopher as her son instead of her brother. "Christopher, take our picture."

He gave his cone a long lick and didn't move from his spot on the wire chair.

"Boy, get up and take this picture."

"What am I going to do with my cone?"

"Throw it away. Remember? You don't like ice cream," she mocked.

He tossed what was left in the trash and wiped his hands on his new jeans. New shirt. New everything. She couldn't have him running around like an orphan. They'd left and hopped on their morning flight without so much as a toothbrush. The fire had conveniently destroyed his old life. She'd bought him everything he was wearing, brand-new.

"I just love your music, and your movies. You are off the chain."

Sirena looked up at the lady, who looked like a lifetime member of the Dark and Lovely club. Straight off the box. Her coif was curled under right at her ear. She didn't understand why women ran around with these freeze-dried hairdos when they could run to the Korean supply and have hair down their back. No matter the age, a man dug sexy strands down a woman's back. What was so hard to understand? You were either in the game or out.

"Cheezz," she sang out with Miss Dark and Lovely.

Christopher fumbled and gummed the silver casing with his sticky fingers. "It won't do anything."

"Let me show you," the woman offered. "Here, just push this button, okay?"

Now it was a game. Christopher seemed to play dumber by the minute. "This button?"

"Boy, I swear, if you don't snap this picture . . ." Sirena went back to smiling. After a few seconds of him holding up the phone but doing nothing she snatched it from him and handed it back to the woman. "I'm sorry. Maybe next time," she said politely, though she wanted to cuss like a sailor.

"No problem. My friends will just have to take my word for it. I saw Sirena Lassiter. You're even prettier in person."

"That is so sweet. Thank you." Sirena calmly accepted the compliment, though patience was not her strong suit. *Go away!*

As soon as the coast was clear she grabbed Christopher by his arms. "Are you dumb, or is you crazy? What is wrong with you?"

"Let go. I'mma tell Pop."

"Tell him what? That you're acting like an idiot? Besides, he's healing in the hospital, remember? You don't want to make him feel worse by complaining."

He rubbed his sore arms where she'd squeezed. *Big baby.*

Quincy had been parked and sitting in the black Cadillac SUV a few cars down. He'd trotted over to where they were sitting. "I heard him screaming. What happened?"

"He's acting like a little bitch, that's what happened." She put out a message to her fans: *Soon the world will know something important about me, about who I really am.*

Christopher coughed and wheezed. He pulled out his inhaler. When he had enough air to talk he said, "You're the one acting like a—"

"Say it. I dare you."

"Can't leave you two alone."

"Sorry to have disturbed your afternoon nap," Sirena snapped, still typing on her phone. *My life is not as simple as it seems.*

Quincy didn't have a response. He knew when to stop talking.

"I don't feel good, Cee Cee." Christopher's sullen tone cut the name-calling to a halt. He kept pumping on the plastic L-shaped tube, but it was no longer feeding him instant relief. His eyes watered and his face quickly took on a rosy hue.

Sirena stood up, pulling him by the arm, facing the fact. "Come on. We gotta get him to emergency."

A Family Affair

In Bloom was buzzing. Trevelle, Vince, and part-timer Jackie were moving like a heist was going down, loading floral arrangements in assembly-line fashion on the van.

The business contract from the Monarch Hotel was keeping everyone hopping. Then there were the other orders from new customers who'd admired all the grand opening décor.

Trevelle wiped her forehead with the back of her hand. "I haven't worked this hard since . . . I'm going to say, never. I'm working like a Hebrew slave, so maybe it was in another lifetime, 'cause it sure wasn't in this one." She looked at her beaten-up nails. "I have gone to the dark side."

"I need to talk to you, Trevelle," I said. "Please, it won't take long. But in private."

"So the fact that we are buried alive under this mountain of deliveries escaped your vision."

"Yeah, li'l lady, now's not a good time," Vince said. "We've got orders going in five different directions with only one van. Things are looking a little iffy."

"I can see that. It's just that this is real important."

Vince watched us from the corner of his eye. I had to give him a sign that it wasn't about him or his moonlighting endeavors to pay for a ring. In fact, it had nothing to do with either of them. "Go on, we'll keep it moving till you two get back."

"The man has spoken," I said, knowing Trevelle would take Vin's sign of approval over my begging any day.

We went to the front of the store, where it was the picture of tranquility. No one would know we were inundated in the back room. I sat down on the couch, but she stayed standing.

"Trevelle, please."

She hesitated, then sat. "Go on, child, life is short."

"I need to know what you did to find out about my past. I mean, who . . . did you use a private investigator? I need someone who can help me find out everything about someone . . . things you can't just find out by Googling. Like birth records," I said quietly.

This seemed to garner her attention. "Whose records?"

"Do I have to tell you everything? I just need the same person you used to find out all the dirt on me and my husband when you were determined to destroy us."

"That's some attitude, missy. You want my help, but I'm the bad guy?"

"Let's face it, you did a lot of nasty things before you became the reformed flower angel."

"That I did, but that's between me and my Heavenly Father."

"I'm not talking about your illustrious career as a teen prostitute. I'm talking about how you tried to take Mya, and used every dirty trick in the book to do it." I put my hand to my forehead. "Please, I'm sorry. That is not what I want to waste time talking about."

Trevelle stayed silent, waiting.

"It's Sirena. She has a boy with her. She says it's her little brother . . . but I'm scared. I have a feeling she's lying. She and Jake . . ." I paused, feeling the familiar lump in my throat coming to cloud my words. "There's a history between them, that goes deeper than he wants to talk about. And I know . . ." *Swallow.* "I have a feeling—"

Trevelle put her hand on my arm. "Let me ask you something. What does it mean if it's true?"

I was choked up now. Fully ready to lose it. "That would be his son. His and Sirena's son."

"And?"

"A son I can't give . . ." *Swallow.*

Trevelle's compassionate frown made me realize how far, how low I'd sunk. She shook her head. "You are not in control. If he has a son, he has a son. What you want, or wish, won't change anything."

I pressed the corners of my eyes. "It will change everything. What I'm saying is, if it's true, Jake will have to be involved, and maybe—"

"There was a time when I thought I could maneuver people and their actions like puppets on a string." She batted her long lashes. "I'm in a place where I know only one thing to be true: we are only passing through. Do you know why I come here every day, for no pay, for no reward whatsoever?" She cut her eyes in the direction of the back room. "Because I want to feel needed. That's all any of us want, to be needed. It's the simplest, and the smallest answer. You think Jake won't need you if he has a son?"

She didn't wait for my answer. "He's going to need you more than ever. Your support, your approval, your understanding. How you respond will be up to you, but don't interfere. I learned my lesson the hard way, never interfere." She stood up and straightened out her pencil denim. She leaned over and squeezed my shoulder. "Speaking of which, I'm sorry for those things I did that hurt you. When we're busy manipulating, we become blinded by selfishness."

"No . . . I'm over all that."

"Just know I'm here because I wanted to make it up to you, and I didn't know of any other way." She headed back to work.

"Trevelle." She stopped but didn't turn around. "Thank you," I said sweetly.

She put her head down. I could tell she was quickly trying to pull herself together. "Anytime," she said. "I'm not going anywhere."

For the first time, I was glad to hear it.

Vince stood in the archway. "Are we done yet? We've got work to do. Sorry, ladies, but we're going to have to split up. Each of you are going to have to make a couple of deliveries in your own cars."

"I will not," Trevelle exclaimed. "What if someone recognizes me, making flower deliveries like some commoner?"

Vince lowered his eyes.

Trevelle caught herself doing it again. Finally she admitted, "I'd just rather ride with you, even if it takes all day. I don't want to be separated."

"I'll take all the small orders. You and Trevelle can cover the Monarch," I said. I never thought I'd see the day when I was actually helping them be together. Maybe there was light at the end of the tunnel.

Doctor Knows Best

The doctor held the stethoscope to Christopher's chest, then his back. Any blind Nellie could see the boy couldn't breathe. Did he really need to hear it too?

The doctor patted Christopher on his knee, then put the oxygen mask back over his face. "You're going to be fine, son. Try to relax." He faced the nurse. "He needs the shot, then start him on the nebulizer."

"Shot?" Sirena asked. "What kind of shot?"

"He's having an allergic reaction, which is causing the fluid in his lungs. Was he exposed to anything unusual?"

Yeah, clean clothes. "Nothing I noticed."

"Not . . . suppose to have . . ." Christopher took a hard, rattled breath to finish. ". . . ice cream."

Sirena sneered when the doctor wasn't looking. "Is he going to be all right?"

"He should be fine. I'll come back to check on him in about twenty minutes or so."

"Twenty minutes." Sirena looked at her phone. "Can't you give him the shot, and we go home?"

"Actually, you should try to get comfortable. He's going to be here a while. After we get him stabilized, I want to run a few tests and see what he's allergic to. Severe allergies can cause death if not treated quickly. We should find out exactly what he should steer clear of, don't you think?" The doctor tapped his head to emphasize he was the only one with good sense in the room. After he left, the nurse went to work on all his instructions.

Sirena sat on the tiny white stool in the corner and cursed the day that she thought taking Christopher was a good idea.

"Brought you something." Quincy entered the hospital room carrying water and various snacks he'd gotten out of the machine. "How you doin', little man?"

Christopher sat swinging his legs and breathing into his mask like Darth Vader without a care in the world.

"This is going to be an all-day affair. Can you believe it? I hate hospitals. Too many germs and bad attitudes." She stood up and stretched. "I'm going outside for fresh air. Call me if something comes up."

Quincy didn't say it, but she knew what he was thinking.

"I promise I will be right outside. I'm not making the great escape."

⟲

The Avery Memorial Hospital was in midtown. The expansive building looked like a contemporary museum with eclectic shapes and abstract statues in the center of the entrance. I parked in the loading zone. The security guard saw my car full of everything from cactus to calla lilies and came over to offer me a hand.

"Thank you."

He helped pulled out the metal folding cart and I loaded it up with arrangements. It was my last stop and I had let the earlier events of the day get buried by my exhaustion.

I pushed the elevator button—two, three times, and still nothing. I was glad I wasn't a patient, although I could admit to being light-headed, even a bit dazed. That would be the best way to explain why I didn't recognize her when the doors opened.

"Flowers, for me? You shouldn't have," Sirena sang out.

I smiled politely and held the doors open while I maneuvered my cart inside. Still on autopilot, I really hadn't bothered looking up. I got those kinds of clichéd comments all the time.

"Venus, you're gon' just ignore me like that?"

The doors were about to close. I put out my hand to stop them. Sirena was standing there with her arms folded and her sharp eyes narrowed.

"Oh, Sirena. I didn't see you. Hi." I pressed the button to hold the doors open. "You're here at the hospital. Are you okay?"

"I'm fine," she said, obviously holding the transgression of not seeing her against me. Who didn't notice Sirena Lassiter everywhere she went? I stepped off the elevator, taking my cart with me.

"I never got a chance to apologize. I really am sorry. I was out of line."

"You were definitely out of line. But I understand. I'd feel the same way if I were you."

There was an insult in there somewhere I didn't have time to explore. "Truce, then." I stuck out my hand.

She kept her arms folded against her ample chest, covering a T-shirt I couldn't read. "I have enough fake people in my life. I don't need another smiling in my face, threatening me with sharp objects when I turn my back."

My mouth dropped. "Fake?"

"So you don't have to pretend. We'll never be BFFs. That's cool with me. As a matter of fact, you're going to hate me even more very soon."

"I don't think that's possible," I said out loud, meaning to only think it. "I mean, really, I don't hate you, Sirena."

"Not really," she mimicked. "We'll see," she said before walking away.

So much for the nice approach. I hadn't realized I was shaking until I went to push the elevator button. My finger trembled, missing the round target three or four times before getting it right. As much as I tried to offer up reasons to not hate Sirena, I did. I hated her. I hated the gut-wrenching possibility that Sirena might have the one thing Jake wanted, truly wanted.

I went straight to the center station. I was used to no one being there so I waited patiently for one of the understaffed nurses to notice me on their rounds.

"Hey, where's Vince?" A large smile topped with red flouncing curls came and inhaled the solid rose bouquet. "I saw the In Bloom T-shirt but didn't see that gorgeous hunk of man. Not that you're not cute as a button," she said.

"Why, thank you. I could use a nice compliment."

"Who we got today?"

I read the clipboard. "The roses are for Jennie Forbes, room 412. This one is for Tina McCray, room 420."

"Perfect." She signed for them. "Tell Vince not to stay away too long."

"Don't worry, he'll be back." I pushed off, heading for the next delivery, wondering if Trevelle knew she had some competition.

For the next delivery I stepped onto the sixth floor and knew by the large murals of zoo animals it was Pediatrics. Children had no use for flowers, but they were far cheaper than what they really wanted, like a new video game. At least this one had a stuffed animal attached.

After waiting at the station, and still no one coming, I decided to find the room for the last delivery myself.

"Knock, knock," I whispered, just in case the little patient was sleeping. I pushed the large door completely open to a dark room, curtains drawn, lights out, and a sleeping boy with a face mask. I put the vase down next to his bed and stopped in my tracks when I saw the husky brown man sitting on the stool like Humpty Dumpty. His thick head was plopped against the wall, sleeping with his mouth hung open. I'd know Sirena's bodyguard anywhere since he'd been in my nightmares for the past few sleepless nights.

I had figured Sirena was visiting a sick friend or relative. I would've never guessed it was the boy. I'd seen them just hours ago having a sunny leisure day eating ice cream. I looked at the flower delivery. The card was sticking out. I hadn't been the one who made the arrangement so I didn't know what it said. Plain as day: Christopher Lassiter. I opened the card to read who sent them. *Get well quick, JP.* Here we go. He obviously wanted to start the bonding process.

I leaned over his bed and stared intently at his face.

Was this Jake's child? The oxygen mask was blocking his nose and mouth. His eyes were closed. I smoothed a hand over his soft hairline. His eyes fluttered open, startled. "Sweetie, it's okay." His face was panicked.

Quincy woke up too, hearing the boy's stricken moan.

"What the hell is going on?"

"I was just making a flower delivery." I inched toward the door, before darting out fast as I could. I left my cart behind. I punched the elevator button. "C'mon." I wasn't sure if he recognized me in the darkened room with my In Bloom hat and T-shirt, but if he did, I was about to be wrung by my collar.

"Hey," the bulging belly yelled. "Whatthahell kind a security y'all got?" He chastised no one in particular, standing in the empty hallway.

The doors opened just in time. I jumped on the elevator, surprisingly relieved in more ways than one.

Bargain Hunter

Jake sat quietly, staring at the seat where Earl would be sitting in just a matter of minutes.

"We need a face-to-face," Earl Benning had said. He'd called and said he was in Atlanta and, "This won't take long."

No doubt he wanted to discuss Sirena and the meltdown with Venus. Maybe accuse him of being the cause of it all, the man in the middle. Probably wanted to make it clear if anything like that happened again, he'd be banished from the world he so loved. Movies. Music. Entertainment. He'd warned himself it wouldn't last. He only hoped the door wasn't closing on him so soon.

Maybe he'd go ahead and show Earl all the messages Sirena had left, begging Jake to meet with her, texting her undying love and hope for them to have a future. Then he'd see it wasn't on him. But either way he'd be the one who fell on the knife. Earl Benning would have to get rid of Jake. And he didn't want that. Making movies was a dream come true. Doing music again, his way, was also a promise delivered from the universe. Something he'd prayed for, at least on the top of his list. Now all of it was happening and he still held no control. Getting pressure from all sides. Venus wanting him to quit . . . or at least keep his distance from Sirena. Earl Benning probably wanting the same. Hell, Jake even wanted to be free of her. But it seemed they were intertwined. Like the universe had fused them together and there was nothing anyone could do about it.

"Sorry I'm late, JP. Good to see you, man." Earl Benning peered down at him, all white teeth and expensive onyx-rimmed glasses. The coffee shop was Earl's choice. If they went to an upscale eatery, they risked the chance of Jake being recognized, then Earl being recognized and harassed by someone offering up their latest greatest masterpiece on a homemade CD.

Jake found it hard to look Earl in the eye, especially after all the messages Sirena had left, claiming she wanted to fix things between them. Make up the past and move to the future. Cryptic messages. Delusional. Dare he say insane? But that was Sirena, dramatic, over the top, and determined to get her point across.

"Listen, I have to apologize to you and your wife. I wanted to do it personally."

Jake was surprised. "Yeah, man. No problem. Sirena and I go pretty far back. Buttons got pushed. All water under the bridge."

"She can be a handful."

"So can my wife," Jake admitted and instantly felt guilty, like he was throwing Venus under the bus. Knowing it wasn't her fault. But he was doing and saying what he had to. "She felt bad about the whole scene."

"I have to tell you, we're putting a lot of money into this next project. Any negative publicity would be detrimental." Earl never took his eyes off Jake. He leaned forward on his expensive suit elbows. "You two have an amazing chemistry. As you know, people aren't good at separating fact and fiction. It's important that we run with the magic you two have for as long as we can . . ."

Jake felt pins and needles climbing from his fingertips up his arms, through his spine, rendering him speechless.

"Your wife is going to have to stay clear of all promotional events. I absolutely know it's bold and rather rude of me to speak on this subject, but when we're talking a fifty-million-dollar film budget, we can't have that jeopardized. We need people to forget you're even married. Sirena can't look like the bad guy, the third wheel appearing to be involved in some kind of love triangle. Something like that would tarnish her reputation. Now we both know, she doesn't have the ability to come back from being labeled a home-breaker." He whispered, "Maybe if she was from the other camp . . . but let's face it, our people don't get a whole lot of second chances."

Jake nodded, still unable to say a word. He licked his lips in anticipation, relieved this was all he had to deal with. On a scale, it was minor.

"Please don't take this personally. I've never met your wife and I'm sure she's lovely, but she'll have to take one for the team."

This was business. Jake knew he was walking a fine line, seconds away from saying something he'd regret. This man was essentially his boss. Earl Benning would pull the plug on Jake co-starring in Sirena's next movie. Kill the music, or anything else on the horizon. Knowing this kept his mouth shut.

Earl realized Jake still hadn't said a word and became uncomfortable himself. "I can understand how you feel. I'd be pissed if someone was trying to tell me how to handle my woman. But you'll thank me later. After this next film solidifies your place in the industry, you can pick and choose. Maybe you work with Sirena again, maybe not, but you'll have your own name to stand on." He extended his hand. "My plane is waiting. Believe it or not, I came all this way just to see you."

Jake shook his hand. "My wife will understand," Jake said, knowing he'd never tell her about this conversation anyway.

Earl left without having a sip of coffee. He jumped into the car that was waiting, engine running. Delivering his warning took all of ten minutes. Message duly noted. If it didn't have to do with business, Jake wanted nothing to do with Sirena anyway.

When the phone vibrated on his hip he figured now was as good a time as any to tell her exactly that.

He pushed the button for the call to come through his earpiece. "Yeah," he said bitterness dripping from his voice.

"It's about time."

"I just got through with a meeting with your Mr. Benning."

"He's *our* Mr. Benning."

Her sarcasm tipped him closer to the edge.

"I don't know how much more of you and him I can take," Jake said. "On one end I have him telling me to lose my wife so I can appear to be into you, and on the other end I have you wishing it were a reality. Can you tell me what kind of freak show you two are running?"

"The minute you tell me we can be together, he's history. He doesn't control anything, Jay. I'm the one making him and his label at Rise Records. He is nothing without me."

"That's not what I was asking you, Sirena. I'm not interested in stepping between you and him. I just want you to know that. If we're going to continue working together, it's got to be something you agree to."

She stayed quiet for a few seconds. "I think there is something you'll be interested in, Jay. Something I should have told you a long time ago." The next words that left her lips landed directly between his eyes.

He sat, still stunned, unable to move. He pushed himself to his feet. He'd been hit all right, with a bomb that had landed right in his lap.

"A son?"

"Yes. I know it's crazy, right? But after all this time, I couldn't keep it from you any longer."

⊙⌒⊙

He was already on his way to Avery Memorial Hospital when his phone vibrated. He prayed it wasn't Sirena again. All he wanted to do was see the boy for himself.

Venus. "Hey," he said sheepishly, wishing he could tell her everything, but knowing he couldn't. "I needed to hear your voice."

"I have to tell you that I ran into Sirena. She was at the hospital when I was making deliveries, I guess she's still there with her . . . Christopher."

That's not what he wanted to hear. His knees felt wobbly. "What happened?" he asked hesitantly, scared of the rest of the story. Their shaky ground would surely crack, unable to maintain this added weight.

"Nothing happened. I promise. She was at the hospital with her baby brother." She said it slowly, as if it were a code word for something else.

"So is everything all right?" he asked, getting impatient.

"Fine, I guess. I saw him . . . her baby brother. The flowers I delivered were actually for him. The card said, 'Get well quick, JP.'"

"Me?" He rubbed his eyes and temples at the same time. Sirena was an endless bag of tricks.

"I didn't think you sent them," she said quietly. "Do you know why she would do something like that?"

"Probably just to make him feel better. He's probably my biggest little fan or something," Jake said, almost holding his breath.

"That's what I thought too. But Sirena was cordial. I didn't get upset, I just wanted to tell you that I saw her and . . ."

"And what?" He released his breath, then inhaled, holding it again.

"She thinks I hate her."

"You do," he nervously chuckled. "But seriously, you two need distance." He thought about Earl Benning's warning.

"Jake, I want you to know that I don't hate her. Don't let my fears or insecurity block you from any decisions. Okay?"

The irony of this conversation was starting to make his head swirl.

"I just want you to know how I feel. I love you and will always love you," she said.

"I love you too. I'll see you later tonight," he said.

"Yeah, much later. I still have to go to Miriam's wedding re-hearsal."

"What time?"

"It's at six, so I should be home around eight."

"Perfect," he said, more for himself. Now he would have plenty time to see Christopher. *His son.* If he really had a son. It was more than possible. It could be true. All this time he'd hated Sirena for what she'd done. Turned out she hadn't gone through with it. The thought made him smile and almost forget about being caught between everyone else's wants and needs. His wife just told him not to make any decisions based on her fear or anxiety, as if she knew.

He had a son.

Hit and Run

The bridal party lined up in twos. I couldn't take my eyes off Miriam's cousin, Jeanette, who was right in front of me. She seemed out of sorts, not really paying attention to the hired coordinator provided by the Monarch Hotel. They were paying top dollar, after all.

"Please keep pace with the tempo of the music. Do not rush. We only get married once."

Everyone snickered. The coordinator even laughed at her own joke.

"Please proceed."

I looked over at my escort, a friend from Ben's work, a physician with huge eyes and a wiry 'fro. We were some pair. I could already picture the wedding photos. Right then I decided to do some serious conditioning when I got home and tie my hair down in a cute one-sided bun.

He looped his arm through mine and we started walking. Ben was at the end of the aisle. Jeanette and he hadn't stopped looking at each other. She was almost in tears, that much I knew.

When I got to the end of the walkway, I leaned into Jeanette's ear. "Are you all right?"

"Yes, thank you. Just a little nauseated. I'm pregnant. You can't tell in this dress, can you?"

Cut. Stop the tape.

I dropped my pretend bouquet and walked the three steps in front of Ben. "Can I talk to you, now?"

"Can this wait?" The coordinator flagged a hand. "Can we get through this dry run? Please."

"No. I'm sorry. It's important."

Ben was confused. His shiny brown bald head was covered with beads of sweat. He wiped with his handkerchief. "We'll be right back."

"I suggest you're back before the bride makes her way down the aisle because we're not stopping."

"Pushy," Ben tried to joke.

I led him down the large corridor to the other side of the hotel. We stopped in front of a huge window overlooking an endless hedge of pink budding roses. The garden was meticulously manicured, along with everything else at the Monarch.

"I know about you two—or, as we say, 'baby makes three,'" I said, risking going overboard, though it really wasn't my place.

His eyes closed, revealing I'd hit the target. "How . . ."

"I saw you two checking into this very hotel. I never said anything to Miriam, but I can't live with this on my conscience. Jeanette's in there standing up for your wife as her maid of honor. Is it me, or is that plain foul?"

"I can't undo what's already done," he said. "Miriam is a good woman, a good mother. I can't hurt her by telling her the truth."

"I know she loves you. Sometimes that's enough to overcome anything."

"She deserves a better man than me. If she finds out about Jeanette, she's going to leave me."

"I'm sure you are a lovely person who simply made a mistake. We all make mistakes. This ceremony is supposed to be about starting over. Fresh, renewed." I shook my head and didn't want to tell him what I thought he should do. It was up to him. "I'm going to get back. You take your time."

Rounding the corner I saw Miriam standing at the entrance, waiting for her cue from the coordinator. Lizzie was in front. "Can I go now, Mommy?"

"Yes, go." She turned when she saw me approaching. "How am I supposed to walk down the aisle with no groom? I hope this is not an omen of things to come."

Thank goodness he was a few seconds behind me.

"Right here," he announced, moving past us to take his place at the end of the aisle.

The coordinator snapped for Miriam to follow. I took my place with the other three bridesmaids and immediately saw Jeanette was missing. Miriam didn't seem to notice. Neither did Ben. They were gazing into each other's eyes.

"You two know your vows? We're on the clock tomorrow. Blah, blah, then you turn, wait ten seconds for pictures, and then you walk." She snapped her fingers. "Everyone, follow in twos this time with a quickness."

For what it was worth, I felt like I'd finally done and said the right thing. One good deed to put a dent in my basket of bad karma.

"It's going to be a beautiful ceremony, Miriam." I hugged her. "See you bright and early." I waved at Ben. He blew me a kiss and mouthed the words, *thank you*. Thank you for not ratting him out, thank you for letting him get away unscathed. He'd have his own karma to deal with, as I had mine.

Easy Come

Sirena sat on the patio of the hospital, waiting patiently for Jake's arrival. The doctor still hadn't released Christopher, so it was the perfect scenario. She'd even challenge Jay to have a paternity test, right there in the building where there was a lab ready and waiting. She wasn't afraid of the results. At this point she was ready to put it all on the line for a chance of a new life, a real life, one that wasn't surrounded by people and things that didn't matter.

People who wanted to use her or take her for granted no longer mattered. She couldn't remember the last time she'd met someone who wasn't all take without any give.

"Where is he?" Jay stood at the center of the courtyard, near the fountain. He'd arrived like clockwork. The lights coming up from the water were enough to see him, but not his face. The leather jacket and jeans was her favorite look on him. It felt like months since she'd seen him last, yet it had only been days. When she got close she could see he still wore the JP swirled initials she'd given him as a gift on the last day of filming *True Beauty*. All the signs were there. No matter what he said, he still cared and maybe even loved her.

"I'll take you to him, but first you have to make me a promise."

He lifted his hands. "Nah, I don't want to make any deals, Sirena.

I've had enough of that. There's nothing to be discussed. If he's my son, he's *my* son."

"Just hear me out."

"I've been hearing you. You've been lying to me every time you open your mouth. So how am I supposed to believe you now?"

"Whether you believe something or not doesn't change the facts." She stopped in front of him. She touched his face. She could tell he wanted it to be true.

He quickly pushed her hand away. "Where is he?"

"Wait a minute. Okay? All I'm saying is that I still love you. I know it's going to take a while for you to trust me. I wouldn't trust me either. But you have to know—"

"All I want to know, is where is he? Tell me or I'll find him myself."

"He's on the sixth floor. The doctor wouldn't release him because of tests. He's extremely allergic to dairy products, grass, nuts, and tomatoes." She coughed out with a laugh. "What are the odds of that?" These were all the same things she remembered about Jay's allergies. Funny how it all came back to her as the doctor announced them one by one.

She'd almost jumped for joy while poor Christopher lay on his stomach, his back was riddled with itchy red hives—reactions to the shots the doctor had given him. Proof.

"Let's go." Anticipation seeped from his pores. He followed silently.

She had him right where she wanted him. She couldn't be swallowed up in regret about the past. All that mattered was here and now, their future.

The doors closed on the elevator. The fluorescent light now gave her a good look at his clean-shaven face. He still looked so young, so boyish, and yet he was more of a man than any she'd ever met, including her father. Larry Lassiter had been too weak to handle a woman like her mother. All those times he'd tell Sirena she was just like her, it meant he couldn't handle Sirena either. But Jay could. He was strong enough to handle anything. That's why she knew, in the end, it was all going to work out.

"Who else knows about Christopher?" He finally broke his silence as they rode up.

"My father is the only one. At the time he didn't think I'd make such a great mother, so he was more than willing to take him off my hands. It was a sealed adoption. That way no one could ever do a background check on me."

"Why was it so important no one knew? People, women, have babies every day. No one cares."

"I cared. I was only nineteen. I was on the rise. You think a major label would've signed me for a record deal knowing I was pregnant? Come on, you can't be that naïve."

He shifted his eyes and sighed like she was a hopeless case.

"I'm not trying to hear your holier-than-thou bullshit, Jay. Not this time. You think I was going to be sitting at home, holding a baby while your ass was traipsing across the country, getting your groove on city by city?"

The doors opened in time. She could tell when she'd touched a nerve. His cool demeanor cracking in tiny pieces. No doubt this was a conversation she didn't want to have, but it had to happen so they could move forward.

"I'm sorry for every lie I ever told you. You remember now, don't you? When I told you I was pregnant, what did you say to me?" She didn't wait for an answer. "You said, 'Are you sure it's mine?'"

"Keep your voice down." Jake looked around. "What did you expect me to say? I find you on the floor with Tommy, how was I supposed to know what was real or not? Then you disappeared. I was broke, Cee Cee. You broke my heart," he finally confessed.

"Well you broke mine too. So I guess we're even."

He shook his head, no. "Just tell me where he is. What does he know? Does he know who I am?"

"I haven't told him anything. He's my little brother, plain and simple. I wanted you to know who he is, and that you have a son. And that we can be a family in our own way. I'm not going to agree to be his mother unless you agree to be his father."

"What?"

"My dad had an accident. He's not going to be able to take care of Christopher anymore. We can . . . I thought you and I . . ."

"Stop. Stop. Wait a minute, Cee Cee, listen to me, stop with the plans." Jake realized he was the one who needed to lower his voice. "One step at a time, okay?" He washed a hand over his face. "Take me to Christopher. Right now. That's about all I want from you."

"No. Forget it." She stood with her arms crossed over her chest, which rose and fell in panic. "You have to promise first." She never cried, not real tears anyway. Yet her heart was beating wild and frantic with fear. She knew she couldn't control it. She stuck her fingers to her eyes to try and put a stop to the useless emotion. "You have to promise you'll at least give us a chance. Or you can forget this whole day ever happened. Turn around and walk right out of here. Go!"

"Excuse me," the nurse interrupted with her hands raised. "This is a hospital, children are sleeping. Y'all need to take that outside." The nurse raised her eyebrows with awareness. "Oh my goodness, tell me you are not Sirena Lassiter. Oh, please, I'm so sorry." She clutched the cross hanging around her neck. "I only started my shift about fifteen minutes ago, but I was told your baby brother was here. He's doing just fine, room 612, straight down on your—"

Jake had already started in that direction. Sirena grabbed his sleeve. "No. Wait."

"Hey, wait a minute now. Do I need to call security?"

Sirena waved the nurse off. "No. It's fine."

Jake started walking again. She ran up ahead of him and blocked the doorway of Christopher's room. His sad dark eyes did something to her heart. He was disappointed in her, yet again. He easily pushed past her because she'd already given up.

Quincy slowly rose from his short stool. " 'Sup, man," he said, puzzled by Jake's arrival. Sirena came in right behind him. "Hey, man, I didn't know that was your wife." Not sure what was going on, he searched their faces.

Jake barely looked in his direction, instead leaning over Christopher, who was sleeping from all the antihistamines. It'd been a long day for the little guy. Jake touched his face as if he couldn't believe he was real.

"Hey, man, are we cool?"

"Tell him to get the hell out." Jake refused to talk directly to Quincy.

"Give us a minute," she said, almost too politely.

For a few seconds her bodyguard didn't move, not sure if there was some secret code he wasn't picking up on.

"Just go," she snapped.

Quincy put his fingers to his lips. "All right. Take it easy," he whispered.

Just go, she mouthed. She didn't want Jake disturbed.

Look at him, she thought, taking it all in. The satisfied wonder on his face, like a kid getting the first real toy he ever wanted. Nothing else would do. No other gift could be greater. He kept his eyes on Christopher, studying every curly strand of hair on his head, then his eyes, his nose, those soft lips and strong chin, confirming what he wanted to know. Could he really have a nine-year-old son?

"His birthday is June eleventh. I held him all day, staring into his sweet tiny face, thinking he looked just like you. I mean, he does, when you were his age. Don't you think?" She was winging it now. She had no idea what Jake looked like as a child. In fact, what she really knew about him could fill a thimble. All she knew for sure was that he was the only man she wanted to spend the rest of her life with. "I never had a single day of morning sickness—isn't that weird?"

What she'd felt was worse than morning sickness, like something had crawled inside her and she couldn't get it out. By the time she'd gone for her abortion, she was told that the fetus was too far along.

"He was no trouble at all. Seven hours of labor. The nurses said it was the shortest labor they'd ever seen for a first child."

Actually, seven hours had gone by quickly once she'd been hooked up to a morphine drip; before that she was cursing and wishing for death to take her out of her misery. Once she was infused, she could no longer feel the lower half of her body. Everyone in the room yelling, *push,* and all she could think of was getting back in the studio. Putting her lyrics to the music waiting for her after a five-month hiatus.

Later, she lied and said she was in rehab, because that's what famous people did. Being addicted to a substance, having a breakdown was more acceptable than giving birth. No one would admit it, but it was true. You could always come back after a stint in the loony bin, but being a mother was forever. It changed everything.

"You can touch him, Jay. He's real."

He put out a hand and laid it on Christopher's chest. The boy stirred but still didn't wake up. Sirena felt like shaking him awake. Now would be a good time to show off his good manners, his smarty-pants pronunciation of every word, his honesty and innocence, the things Jay would appreciate.

"So what now?" he asked, still having his eyes on Christopher.

"That's up to you," Sirena offered. The underlying message was simple: She now had something he wanted and he'd have to go through her, literally, to get it.

"Let's go outside," he huffed. He grabbed her by the arm and half pulled her. Quincy caught a glimpse of them coming out like it was a hostage situation and she put up a hand for him to stay back.

It was negotiation time. She figured she had one shot and she'd better make it good.

It's a Jungle out There

"What are you doing out here?" Pauletta knocked on my car window where I sat, parked in the garage. "Suicide's not worth it, child."

"Mom, seriously."

"Well, how am I supposed to know? This generation takes everything so seriously. Nothing's that bad where you need to off yourself."

I pushed the door all the way open and threw one leg out, about all I could manage. "I wasn't going to turn the engine on. I just needed to decompress. I had a hell of a day."

"Yes, I know. The minute Jake walked into the house with that boy, I knew there was trouble."

"Boy? What boy . . . Christopher?"

"Umm-humm, but it's not the end of the world," my mother announced. "When a man brings home another woman's child you already know the situation. You need to be understanding. At least he wasn't conceived while you were already married. That's the worst."

Energy surged through me. I could suddenly move with great intensity and speed. Darting from room to room, I found Christopher and Jake in the kitchen. Mya sat there, too, eating a sandwich and French fries.

"Mommy!" Mya jumped up when she saw me, rushing into a big hug.

"Hi," was the best I could do, for all of them.

Jake stood up from the table and extended his hand. "Come here. I want you to meet someone."

I took ahold of myself and took a few unsteady steps. I stood at the edge of the table. Jake was so proud and I was so confused. Everything was happening so fast.

"Christopher, this is my wife, Venus."

"Hi there," I said, my voice shaky. I looked to Jake to tell me what else I was supposed to say. *Welcome to the family?*

"He's going to stay with us for a few days." Jake put his other hand on top of Christopher's head. "His dad had an accident and Sirena needed help while she took care of a few things."

"Oh, wonderful." I gulped air, swallowing Jake's pack of lies. So hard because Jake never hardly lied about anything. If the truth hurt, so be it. But that seemed to change once Sirena entered the picture. I squeezed his hand, giving him a tug.

"How're you all doing in here?" Pauletta came behind us. "Christopher, would you like some more tuna salad?"

"Yes, please," he said. The only words I'd heard out of his mouth.

"A boy after my own heart. I love me some tuna salad."

"Me too," Mya chimed. "Love tuna." She seemed happy to have the company. She'd been sequestered too long away from her friends at school.

Jake and I went upstairs. He closed the door and cupped my face with his hands. He kissed me gently then held me tight, afraid to let go. "I have something to tell you."

"Say it."

"Christopher is actually Sirena's son." He stopped there.

I was waiting for the rest. "And . . ."

"You're not surprised?"

"Not at all. I just knew. I saw them together and it just seemed obvious." Still waiting for the rest. "Why is he here?"

Jake sat on the edge of the bed. "Sirena says he's my son."

"And you believe her, just like that?"

"I want to believe her, but I don't know. I convinced her to give me some time with him, sort every thing out later."

"Later? Why is he here? Why are you involved if you don't really know?"

"Because I don't really care. I'm not about to start a biological investigation of whose sperm made it to the egg first. I just don't care. If he needs a father, fine, I'll be his father."

"I knew exactly what she was up to the minute I saw her traipsing around town with that boy. I just didn't think you would fall for it hook, line, and sinker. I thought you would need to talk to me about it. But I come home, and he's sitting in our kitchen. And you're talking about, you don't care. What do you care about, exactly? What matters to you?"

"What matters is that I love you and you love me."

"What the hell does that mean?"

Jake paused to gather himself, as if to find the words to convey his fear. "You and I have wanted a child together and we weren't able to have one, no matter what the reason. Now, I'm not trying to get all mystical on you but this child is here, no matter how he got here. He is sitting in that room."

"Jake."

"Wait, let me finish." He put his head down. "My heart felt like someone ripped it out of my chest and stomped on it when I stood there in that hospital room and our son was born without a breath in his body. I stood there helpless. For the first time in my life I didn't know what to do. I didn't know how to fix . . ." He trailed off. "I couldn't make it right."

"What about all that time you made me feel like I was overreacting because I couldn't get over it? I forced myself to move on even when I wanted to keep mourning." I sniffed back tears. "I moved on. This boy isn't going to fix anything."

"How do you know?" Jake's breathing changed in a way he hadn't felt in a while. He'd stopped having asthma problems since the move to Atlanta. But right about now he was laboring for each breath. He got up and opened the side drawer. He inhaled with two squirts.

He could see from my expression that I was concerned, but he had to finish saying what was on his mind.

"We all hurt in different ways. Just because I didn't seem like it hurt me, it did. I felt responsible for every tear you shed. Now this child has come into our lives and I know taking him in without knowing he's my son seems foolish, but I looked in his eyes and I knew he was my son. I didn't think of checking blood samples to confirm what's in my heart. It's the same way I looked at Mya the day she was born. I didn't care if she was Airic's or mine, she was my daughter."

Uncontrollable tears streamed down my cheeks. I couldn't hold them back. "I just wish you would've talked to me first. Remember when I said you don't have to worry about me? That I wanted you to make decisions without fear of my judgment, because of how much I love you? That was your chance to trust me, and for us to be a unit for once. I'm so sick of you and me running around in separate directions. We're not in sync and we haven't been for some time."

"Don't start with me about not being in sync," he said. "There's nothing wrong in this relationship, at least nothing real."

"So I'm imagining it?"

"All I'm saying is, anything wrong can be fixed if you talk to me about it."

"I tried. I told you how much anything to do with Sirena drove me crazy. And now this. I thought you'd see right through her manipulation, her scheming. I don't want to have Sirena's son in my house. I wanted Sirena to go away, and now with this child, Jake, we will never be free of her." I slid to his knees, taking ahold of his face. "Please don't do this. I don't think our relationship is going to survive this right now. I'm just asking for a little time, just a little."

"You never wonder about my love for Mya, but you know other

people look at me strange when I claim she's my daughter, and I don't care. They look at me the way you are looking at me now, because I know she looks just like Airic. I don't have a birth certificate or a blood test. So what," he exclaimed. "Our ancestors never gave a damn about who the *real* daddy was and all that bullshit. When a child came into a man's home, he loved and raised that child as his own. That's all that mattered."

"Funny, I don't remember you feeling this way when I wanted to adopt Ralph. I very specifically remember you being against the whole process."

"I wasn't against it. I knew we weren't going to be ineligible. I knew it was going to break your heart and I didn't know if you could make it through that kind of pain again . . . losing a child. I regret that we couldn't adopt Ralph. But here's our chance to be a part of this little boy's life. I think we should take it."

I heaved a sigh of defeat.

"I leave for filming in a few days. We don't have to make a decision right here, right now, but I want you to think about what I said and how I feel, and then we can discuss it again."

"It looks to me you've already made your decision—for both of us." I stood up and wiped my face.

We looked at each other and Jake already knew what my decision was going to be, whether it was now or weeks from now. But what could he say that he hadn't already said?

He didn't need me.

"Mommy, I like Christopher." Mya sat next to me in the passenger seat. First day back to school since the ultimatum of us or them. I'd held my ground until it became apparent I was going to lose this war too.

"Yes, he's a sweet kid," I said truthfully. It was his mother who rubbed me burning raw.

"Daddy said Christopher was kind of sick, but when he got better we were going to go to the aquarium."

"That would be great." I looked over her head, apprehensive about letting her go back to school.

She must've seen through my calm-mommy demeanor. "I'm going to have a great day," she announced. "Because good days happen when you just be yourself."

"Oh sweetie, yes. You're right about that." I kissed her forehead. She was repeating what I'd been singing as a mantra since she could understand my every word. *Just be yourself.*

The children were filing through the tall brick arch. "There goes Jory," I pointed.

Mya gave me a fast peck. "Bye, Mommy. See you later."

"I love you," I said, waiting for her usual response of *I love you double, triple, quadruple* until we ran to infinite possibility. She slammed the door and took off running, screaming Jory's name. They fell into each other's arms like long-lost friends. He didn't care about his little first-grader buddies giving him the evil eye. He and Mya entered the building side by side.

"Boo." The voice startled me from my rolled-down window.

"Robert." I released a sigh, actually grateful to see him.

"Well, well, long time no see. Mya wasn't at ballet practice or school. I was beginning to think you left town."

"I definitely felt like it. Between my bathroom brawl, and Mya being attacked at school, I could've stayed under the covers for a good long time."

"But you didn't. That-a-girl."

"Thanks for the vote of confidence."

"Speaking of votes . . ." He grinned. "Holly is still planning to commandeer you for a few fund-raisers. I'm up for re-election next year. These good looks can only go so far."

I took a long deep breath. "Just one more thing on my crowded plate. But I honestly think I'm going to have to pass." He'd understand if I told him Jake and I were on rocky terrain and I wasn't sure if our marriage was going to survive. I could explain that Sirena was the Big One I'd been preparing for all my life but the truth was, you can't ever prepare for an earthquake of this magnitude. When your foundation starts to crumble, there's nothing to do but hide and pray for it to be over.

"Not even for li'l ol' me?" Robert asked.

I couldn't resist his pout, which came out more sexy than sympathy-ridden. "I'll see."

"That-a-girl," he said, this time putting a one-handed squeeze around my neck. "There's always a little fight left in ya."

"You just reminded me I'm due for a serious massage."

"I can accommodate you," he said and winked, giving one more squeeze for good measure.

I put my head down, and before I knew it I was gushing with tears.

"Whoa! Hey, what's going on?"

"No, it's nothing. I'm just dealing with some issues. It's not anything you said."

"Oh, yeah, I can tell." Robert's dry wit usually made me smile. Not this time. "Anytime a woman bursts into tears after I try to flirt with her, I know I'm doing a bang-up job."

"Really, I'm okay." I started my car and exited the school parking lot. Falling into Robert's consoling arms was tempting, but it wouldn't stop the tremor rolling through my life.

Cry Me a River

Trevelle stared at the back of my head, waiting for me to turn around, but I couldn't. My eyes were rimmed with redness from crying. It was an all-day, all-night leakage. Always on the verge of tears, from the minute I woke up to the minute I fell asleep. Jake had gone to Vancouver to film his new movie with Sirena. It made it easier not to have to voice what I was feeling.

"At some point you're going to have to get off your high horse. Obviously you hate yourself."

"I don't hate myself. I'm just sad that this is what my life has come to. My husband left me."

Trevelle giggled or snickered. Either one was rude. Then I turned and faced her, ready to give her a piece of my mind. She pointed. "Aha, caught 'cha." She came and wrapped her long arms around me and squeezed. "You have made a mess of things."

"It's not my fault. It's Jake's fault. He knows that woman is manipulative and scheming. He should hate her, like I do. And now, he wants me to raise her son. I thought I could—for a minute, I believed I could do it. But I can't live like that."

"Jake hated Airic, but he's raising Mya."

"You know, I'm about sick of that tit-for-tat argument. It's different. This is all completely different."

Vince came in and set down a couple of boxes while Trevelle

and I were still in the middle of an embrace. "Now that's what I like to see, my two favorite girls bonding."

"She's in need of many hugs," Trevelle said before untangling her bracelet from my hair.

"One big happy family," Vince said.

The word *family* made me gush with a fresh set of tears. I ran to the bathroom and took a handful of tissue off the roll.

When I came back out, I saw Vince on bended knee in front of Trevelle. He was holding up a black case. I approached slowly and stood over him like an invisible spirit. Which wasn't hard, since they both pretended I wasn't there and proceeded uninterrupted.

"Would you do me the honor of being my wife?" His hand shook while he opened the box to reveal a gorgeous—however modest, for Trevelle's taste—engagement ring.

She kept both hands over her mouth. Vince finally stood. "My knee can't take it anymore. What's it gonna be, you're in or you're out?"

Now I was directly between the two, staring up between the two of them like a tennis match.

"Vince, you know I care deeply for you. But we, you and I are—"

"What? You're black, and I'm white."

"No, of course that's not what I was going to say. Our backgrounds. Just different."

"I busted my ass to make enough money to buy this ring, woman. I respected you enough to want to show you I'm sincere. I love you."

"I love you too," she admitted with a trembling bottom lip. "But . . ."

"You got some nerve." This time it was me speaking. They both looked at me as if realizing I was there. "You just got through telling me to get off my high horse. Seriously, Trevelle. Your advice isn't worth a hill of beans."

"Now this is different."

"Ahuh," Vince and I said at the same time.

"It's very different. Vince and I have only known each other for a year."

"But long enough for you to know how different you two are. Please, go on."

"I'm afraid," Trevelle announced. "I'm scared of being hurt again. I'm scared of giving my heart to you."

"Would I hurt you? Look me in the eye and tell me, do you think I would ever hurt you?"

"Not intentionally. But I'm sure that's what Jake told *you* too," she said, facing me.

"Leave me and Jake out of this," I growled.

Vince went back down on his knee. "Trevelle Doval, I promise to love and protect you for the rest of my life. Will you marry me?"

"On one condition," Trevelle said, cutting her eyes toward me. "If you work things out with your husband. Open your heart and mind to that little boy, and be a family."

"This is a setup."

Vince looked up at me. "You're either in or you're out."

"You first," I said to Trevelle, knowing she'd never take the bait.

"Mr. Capricio, it would be an honor to become your wife." She tilted back her head. "Dear God, please let this man be the one."

Vince stood up. "The only one." He swooped her up in a big hug.

I clapped and cheered as if they'd just said their I do's. "I can't believe it."

"Now your turn. Go get your man. Stop acting like you know everything." Trevelle touched my face. The jangling of her many bracelets used to drive me insane; now it was a sentimental sound that reminded me I had a friend.

"There's only one problem—he's in Toronto, Canada, remember? Filming a movie with Sirena. So I figured . . ."

"Don't assume anything. A man will tell you exactly what's on his mind. You just have to listen," Vince said in a more fatherly tone.

"Oh cry me a river," Trevelle interjected. "Whatever you figured, you figured wrong. You need to tell him you love him and can't live without him, and everything else will fall into place."

"Said the woman who hadn't wanted to accept his first proposal," I said.

"That was all a ruse. I've been waiting for him to get down on one knee since January."

"Ooh, what happened in January?"

"Remove your mind from the gutter and get on the next plane to Canada, will you?"

"Yes, ma'am." I gave Trevelle a salute and pecked Vince on the cheek. "Thank you, guys. I'll call and let you know how it goes."

Ray of Sunshine

With that optimism, I headed for Canada. My mom and dad stayed with Mya. The nine-hour flight left me restless and full of anxiety. What would I say when I saw him? Would he be happy to see me? I called ahead only to reach Jake's voice mail, which I'd hoped he checked by the time I was there. He kept his phone off during his all-day filming schedule. Our conversations had been brief and brooding. I hated myself for having been so selfish. Not being able to welcome the boy into our lives the same way Jake had opened his heart to Mya, knowing she wasn't his biological child.

But I had a plan. I was going to make everything right.

"Taxi? Do you need a taxi?" The Ethiopian driver nearly blocked my exit of the double doors at the airport. He stretched his skinny arms out wide. "This way, I have a taxi for you."

"No, thank you." I had a high hope that someone would be standing outside with my name scribbled on a drawing pad, VENUS, Mrs. Parson, Mrs. JP. Hell, at this point I'd take, Bitch with Attitude.

There was no one. Jake probably hadn't gotten my message. Him not wanting to hear another one of my whining messages, he probably had no idea I was standing on the airport curb nearly ready to start sobbing. The cool clear air was a sweet awakening. Maybe I'd made a mistake. What in the world was I doing listening to Trevelle Doval anyway? *Go get your man.*

"Mrs. Parson?" A young woman with large sunglasses and puffy pink cheeks stood in front of me. "I'm Gertrude, Mr. Parson's assistant. I am so sorry to be late." She was a strawberry blond curly-headed girl wearing a bulky sweatshirt that said PEACE. Her jeans skirt nearly touched the ground. She smiled.

"I'm just glad you're here." I hugged her. She appeared miffed, but grateful this wouldn't affect her coveted personal assistant position, even if it only lasted as long as the filming of the movie.

"Can I get your bags, eh?" Her Canadian tweak on the end of her sentence was the only reminder I was in another country. That and the icy cold wind that whipped across my face. The sun was high and bright and I was still shivering. I pulled my trench collar up around my neck and face.

"No. All I have is this." I showed her my bag, a gift from Burberry to Jake. Free things came all the time—watches, hats, jeans, T-shirts—all in hopes he'd be caught wearing it in a paparazzi pic worth a million in free advertising.

I slipped into the front seat of Gertrude's cube-shaped vehicle and we were on our way. The downtown city was big, metropolitan, and clean. She drove me straight to a hotel. The valet rushed to open my door and I pushed the lock. "I thought we could go straight to the filming. I was hoping. I mean . . . I haven't seen my husband in a week, and I miss him."

"JP—Mr. Parson—asked me to take you straight to the hotel."

"I'm sure he thinks I should go rest, but I'm not tired. I don't think I'd survive sitting inside that room, just sitting. It was a long flight. I promise not to get in the way."

Gertrude looked torn. She understood perfectly well my situation, but there was her concern of not following orders. "Okay, then." She picked up her cell phone and thought about calling someone for a second opinion, then laid it back down. "I guess it'll be all right. We'll just drop in so you can say hello, then I'll bring you back, or take you to the City Center. There's great shopping there. Most wives love the City Center."

"Great plan." I waved at the zealous valet, who was still trying to get the car door open.

☉☉

"What're you doing here?" Jake's eyes widened, then darted around over my head where I stood outside his trailer. He pulled me up the few steps and inside. He hugged me fiercely tight, then again asked, "What're you doing here? I told my assistant to take you to the hotel."

I was frozen with disappointment. "You're not happy to see me?"

"I am. It's just . . . I'm working, babe. It's hard to focus as it is."

"Understandable. I just wanted to see you and tell you I am sorry for not being on board right away. I love you unconditionally. I had a change of heart and would like to be involved with Christopher."

"That means so much to me," he said. "Okay, we'll talk about it some more at the hotel." He picked up the walkie-talkie–looking phone and squeezed the side. "Gerty, can you come pick up my wife and take her to the hotel?"

"Yes, sir." Gertrude responded like a military command. "Right away."

I swallowed back the lump in my throat and tried not to take it personally. I leaned in and kissed his cold lips, ignoring the tickle of his mustache he'd grown for the part. It was the easiest way to transition from the young character to the older one. I'd read the script, set in the Roaring Twenties in Harlem. I'd counted the kissing scenes with Sirena as Sarah, the woman he couldn't resist, though she continually put him in danger. How apropos.

We both jumped with the banging on the door. "Must be her."

He swung it open, then pulled it close and talked low. I couldn't see who it was. Then her distinctive laugh. Sirena.

I moved to the tiny window and peeked down through the mini-blinds. She stood in a bathrobe, her hair upswept and sophisticated, her shiny red lips perched in a smile.

Before he came back inside, I moved to the sad rendition of a couch. I smiled and tried to look relaxed and unfazed. No pressure. "Is Gertrude coming?"

"Yeah, she'll be here any minute. Sorry about that. It was Sirena."

Big smile. No stress. This time the knock was softer, almost timid. I stood up, knowing it was my ride. "I'll see you later."

"Yeah, babe. But understand I'm at the mercy of these guys. I don't have a set time."

"No, I understand. As long as you come eventually. Whenever you get there is fine." I was the picture of a loving, understanding, secure wife married to a movie star with an upcoming love scene with the woman he may or may not have fathered a child with nine years ago. I kept it together right on out the door.

Gertrude handed me a bottle of water. "Is everything okay?"

"Just beautiful."

Mistaken Identity

I sat on the edge of the hotel bed and then fell backward with exhaustion. Gertrude had taken me shopping as if her orders were to make me shop until I dropped. My feet throbbed along with my back and neck. I stared at the ceiling, studied the design of the moldings. So much work involved to make something look so simple. Kind of like being married. No one knew the work involved.

I stripped off my clothes and hopped in the shower. Later, dripping wet, I opened my suitcase and pulled out my secret weapon. I held up the long strands, the wig I'd bought before leaving Atlanta. I had planned to give him a show. One night of freaknik was the quickest way to a man's heart regardless of how much they denied it.

After having lectured Miriam on being herself, here I was following suit. Embarrassing. I pushed the wig bag in its velvet pouch. How desperate was I? A woman in love was capable of just about anything.

The sun had set and threatened to rise again by the time Jake came to the hotel. I listened while he showered. There was an art to his bathing, a rhythm. If the water ran too long with no movement, I knew he was in there thinking. The water streamed steady with no sloshing movement. He was thinking. He was acting a bit pent up. But who wouldn't be after a long day of hard work?

When Jake came out, still moist from his shower, I was lying across the bed in the matching lace bra and panties. I was posed on my stomach for full effect, wearing the red five-inch-heel pumps from the premiere, the ones I'd vowed to never wear again. My new hair cascaded down my back and I waited for him to say something.

"Baby, damn." His palm cupped a handful of cheekage. "Damn," he whispered again, sliding his fingers where even the panties couldn't reach. "Nice."

"How nice?" I arched my back, then stretched in a nice catlike pose.

His towel was on the ground, followed quickly by my ensemble. The high heels and the wig were the only survivors. I'd kept them on the entire time, proud of my new set of skills.

Jake fell into me as if he'd never had me before. I held him tight and kissed his neck. He pumped and surged until we both collapsed. A faint taste of salt from our aerobic lovemaking stayed on my lips. I remained still as long as I could, not wanting to disturb his recovery time. His weight was crushing me. I tapped him lightly on the shoulder. "Why didn't you say something about my new hair?"

He rose up on his elbows. "I missed you." His dark shiny eyelashes blinked slowly. "Honestly, I didn't even notice this . . . thing." He stroked his hands through it, then made some kind of face between confusion and wonderment.

"Well, you certainly acted like you noticed."

"You're the only thing I'm hungry for."

I kissed his smooth strong chin. I scooted from underneath his weight since he wasn't giving up peacefully. I still had on my high heels but hadn't noticed until I attempted to get on my feet.

"Don't take them off." He caught me just before I was about to step out of them. "Please," he said. "Just till you get to the bathroom. Then do a little pose." He grinned with his hands resting behind his head. The sheet barely covered his precious loins and I had a sudden flashback of the pictures on the Internet.

This was no time to reincarnate the past.

"Oh . . . now I'm auditioning?" I played along. "I thought none of this getup mattered?" I stood up, took a few steps, then did a mild swirl of my hips. I lifted my arms and belly danced slowly. "Don't say I never did anything for ya, boy." I pole danced without the pole, slinging my new hair every which way.

"I would say you've done everything for me." Jake's mega-watt smile turned back into a lazy grin. "I love you, baby. You're my life."

On that note I felt like jumping back into bed. Tears sprang from my eyes and I turned quickly so he couldn't see. "Wow, if I'd known it was that easy I would've whipped out the wig and the high heels a long time ago."

I heard the bed creak slightly. He got up. His arms wrapped around me from behind. "Baby, it's all you. Wouldn't have mattered what you were wearing."

"Thank goodness. Then I'll take it off." I went to peel back the long shimmering wig and he stopped me.

"Not yet." He looped the hair over one shoulder and nuzzled the back of my neck.

Prickly hairs rose with my awareness. "But I . . . thought . . ."

"Just keep it on for a few more minutes," he breathed hotly around my ear. His nature was at full direct attention.

I closed my eyes and let the warmth overtake my mind and body. I didn't want to hear what he was really saying. But it was work-ing. His hands trailed, starting at my shoulders, smoothing over my breasts, past my waist, and down to my thighs. He turned me around, facing him. His soft lips glistened light pink from having kissed and suckled all over my naked body.

He pushed me back onto the bed and roped my legs around his shoulders for round two. I held on for the ride. He hadn't made love to me this way in some time, pulling me deeper against him with every movement. His muscular shoulders driving with every thrust. I tried to take hold of his face so that he would look at me but his eyes stayed closed. Faster and harder, he rose into a crescendo, then dived with reckless abandon.

His jaw tightened and released as he moaned out his satisfaction. Within moments he was snoring lightly right beside me.

I threw on my trench and grabbed my bag and was out the door. I'd left him sprawled naked, entangled in the sheet. Leaving without awakening him wasn't difficult. Jake was exhausted and needed every drop of sleep.

When I got to the airport I called and left a message on his phone, knowing it was still turned off. "Hi, baby. I'm going home. I'll see you when you get there." I paused, waiting for smarter words to leave my lips but there were none. Only the truth. "You don't need me here. I'm just in the way."

I shouldn't have come, I wanted to say. *The woman who arrived was not me. She was a desperate wife who needed your approval. I only need your love. That's not me.*

The trip was a dismal failure. It was in his eyes that he hadn't wanted me there. Inside the airport bathroom, I caught a glimpse of myself. I'd forgotten the silly wig was still on my head. So much for the great experiment. The false tresses may have won Ben back for Miriam, but for me it only won the part of Jake I could do without. I needed his heart, not just his desire. I needed his goodness and honesty. I needed him to say he loved me and that we were going to be fine. Every family has its ups and downs. Every husband runs into his old lover, who happens to be voted the most beautiful woman. Every wife finds herself lonely and insecure at some point. But we all get through it. And what we find on the other side is ourselves, better, stronger, and ready for a fresh start.

I tossed the mop of hair in the trash. I undid the rubber band and poofed out my natural ball of wonder.

"Now there's the girl I know and love," I said smiling.

I slept all the way home, only waking when the plane's wheels touched the ground.

Jake awakened with a start. The hotel room was quiet. The entire night had felt like a dream. He relived the intense lovemaking, already feeling himself growing again. He'd needed the touch. Her visit was right on time. He rolled over to see the bathroom door was open and the room was empty. Maybe she'd gone to get coffee. He sat up and looked around, noticing there wasn't a trace of her. The woman with the sultry hair, sexy high heels, tiger thong, and bra had been a figment of his imagination.

He closed his long lashes and washed a hand over his face with the realization she'd been really there but now was gone. What had he done this time?

He might catch her before she got on a plane. He moved rapidly putting his pants on, shirt, socks, and shoes. He moved like a man with a mission, ready to give chase, and then he stopped in his tracks. Men stood posted outside his hotel room, pointing cameras at him like guns. The only thing they didn't say was *freeze*.

What they did say, "You're busted, JP. Who was she? It's easier to tell us." One of them gave a wise guy smile. It was a United Nations of paparazzi.

The black one with an English accent interjected, "Or we'll have to start guessing. I say it was his co-star, Sirena Lassiter." He opened up his camera viewer. "Yep, looks just like her. But who can really tell with the sunglasses and long flowing hair? Bangin' body, though, chief."

"Wait a minute. You guys got it all wrong." Jake's shirt was still open from having thrown it on. He raised his arms like he was under arrest, or giving in. Either way, he needed to clean it up. "That was my wife. Plain and simple. Her name is Venus and you guys know that."

They all laughed. Pictures of his wife were worthless and they all knew that too.

He was at their mercy. If they sold pictures of lies, saying it was Sirena, they'd make top dollar. Only Jake would be in trouble with Earl Benning and the rest of the execs at Rise, putting his career very close to death's door. Earl made it clear he didn't want any scandal that made Sirena a marked woman. If the scarlet letter of shame landed on her back, he'd hold Jake personally responsible.

"Seriously, it was my wife," he explained pointedly. "She came to surprise me. The hair, the high heels, and trench—you know what I'm saying? The sexy-spy thing. You know what I'm saying?"

"That's not as much fun, JP. In fact, if that was your wife, the pictures wouldn't be worth half a cent," the Asian one with his hat half slanted said coolly.

"Dude, I'm telling you, this is a case of mistaken identity." Jake pulled out his phone. He raised it up. "She left me a message. I'm on my way to find her at the airport. Now why you want to mess with a man's life?" He shook his head. "Enough, all right? I gotta go. Y'all have a great fuckin' day," he said, sliding past them and daring one of them to touch him.

He knew from the minute he set foot inside the airport, he had no idea where to find her. It was only in the movies when you caught the woman you loved, right before she stepped on the plane, and told her you loved her and couldn't live without her. It was only in his mind that he thought he could convince her anyway. He'd tried to make her believe how deep, and how much he loved her for so long, he was nearly weary.

Maybe this time he'd give her what she wanted. He turned around and walked out. The plane flying overhead sounded loud and ominous, as if she were staring down at him that very moment. Maybe it was time to let her go if that's what she wanted.

Last Call

Jake couldn't get the scene right for the sixth time.

The director seemed to yell, "Cut!" every time Jake opened his mouth. "Okay, really, JP, you're killing us. Everybody, let's wrap and move to the next scene."

Jake helped Sirena out of the cold bathwater. She wore a one-piece, flesh-toned suit, but it left nothing to the imagination. "What's the problem, man? I'm freezing my ass off and you can't spit out two lines?"

"My head is somewhere else."

"Are you still tripping over those paps at your door? Welcome to my cold-ass bathwater—they're everywhere."

"Not just that . . . listen, I need to head home." Jake's hair was parted on the side. His twenties-style pleated pants and suspenders still hung around his muscular abs, but he was quickly pulling the wet wife beater that was supposed to be soaked with perspiration over his head. "I have to go check on Venus."

"Are you serious?" Sirena's eyes narrowed and cut left to right to make sure no one else heard the ridiculousness spouting from his mouth. "We are in the middle of shooting a film. You can't run off chasing your insecure wife every time she loses her damn mind."

Jake nodded. "Thanks for the spectacular advice. But until you're with someone longer than the six o'clock news, don't try and tell me how to run my relationship."

"That's what you call it? A relationship? Okay," she scoffed. "You're a babysitter. You talk about me, not knowing how to be in a relationship. I can tell you one thing, I'd know not to show my ass every time we were having an issue." She pulled the towel around her shoulders and gave another quick gaze around the set. She lowered her voice. "Jay, please don't go. This could hurt your career. They could fire you."

His eyes sparkled with the acknowledgment, as if she'd hit a nerve. "Cee Cee, having notoriety, fame, money don't mean a hell of a lot when you don't have the person you love. One day you're going to know that." He turned and started walking away.

"I already do," she shouted. This time she didn't care who heard. She rushed to catch up with him in her bare wet feet. "You don't think I know? Why do you think I'm standing here in front of you? You think all this is happenstance? I just happened to pick your name out of a bit ol' hat to be in *True Beauty*? Then I just happened to push the director into casting you for this one?" She pushed the wet tendrils of hair out of her face. "That's love, Jay."

"That's not love, sweetheart. It's bribery."

"Well, how about we upgrade to extortion? You walk out of here, you'll never see Christopher again."

"If that's what you want, so be it." Jake turned around and kept moving.

Have and to Hold

I fluffed Miriam's veil and made sure her train was straight. She turned around and faced me. "Why have you been so quiet?"

"I'm focused. There's a difference."

"You still haven't talked to Jake yet?"

I shook my head, no. Two days and counting. "I'm not about to talk about this on your big renewal day. It's your time to be happy, not thinking about my marital woes. Now turn back around, you ruined all my straightening."

Miriam faced me again. "When he's finished filming you guys will get back on track. Mark my words. Things will get normal again." She fanned out her arms. "Now how do I look?"

"Like a happy bride. Beautiful."

"Okay, ladies. Time to get the show on the road." Judy, the wedding coordinator, stepped between us. "Line up, girls," she said to Lizzie and Mya. "And where is our maid of honor?"

I had noticed Jeanette was missing, but was afraid to ask for fear I'd leak more concern then I could control.

"She's late," Miriam chimed in.

That was an understatement. Wondering if she'd gotten confirmation of her pregnancy or not, I finally spoke up. "Is she doing okay?"

"There she is," Judy announced. "Come, come. Line up."

Jeanette was wide-eyed but obviously had just finished a good cry. "Sorry I'm late." Her dress was shifted awkwardly. She worked quickly to get herself together. Her long black hair hung slightly over her face. We were all supposed to wear a gardenia pinned back.

"Goodness, gal, you look a mess," Miriam whispered. "What's wrong with you?"

"I . . . need to talk to you," Jeanette stuttered.

"We are on the clock, ladies. All this sentiment will have to wait." Judy clapped her hands and snapped. Any minute she would stomp her feet. "Let's move." She herded everyone to the door.

Jeanette hung back.

"Maybe you should talk to her after the ceremony," I gauged before saying more. She knew immediately that I was privy to the situation. "You know, it's not like this day changes anything. They were married before, and they'll still be married whether you speak up or not. Maybe you can just let it wait." I pushed her hair behind her ear and placed the bobby-pinned flower. "Let her have this day."

The bridal party headed out. I got in line with my escort and we started down the hall, shoulders back, head out of Miriam's business. She'd be endlessly hurt if she knew I knew, and never said a word. The music started and Judy snapped for our attention, and from that moment I drowned out the gnawing guilt and took one pointed-toe step at a time.

The small crowd clapped and cheered for the bride and groom. I was swept up and relieved all at the same time. Glad Jeanette decided to stay behind. Miriam barely noticed. She spoke her renewal vows. Ben recited his. The harpist played a sweet romantic melody while their pastor announced them husband and wife *again*.

Ben hugged Miriam and kissed Lizzie. They were a beautiful family all dressed in white. After a few perfect pictures we gathered in the courtyard for the reception.

"You look beautiful."

I turned around, surprised to see Jake, flawless in a pinstriped suit, white shirt, and black tie. "You look beautiful too," I said. "Damn." I walked toward him. "I may not have told you before, but the mustache is working for you."

"Yeah, you like that older man feel?"

"It suits you," I purred, stepping into his arms.

"You just showed up, sexed me all good, then walked out the door. Okay," he chuckled. "Don't ever do that again. You had a bro-tha sprung."

"Just wanted you to know what it felt like." I kissed him softly on the lips. "I promise not to ever do that again. In more ways than one, you have no idea." I accepted the shame, then tapped his nose. "What're you doing here? You're not finished filming?"

"I told the director I needed a minute. He said take two. I have to be back Wednesday morning. You still got the wig?"

I smacked him on the shoulder. "Have a little shame."

"None. I have absolutely none."

"Well, I do. I'm sorry about being so selfish. You are who I want to be when I grow up."

"I got news for you, *you're* already who *I* want to be. The way you jumped into motherhood, the way you would sacrifice anything for Mya, it makes me love you even more."

I was beginning to feel the familiar lump in my throat. "Thank you," I squeaked out. The sun was beginning to set. Jake held me even tighter, not realizing my shivering wasn't from the weather, but because he was near.

"I understand about your feelings toward Christopher. I was wrong to just drop that on you."

We started slow dancing even though the small band had begun to play "Dancing on the Ceiling," by Lionel Ritchie. We rocked steady side to side. "I read online about the problems you were having on the set from *Life 'N' Style*. That crazy reporter, Melba Dubois, must have a bug up her butt. She sends minute-by-minute tweets of your every move. I cracked up when I saw the mystery woman wearing a trench and sunglasses and the headline, 'Busted.'"

"I tried to tell them it was you."

"I hope she got fired."

"Let me explain something," Jake said, feeling his opportunity. "I was given strict instructions from the execs for you not to run into Sirena. I was nervous about you seeing her and her seeing you. That's probably what you sensed. I wanted you there, but I was threatened not to put Sirena in a position to look like a home-wrecker."

I scrunched up my nose. "Seriously? She was doing a fine job of that all on her own."

"Number two, I was feelin' the animal print and heels, and the hair." He threw back his head. "Damn if I'm not guilty, but baby, you were smoking hot. I swear, who you are, is who I want. I don't give a care whether your hair is straight, short, chopped, or bald to the scalp. You are the most gorgeous, lovin', sexiest woman, and you're mine."

I wrapped my arms tight around his collar while he lifted me off my feet. I was about to continue the lovefest with my own set of compliments when the sound of screams and a gunned car engine turned our heads.

A speeding car came out of nowhere, taking down a few rose-bushes with it. We all watched in horror as the car didn't slow down. Screaming guests and the bride yelling at the top of her lungs didn't impede the car's progress. In fact, it sped up.

Ben was sideswiped, throwing him on impact. The small car ran into the hedges.

"Oh my God, Ben." Miriam ran to him. He was bleeding from his head and his leg looked twisted.

The pandemonium only got worse when Jeanette got out of the car screaming, "I hope you're dead, you coward. I hope you die." She staggered to where he lay on the ground, standing over him. "You're nothing but a liar and a coward." She held her own bleeding head where she must've hit the steering wheel.

Miriam was mortified, kneeling under Ben's head, dripping blood all over her starched white fluffy gown. She put out a hand to keep Jeanette from getting any closer. "Stay away from him. What are you talking about?"

"He's been paying for my apartment, taking care of me. Telling me the whole time we were going to be together. He kept telling me he was going to tell you before this fake ceremony, but he's a coward." She sneered, blood dripping from her busted lip. She held her stomach in pain and slumped down. "I think I need an ambulance."

Miriam let go of Ben's head. He moaned in agonizing pain when she let it hit the tight hard lawn. She stood up and pulled the wig off her head and slapped Ben's face and head with it. She took the brand-new ring and dropped it on top of the mound of hair. "Did it have to be my cousin?"

She took Lizzie's hand and headed back into the hotel, leaving a bruised and battered Ben and her distraught cousin to fend for themselves.

"Is Daddy going to be all right?" Lizzie asked.

Miriam didn't look back. "We have a beautiful suite. No sense in letting it go to waste."

"Somebody call an ambulance," the crowd all seemed to say at once. I watched Miriam stomp off across the grass, not caring whether Ben's injuries were serious or not.

Jake held on to my hand. "Come on, nothing we can do here."

"No, I should stay and at least wait for the ambulance. I kind of feel responsible."

"You?" Jake reached out and hugged me. "This I have to hear."

⟲

We talked on the drive back home. Eventually I had to bring up the last and final subject. The one we both had been avoiding.

"So what about Christopher? You did promise to take him and Mya to the aquarium."

He pulled into the driveway. "Yeah, well, I don't think that's going to happen." He pushed the button and the top on the convertible pulled back. The black sky and stars glittered overhead. Jake took my hand. "Sirena told me if I left the film shoot, I could forget about having a relationship with Christopher."

"I'm sure she was just angry because you were chasing after me."

"Sirena has to be in control. I was a fool to think I'd be able to have him in my life without her calling the shots."

I stayed silent. Determined not to pass any judgment.

"Regardless, I'm glad it went down now instead of after I got attached to him."

Still silent. Too late for that. Jake never made a decision lightly. Putting his heart and mind into every move. He wouldn't have taken the chance to bring Christopher home with him, if he hadn't weighed it carefully. He wanted a son, simple as that. No one understood more than I.

"Maybe she'll come around." I leaned over and kissed him. "I did."

"Yeah, but my magic mojo only works on you."

I shook my head. "If that were true, you wouldn't have so many fans. There's a light about you. I'm going to have to get used to sharing that light."

Hide and Seek

The next evening Jake was picked up in a town car. He came down the stairs wearing a crisp midnight-blue shirt unbuttoned at the collar over black slacks. He broke into a smile the minute he saw me and Mya waiting by the door.

"I hate to leave you two."

"Daddy, when you coming back?"

"In a week or two, baby." He picked her up. She smashed her face into his neck and held on tight while he twirled her around. "I will call you every night, sweetpea."

I waited my turn. I scooted against him and felt all the anxiety dissipate. We were a family just like we'd always been before this huge movie business, before the Big One. We'd survived.

Mya took one hand, I took the other. We walked him out to the car. The driver held the door open.

"Hold on, wait a minute." Pauletta rushed outside with a bag of her homemade cookies. "In case you get hungry on your flight. Oatmeal cranberry, with that organic sweet syrup you like."

"Agave. Thanks, Pauletta. Not just for the cookies, for taking care of my family."

My mother beamed as if she'd been given the highest compliment. "Thank you, sweetie. It was a pleasure. But I won't be here when you get back."

As soon as the car was out of the driveway, Pauletta leaned against my shoulder. "You've got a special man right there."

"Yep, I know. And so do you." I looked at my dad, who was still waving at Jake's moving car. "I'd say we're both pretty lucky."

"I know that's right," Pauletta agreed. My father had finally won her over. I would miss her for sure.

Champagne Wishes

The film had wrapped and Sirena was feeling proud as a peacock. The director popped the cork of the champagne and the cast and crew celebrated on the set.

She peered over at Jake, who managed to keep his distance unless the camera was rolling. Otherwise he barely looked in her direction.

So be it. This was the movie that would put her on the map. The real map, not just as a popstar celebrity, but a real actress. If he didn't want to come along for the ride, it was his loss. She still had Earl Benning, one of the most influential men in the business. In fact, he should've been there celebrating with them. She peered over her shoulder, checking the entrance.

That's when she saw a few of the extras holding the magazine, gathered around and gawking at her. One of them didn't bother trying to hide her smirk. Goose bumps rose on Sirena's arms, the knowing feeling something was wrong.

"The film is slated for release next summer. I know it's going to be a huge success and you all will be dying to work with me again." The director laughed at his own joke. The basic rumor on the film set was that he'd been an impossible jackass and if anyone ever saw him again, it would be too soon. "To all of you for putting up with me." He held up his plastic champagne glass. "Cheers."

Sirena marched over to the commoners and didn't have to ask. The one holding the magazine handed it over and scurried off.

The cover headline nearly made her fall backward. BABY BROTHER ACTUALLY SIRENA'S SON. There were three pictures Photoshopped like they'd been torn apart, then pasted back together again: her, Christopher in the middle, and a shot of Jake. She flipped it open to the article.

"Did I leave anything out?" Melba Dubois stood close to Sirena, reading over the article with her.

"You lying bitch. You said you were going to write something to make his wife run for the hills." Sirena shoved the magazine at her. "How dare you?" They'd gone way back. Melba had always been her inside woman. Now she had betrayed her.

"I'm reporting a story. I used everything you told me."

"I didn't tell you about Christopher. No one knew about him."

"Your father. Forgetting about him?"

"You went to my father while he's in a hospital room? What kind of scavenger are you?"

"Same kind you are. Everyone wants to be on top of their game, Sirena. You're the one told me to trust no one—whether you're a street sweeper or the CEO of a company, everyone wants to be better than their competition. I scooped this story. I worked hard for it and I got it." Melba's raspy voice went lower. "It was bound to come out anyway. Trust me, I was kind. I told of an innocent young woman who was torn between an abortion or keeping her child. All those pro-choice groups will be new fans."

"What you did was make me out to be a selfish fame climber who would give up her own child for her career."

"If it quacks like a duck—you know the rest."

"Get out of here. If I see you anywhere near me, I'm going to smack that permanent smirk off your face."

Melba rolled her eyes toward Jake. "If things had gone the way you had planned, we'd be having an entirely different discussion right about now. But face it. You've lost him for good this time. No long-lost child is going to bring JP running into your arms."

That was the final straw. Sirena lunged at Melba. The two women scratched and pawed at each other until they were pulled apart. Jake had grabbed Sirena by the waist, and Quincy had Melba.

"I will sue you and your lying tabloid," Sirena huffed. "When I get through with you, you're going to have to move back to the slums in London where you came from."

Melba backed out, putting her extended pinkie and thumb to her ear and mouthing the words, *call me* to Sirena. Only making her more enraged.

Jake held her arm. "Calm down. Stop it."

"Oh Jay, she's told the world. Now everyone knows about Christopher." She tried to sob into Jake's chest but he kept her at an arm's distance.

"Then now you can be his mother. That's all it means."

That's all you have to say to me? Sirena moved the hair out of her face. "Yeah, I guess that's what it means." She glared at him, then pushed him aside and marched to her trailer, glad to be on to the next project. Her life held possibilities that these silly little people couldn't even imagine.

She threw her personal notions in her bag. The knock at her trailer was followed by Earl's voice. "Open up, it's me."

"Thank God," she sighed, falling into his arms. "Did you see that *Life 'N' Style* article? Can you believe what that tramp wrote about me? I have been nothing but good to her, giving her exclusive interviews every damn time she asked . . . I can't believe she did this to me."

Earl came inside. His dark suit hardly had a wrinkle after a four-hour flight from Los Angeles. He took a long hard breath. "Sirena, this is bad, very bad."

"I know it's bad. Don't you think I know that? I need to tweet a heads-up to my fans, so they will feel empowered with information instead of feeling like I was hiding something." She paced, then sat down to zip up her boots. "I can't wait to get out of here. Relax on your private jet and head to Saint-Tropez." She looked up. "I'm sorry I didn't tell you about Christopher."

"I'm sorry too." He was still standing. He turned his back to her, seemingly looking for the right words. "We're going to have to postpone our nuptials. This thing needs to blow over. I have a lot to do, a lot of damage control. Now's just not the right time." He grasped his hands, then rubbed them together like he was washing himself of her and the mess she'd made.

"Damage control . . . what are you talking about? I'm still the hottest game in town." She stood up, putting her finger in his face. "You're playing dangerously close to me walking out of this relationship."

Another deep breath, as if he was getting closer to his goal. "That may not be a bad idea. Look, a son, you having a child, changes things for us. For me," he admitted.

"Nobody asked you to be his daddy," she spat. "He's at my house in Atlanta being very well taken care of. What's that got to do with you, or our relationship?"

Earl adjusted his sleeves. "We're getting nowhere and I'm short on time. I have a film that just went overbudget, bringing the production cost to sixty million. I have a star who might now be crowned the worst mother of the year, thereby making that sixty million the biggest loss of the company's history."

"Then wouldn't it make sense that we got married? You'll make an honest woman out of me and we'll raise Christopher, appear to be one sweet loving family." She opened her arms. "There you go, damage control. I'm going to make you the happiest man on earth. Do you know what any man would give to be in your shoes?" She moved toward him, her perfect bronze thighs bulging under the robe.

"Just stop. Okay, like I said, we're going to have to postpone. That's it. So you play dumb on your own time." He stormed out and down the trailer stairs in his expensive Ferragamo loafers, taking determined strides out of her life. She would never forget this humiliation. One day he would need her, long before she would need him.

Sirena crouched down in misery. Humbled to the core, but she wouldn't stay there long.

She'd show Earl Benning damage control.

The next day began with step one: she lined up interviews with every morning show that would have her.

Step two, she packed up Christopher's few belongings and drove him to Mr. Holier Than Thou's residence. Jay asked no questions—in fact, he hardly looked at her, and that was okay with Sirena. Freedom always came at a price.

Step three, she vowed to work even harder. In her head was a list: win an Oscar, break a record for most weeks on the *Billboard* chart, make more money than Oprah. Why not?

Fistful of Fears

"Open it." I stood over Jake and waited patiently for him to open his eyes. I placed the small black velvet box on the pillow. Inside could've been a bracelet or a watch, but it was neither.

"Babe, what time is it?" He leaned over and did a one-eyed view of the nightstand clock. "Six forty-five?" His head rocketed under the pillow. It was a Saturday. After having 5 A.M. wake-up calls during filming, and coming home to Christopher and Mya running around the house at all hours, he made it his business to sleep until midmorning.

I shook him, then kissed him on his chin. "You will love it, I promise. Listen, I gave you a whole fifteen minutes extra, considering it took me that long to find a suitable box."

This piqued his interest.

"Open says me." I handed him the box.

He flipped it open. The plastic casing shaped like a thermometer lay faceup. The dashed pink lines glowed miraculously. Jake's eyes still hadn't left the box.

"How . . . baby?"

I nodded my head up and down slowly. He reached out, pulling me in for a long kiss.

"I must've used up five tests 'cause I still couldn't believe it. But it's true. As for how, I'm guessing it was the wig and stilettos." I grinned, remembering the powerful lovemaking.

He pulled me down on top of him. "Baby," he said, holding me tight, "I got you, I got Christopher and Mya, and now . . ." He trailed off. He took a deep breath, looking me in the eyes.

"I'm not afraid. I know it's going to be okay." I raised my balled fist, then dumped the imaginary contents. "No more fear. No more bad karma. We deserve every good thing this life has to offer."

We cuddled for a good few minutes before Mya and Christopher busted in.

"We made happy-face pancakes," Mya said. Christopher was carrying the tray.

"Does no one sleep around here?"

"Life is too short to sleep," Christopher said. "My pop always says, you can sleep when you're dead."

"Oh man, that's some philosophy." I kissed him on top of his head. He was such a mature little guy. But a vulnerable child all the same. He missed his pop and we'd already taken him to visit twice. The nurse did say he got better with each visit. Sometimes, people got better when they had hope. I slid my hand over my already rising belly. I would say Christopher had that effect on me too. He gave me hope.

TRISHA R. THOMAS is an NAACP Image Award for Outstanding Literary Work finalist. She's a Literary Lion Award honoree by the King County Library System Foundation and was voted Best New Writer by the Black Writers Alliance. Her debut novel, *Nappily Ever After,* is now a Netflix movie. *O, The Oprah Magazine* featured her novels in "Books That Matter" for delving into the self-esteem of young women of color and the insurmountable expectations they face starting at an early age. She lives in California with her family where she continues to write the Nappily series.